Estelle Thompson has written fifteen novels, which have been translated and published in German, French, Dutch and Italian, as well as one non-fiction work. She has written for various magazines in both the UK and Australia, including *Woman* and *Woman's Weekly*.

She is a retired dairy farmer, and now lives with her brother on his farm in Queensland, Australia.

COME HOME TO DANGER

Charles Waring has come home to Queensland to attend his mother's funeral and his remark, intended only for a family friend to hear, is inadvertently overheard by several other people. The chain of events which follows convinces Charles that his mother was murdered because she knew a terrible secret from someone's past, and he finds himself in a deadly game of cat-and-mouse as he tries to unravel the mystery. Meanwhile, he must face the certainty that someone among those he has come to care about poses a cruel threat.

Books by Estelle Thompson
Published by The House of Ulverscroft:

THE MEADOWS OF TALLON
FIND A CROOKED SIXPENCE
A MISCHIEF PAST
THREE WOMEN IN THE HOUSE
THE HEIR TO FAIRFIELD
A TOAST TO COUSIN JULIAN
THE SUBSTITUTE
HUNTER IN THE DARK

ESTELLE THOMPSON

COME HOME TO DANGER

Complete and Unabridged

ULVERSCROFT
Leicester

First published in Great Britain in 1998 by
Robert Hale Limited
London

First Large Print Edition
published 1999
by arrangement with
Robert Hale Limited
London

British Library CIP Data

Thompson, Estelle
    Come home to danger.—Large print ed.—
    Ulverscroft large print series: mystery
    1. Detective and mystery stories
    2. Large type books
    I. Title
    823 [F]

    ISBN 0–7089–4079–X

Published by
F. A. Thorpe (Publishing) Ltd.
Anstey, Leicestershire
Set by Words & Graphics Ltd.
Anstey, Leicestershire
Printed and bound in Great Britain by
T. J. International Ltd., Padstow, Cornwall

This book is printed on acid-free paper

Acknowledgements

I would like to sincerely thank Chris Gray, of Rumbalara, Mary Puglisi, of Ballandean Estate, and Sam Costanzo, of Golden Grove, for their kindness in assisting me in gathering background information on winery and orchard work, and generously giving me their time. If the book contains any errors in this area it is due to my own failure to correctly grasp what I was told and shown.

My thanks also to Graham and Margaret Rogers, formerly of the Granite Court Motel in Stanthorpe, for suggesting the dramatic backdrop of 'Donnelley's Castle' for the climactic scene. Also to my nephew Barry Thompson for his advice on the area generally.

The help and interest of all these people is greatly appreciated.

Estelle Thompson

1

'I think the worst part is that I just don't believe it was an accident.'

The words fell into one of those lulls in conversation that can occur for no particular reason even in a roomful of people. A dozen heads turned to look at the speaker.

'What the devil do you mean, Charles?' A solidly built man with sandy-fair hair and clipped beard, both greying, swung around sharply to ask the shocked question that was on a number of faces.

Charles Waring looked around him, clearly embarrassed that his words had carried.

'Sorry, Dad. I was just talking off the top of my head to John, that's all.'

'It was a damn funny thing to say at a funeral, even to your mother's solicitor. Maybe especially to your mother's solicitor. You must have meant something.' Geoffrey Waring's voice was bluntly angry.

Charles hadn't moved from leaning one arm on the mantelpiece above the empty fireplace in a weary stance that belied the whippy strength of his tall frame, but there was sharp alertness in the hazel eyes that flickered over the group of people who had been close enough to overhear his remark.

He said slowly, 'Mother knew that road as well as she knew this living-room. She drove over it virtually every day — had done in the eight years since she married Anthony. Yet she simply failed to take that bend and just drove off in the worst possible part of the road. It doesn't make sense. Not to me.'

A dark-haired woman in her mid-thirties said coolly, 'For goodness sake, Charles, you're not suggesting Ursula committed suicide?'

Charles looked at his stepsister. 'Mother? No.' He shook his head. 'No, Miriam, I can't see Mother killing herself. Not unless she had some terminal illness or something. Which she didn't.'

'How do you know?' the man beside Miriam asked curiously.

'There was an autopsy. She was a perfectly healthy woman. After all, she was only fifty-two. No tumours, no coronary problems, no sign of a stroke, blood alcohol level nil.'

The man he had first spoken to frowned. 'So if you question whether it was an accident and you don't believe it was suicide, what you're suggesting is outrageous.'

Charles smiled faintly. 'And as a solicitor you would advise against such unfounded remarks. I know. I'm sorry. I didn't intend it to be a public comment, and I don't even know exactly what I was thinking. Anything other than accident is impossible, I guess. Put it down to shock and — well, the kind of wanting answers that everyone goes through when they unexpectedly lose someone they care about. It can make your imagination run riot. Please forgive me. My father is right: this certainly wasn't the place to begin talking wild nonsense. I'm sorry.'

The solicitor smiled and looked relieved. 'My dear fellow, it's perfectly natural you should be under stress. For one thing, you must be short of sleep — it's a long flight from Canada to Australia. And you hadn't seen your mother for — how long?'

'Three years.'

'I think that all adds up to making it very hard on you. Here, let me get you a drink.'

He moved off, and the little group around Charles dispersed and joined in the general buzz of conversation. Charles stood, looking around the room. Had it been imagination, or had that stupidly timed remark of his produced a reaction in one of the hearers — a reaction stronger than might be expected? You really are imagining things, he told himself.

He didn't think the reaction — if there had been one — had come from his father, in spite of his startled questioning of Charles's meaning. It had been a bit of a surprise, actually, to see his father at the funeral service. Stranger still to see him here in the home Ursula and her second husband had shared, mingling with the other mourners who had accepted the stepfamily's invitation to have light refreshments after the funeral. Still, Charles reflected, to be fair, Geoffrey and Ursula had remained on friendly enough terms after their divorce, simply agreeing to go their separate ways when Ursula finally decided Geoffrey's charm and general good humour didn't compensate enough for his irresponsible use of money and, more tellingly, his frequent pursuit of other women.

Charles's gaze sought out Rhelma Waring, his father's present wife — slender, attractive, dark-haired, with a strange quality of remoteness, a kind of courteous coldness. She was expensively but very tastefully dressed, looking every inch the successful businesswoman she apparently was. She must, Charles thought, be close to twenty years younger than Geoffrey. Charles wondered wryly whether his father was as consistently unfaithful to her as he had been to Ursula.

Although she and Geoffrey had been married five years, this was the first time he had met the woman who was his stepmother. Odd to think of her as that, really: she was probably not more than seven or eight years older than he was. Geoffrey seemed to lavish attention on her.

Charles sighed and walked over to the window to gaze out on the garden and the countryside beyond.

This house had never been his home. He'd been eighteen and studying geology at university when his parents had divorced, and consequently, even when four years later his mother had married Anthony Erskine, who headed a successful trucking business, Charles had never been more than a guest here.

The house which had been his home in childhood and through his high-school years was at the vineyard and winery which had been first his grandfather's and then his mother's property and abiding love. His father had been the proprietor of a menswear business in the town and although, when that had failed through his tendency to financial foolishness, he had worked Glenlodge Winery with his wife, he had never had any enthusiasm for it, never been absorbed in it as she had been.

Had been.

The past tense of the words in his mind gave a fresh twist of pain to the ache of his grief. The alert, intelligent, kind woman who had been his mother was gone, killed when her little Suzuki four-wheel-drive which she always drove to work went off the road as she drove up along the ridge to this house which Anthony Erskine had built for her, perched high on a hill and looking out over the countryside. The car had crashed down over a tier-like group of three enormous granite boulders, rebounding from one to the next in a total metal-crushing drop of about fifty metres, to end up an almost unrecognizable wreck at the bottom. The police had told him that even if she had been using the BMW which had been a gift to her from Anthony, it would have made no difference. Ursula must have died almost instantly. That was the only consolation Charles could find.

Three years since he had seen her. That only made the ache worse. Letters and the occasional long-distance phone call weren't the same, not by a long way. He'd been due to come home in just over a month, taking overdue holidays.

He thrust his hands into his pockets and stared out over the countryside he'd once known so well: the grey-green trees, the whitish soil, the neat lines here and there of vineyards and orchards; and, scattered everywhere, the great boulders which gave the Granite Belt of southern Queensland and part of northern New South Wales its name. So totally different from the lakes and dark-green conifer forests and towering rock-and-snow peaks of the Canadian Rockies where he had been working as consultant geologist with an engineering company.

He'd been wondering whether he might leave it and come back to work in Australia if he found a suitable opening in his profession. But there was no point in that now. He'd be glad to go back to Canada, and as soon as possible. Here, as an only child, he had only a father he hardly really knew, a stepmother he'd only just laid eyes on, and assorted stepbrothers-and-sisters and their partners, all of whom were no more than casual, seldom-seen friends.

'Sorry I took such a long time getting your drink, but I got waylaid.' John Farrell, the grey-haired solicitor who had looked after Ursula's legal affairs for as long as Charles could remember, was at his elbow.

Charles took the proffered whisky with a smile.

'A fine lady, your mother,' John Farrell said quietly. 'I suppose it's an admission that

I'm getting old, but I can remember when she was helping her father run the winery while your father still had his business in the town, and you were just a little fellow. I remember her taking you down to that big pool in the river to teach you to swim. And not just you, but half the neighbours' kids as well.'

Charles smiled. 'I remember. Hentys' pool. Hentys owned the farm. Mr Henty let everybody use the pool for swimming. But he didn't trust kids to shut a gate, I guess — very wisely — because we used to go in from the road by a stile. I remember that because I think I've only ever seen two or three stiles in my life. I wonder if it's still there?'

The solicitor shook his head. 'I couldn't say about the stile, because I haven't been down that way for ages. But certainly the pool's still there, and it still belongs to the Henty family. Young Warren Henty runs the place now, though his father still has an interest in it and works part-time on it. Warren's a pretty easy-going sort of fellow like his father, so I dare say the local youngsters still swim there.'

'I must go down there tomorrow and have a look,' Charles said. 'I believe my stepfamily and I have an appointment in your office tomorrow morning to attend to the legal formalities. But after lunch I'll do the nostalgia bit.'

'Have you been out to the winery?'

'No.' Charles shook his head. 'I think that's one bit of nostalgia I'll do without. That was home, for me.'

'And going back would be painful? A home that's no longer your home?'

Charles shrugged. 'Let's just say there'd be no point in it. I expect to be leaving for Canada again pretty soon, unless something unexpected happens.'

John Farrell gave him a searching look, but changed the subject, and Charles, when someone came up and spoke to John, took the opportunity to put down his glass and unobtrusively make his way out into the garden.

As he did so, he heard a woman in the room behind him say in a puzzled tone, 'If Charles thought his mother's death wasn't an accident and it wasn't suicide, what was he talking about?'

'There's only one thing left, isn't there?' a man's voice answered tersely. 'Murder.'

Charles kept walking. *Was* he talking about murder? He wondered. Well, whoever the man was, he was right, of course: murder was the only thing left.

But it was an absurdity. An ugly absurdity, and he fervently wished it had never crept, unwanted, into his mind, let alone been spoken.

If Ursula Erskine had been murdered, as far as he could see the most probable people who could conceivably have a motive were her stepfamily, and their only conceivable motive would have to be plain old-fashioned money; because, at their father's death, beyond some relatively minor legacies to each of them, he had left the bulk of his estate — including this large house — to Ursula. That had seemed reasonable enough, Charles remembered thinking at the time, because he had financially helped all of his children to follow the careers of their own choice and, being a firm believer in standing on one's own feet, he had wanted them to succeed because of themselves, and not because their father had a reasonable amount of money.

Charles frowned, trying to think back to what he had heard of Anthony Erskine's will. Since he wasn't involved — though he had liked his mother's husband and much regretted his too-early death — he hadn't paid much attention then to the terms of the will. All he could really remember was that it made his mother very comfortably situated financially, and she, sharing Anthony's enthusiasm for independence, had confided in Charles that, while accepting the house, she had placed the money into a separate investment arrangement which she didn't wish to draw on for herself.

He could remember her standing in this house, in the living-room he had just left, looking out on to the garden he was now walking in: a fairly tall woman, slender; curling brown hair like his, but greying; pale with the stress of grief, quietly controlled.

'I can only feel I hold everything of Anthony's in trust for his children, Charles,' she had said. 'Even this house. I'll leave it to his children. I'll go on living in it because Anthony had it built for my sake, and I've been happy here. But Glenlodge is my real home: the orchard, the vineyards, the winery — the house, too, I guess, though I'm happy for the Rushtons to live there.'

Tom Rushton was the orchard foreman.

'Your father had no real interest in the winery, or the vines. He tried, I think, but it didn't work. Anthony had no interest in it whatever and never had anything to do with it, but he was always happy for me to carry on with it. What I make from Glenlodge is mine. I've never felt I had any real right to what was Anthony's. Can you understand that?'

He had understood, because that was the way Ursula was. But even though she never wished to touch Anthony's money, his children couldn't touch it either, while ever she lived. That was the way Anthony had left it. And, as far as Charles understood, that money was fairly substantial, having come from the sale of Anthony's business interests.

But, one of those perfectly ordinary, pleasant people, a coldly calculating murderer? They had all been adults or in their late teens when Ursula and Anthony married, and, so far as Charles could tell, they had all had a very good relationship with Ursula. But he had been away for three years. Much could change in three years.

And if one of them — or one of their spouses — had been desperate for money . . .

Charles shook his head sharply. Rubbish. Ursula Erskine had died in an accident. Anything else was unthinkably absurd. Anyway, it wasn't easy, surely, to fake a car crash. And no matter how well anyone knew a road, they could still meet with an accident on it. It was the sort of thing that happened all the time: a sudden swerve to avoid an animal on the road, an unexpected scatter of loose gravel on a corner; a two-second doze. Any sudden distraction.

Vehicles began to start up and drive away as people, having paid their final respects, their last tribute, to Ursula, gradually dispersed to resume their own lives.

Suddenly, unexpectedly, Charles felt himself half-blinded by tears as the finality of the loss of the woman who had been his friend as well as his mother, washed over him. Although he was staying in his mother's otherwise empty house, he wanted to get away for an hour or so, and not have to talk to anyone.

He strode swiftly to his hired car and drove away. Back down the road that crested the ridge, back past the spot where Ursula had died. He was aware of the car in front of him, but he was driving mechanically, not really thinking of what he was doing, trying not to think of a car toppling off the road, crashing and rebounding from boulder to boulder. He was down off the ridge, almost at the point where the private road to the Erskine house rejoined the main road, when the car in front of him braked and swerved suddenly. Because his mind wasn't really on what he was doing, he was a second slow to react, braking and swerving also a shade too hard, and his rental car slid slightly and clipped a rock with a sound of grating metal.

Charles swore and stopped to get out and inspect the damage, and the driver ahead, evidently seeing in the rear-view mirror what had happened, stopped also and came back — a trim-figured girl in her mid-twenties, with wavy auburn hair and concerned brown eyes.

'What the hell do you think you're doing?' Charles snapped. 'Isn't one accident on this bloody road enough?'

Even as he flung the words at her he knew he was being unreasonable, but reasonableness and his raw emotions of the moment did not go hand in hand.

'I'm sorry,' the girl said. 'But you must have been very close behind. Is there any damage?'

'Oh, it's still driveable,' Charles said curtly. 'But that dent and scrape won't exactly endear me to the car-hire company.'

'I'm sorry,' she said again, 'but a cat ran across the road front of me.'

'Is that so?' Charles said sarcastically. 'Well, *I* didn't see it.'

The girl looked at him for a moment. 'No,' she said with sudden bitterness. 'You're like the rest of them. You'll never see what you don't want to see.'

She got back into her car and drove away, leaving Charles staring after her, anger fading to puzzlement.

2

Charles stood at the window in the solicitor's office and stared down at the street below: cars parked at the kerb, a thin but steady flow of traffic; pedestrians, loitering at shop windows or hurrying purposefully, here and there standing in twos and threes in conversation. A normal smallish town. Once very familiar, now almost alien; though he wasn't really seeing it. He was still trying to absorb what he had just been told.

Glenlodge was his. His mother's winery.

Why it had never occurred to him that it would be so, he didn't know. Perhaps because until a few days ago his mother's death was something so far in the future that he simply hadn't thought about it. And in the few days since, his mind had been on other, bitter things. As her only child, it was perfectly natural Ursula would leave her property to him; yet somehow it had come as a shock that he now owned the place where he had spent his childhood and his early teenage years until he went to study at the University of Queensland.

An attractive weatherboard house with

15

wide verandas, in a garden of trees and shrubs which sheltered it from wind but were planted so as not to block the winter sun. Neat vineyards; a cool, dim winery lined with great oak vats. Expanded, since his boyhood, to include the orchard next door with its large area of stone-fruits.

Ursula herself had grown up there, loved it, inherited it, worked it successfully, expanded it. She, who never drank more than one glass of wine a day, had been entranced by the art of wine-making, and had turned what had once been scarcely more than a back-yard hobby into a small but highly-respected winery. It had been her life, and she had left it to him.

And he didn't want it.

'Will this mean you'll be staying on, Charles?' Someone behind him in John Farrell's office asked the question. Afterwards, Charles was to try to remember who it was, but his thoughts had been in turmoil and although the question registered, the identity of the speaker did not, because it didn't seen important, then.

With an effort to concentrate his mind on the business in hand, Charles turned. His stepbrother and stepsisters and their respective partners were all present to hear the solicitor read and explain Ursula's will.

Charles shook his head. 'There's no reason for me to stay. I'm a geologist, not a winemaker, not an orchardist. I wouldn't know the first thing about it. Selling is the only sensible thing to do. I'm sure I can leave the sale of it in John's hands. There's no earthly reason for my physical presence to arrange a sale, is there, John?'

The solicitor shook his head. 'No.' He looked at Charles for a moment and then looked down at his desk. 'But isn't that a rather hasty decision, Charles? Your mother had built Glenlodge into a very successful business, and she had excellent staff. Certainly she went into debt to buy that additional property, but it was a sound move. A few seasons will more than clear the debt. I believe Glenlodge is a very sound property indeed. Besides, that was your home. You're the third-generation owner.'

Charles smiled wryly. 'Then the third generation would probably send it broke through ignorance. Sorry, John. Sentiment should never be allowed to overrule common sense.'

The solicitor shrugged. 'I don't mean to suggest it should. But I would sincerely advise you to think for a while before you put Glenlodge up for sale. At least I think you should go out and talk to the staff personally. Will you do that?'

'Perhaps.' Charles was non-committal. 'But not today. This afternoon I have promised myself one bit of sentimentality, remember? I'm going down to look at the swimming-hole in Henty's place.'

There was some further discussion of legal formalities, then the family of Ursula Erskine trooped out of the office, down the stairs to the street, where they paused uncertainly.

'What,' Charles asked, 'is everyone planning for the rest of day?'

'I think we'll go home,' Miriam said. 'Douglas doesn't want to leave his partner with the whole practice to deal with for any longer than necessary. He always has this dreadful feeling there'll be an outbreak of broken arms or appendicitis if he's away for more than a day without arranging a locum.' Her tone was affectionately teasing.

Douglas Wentworth smiled. A tall, slim man with greying dark hair, Charles scarcely knew him and always felt that behind the blue eyes that smiled readily and made his patients feel relaxed and at ease there was something the world was not supposed to see — not anything sinister, just a man few people were meant to discover. Douglas said easily, 'Well, Ted's not as young as he was. But,' he added, smiling at his wife, 'the real truth is that Miriam can't bear to be parted from the horses for long.'

'I have to talk to a client who wants a house designed for an awkward block of land,' Sandford Erskine said. 'Tell you what: why don't we all have lunch together here in town? Jill has the afternoon off from the clinic, haven't you, kiddo?'

The youngest of the Erskine family, Jill, at twenty-five, was some eight or nine years younger than Sandford, but with the same fair hair, blue eyes and lean build — neither of them especially good-looking, but with a lively good humour about them which was attractive.

'Well, yes, I do have the whole day off, and I know a top spot for lunch, but it depends whether you're shouting, Ford. If we're all buying our own, I know a good sandwich bar which I frequent in the depths of my poverty.'

'Have no fear, baby sister,' Sandford said cheerfully. 'It's my treat. Will you all come? Please? Not quite so cold as all dispersing in the street and leaving Charles alone. I know we've all lost a friend,' he added soberly, 'but it's a bit more than that for Charles, and he has no one to share it with him.'

There were quick murmurs of agreement, and Charles felt touched by Sandford's

19

thoughtfulness. The exuberant, happy-go-lucky stepbrother his family called Ford had just shown a side to his personality Charles had not suspected, though Sandford's success as an architectural draughtsman and builder made it clear that cheerful good humour was by no means his only trait.

Conversation over an excellent lunch was easy and relaxed, and gave Charles his first real chance since returning home to observe his stepfamily. In fact, he reflected with a touch of something like surprise, it was probably the first time he had ever seen them gathered together, the first time he could think about their personal relationships. They were, as far as he could gather, on very good terms with each other.

Certainly, he thought with a touch of bitterness of which he was instantly ashamed, they had enough reason to be cheerful. An unworthy thought, he decided, since they had indeed regarded Ursula with genuine affection. But they had also just learned — or had their belief confirmed — that each of them, each of Anthony Erskine's children, had inherited a full one-third share of the considerable money he had left to Ursula in the first instance.

She had invested it well, and then in turn had bequeathed it to them, along with the house where she had been living until her death — the house to be sold and the proceeds shared, unless one of the three Erskines chose to keep it and buy out the other's shares.

'Of course,' Miriam had said immediately, 'Charles must feel free to stay in the house as long as he chooses — either until he goes back to Canada or has time to make whatever arrangements he likes. It's much better to have the house occupied, anyway.'

There had been immediate agreement from the other family members.

During lunch no one made any reference to what had transpired in the solicitor's office, whether out of respect for Ursula or regard for Charles's feelings. But, he felt, they could not fail to be thinking about it because, while not by any means a fortune, it was a significant inheritance, and he was sure none of them had known that Ursula had left their father's money untouched. What would they do with that money, he wondered.

He thought about Miriam, the eldest, with her passionate love of horses and racing, who owned a small but highly regarded thoroughbred stud; everything about her was intense, focused. For her, it would be something with the horses. To guess about the dreams of Sandford — cheerful,

21

easy-going Sandford — or Jill, the veterinary surgeon, with the good-looking fiancé, would be much more difficult, though doubtless they *had* dreams. Everyone has some kind of dream, Charles mused. And then thought at once: if that's true, what are my dreams?

As they dispersed after lunch, Miriam said, 'Will we see you before you go back to Canada, Charles?'

He shook his head. 'I don't really know. I'm due for holidays anyway, so I might stay on for a bit. I might even think of trying for permanent work in Australia, maybe with a mining company.'

He wondered afterwards what had possessed him to say it when he had no intention of doing any such thing.

'You'll keep in touch anyway, won't you?' Sandford said.

'Don't just wander off into the sunset in the Rockies or something, will you?'

Charles smiled. 'I'll keep in touch.' The sort of thing, he thought, you say to people you meet casually on a holiday, and never follow up. He wondered if it meant anything more to these people than that, and found he rather hoped it did.

They said their farewells and he went out to his hired car and drove back out to the house which now belonged to his step-family. It seemed echoingly empty, and he was grateful when a raucous parrot-voice reminded him he had his mother's two pets to look after while he was here: Aristotle the galah, and a black-and-white cat called Marmaduke. Jill had asked him to care for them until she could find homes for them. 'I'd love to have them, but I have a flat and no pets are allowed.'

He'd assured her he would be happy to care for them while he was here, and it was true. He had always liked animals and birds.

He went out to Aristotle's outsize cage and checked seed and water levels and talked to the bird which Ursula had rescued when she had found it on the roadside, apparently struck by a passing car and suffering permanent wing-damage which meant it would never fly again. Aristotle fluffed his pink and grey feathers and regarded Charles curiously with bright black eyes. 'Hello, larrikin,' he said.

Charles smiled and turned to find the cat sitting in the door-way surveying him gravely, and he felt a quick tightening in his throat. Since Ursula's death, Marmaduke had endlessly searched through the house and garden for her, a silent, puzzled small searcher, seeming somehow heart-grabbingly fearful that his loved human companion was not coming back.

'I know, old chap,' Charles said quietly, walking across to pick him up and carry him indoors. 'Don't worry, something will be worked out for you.'

The cat accepted the attention with neither resentment nor enthusiasm, but he sat and watched as Charles changed from his suit into jeans and shirt. Miriam and Douglas had been staying in the house since they had been called when the accident occurred, but they had taken their luggage when they had left to go to the solicitor's office, saying they would return home. Sandford and Antoinette had a house just outside the town of Stanthorpe, and Jill had her own flat there.

'You guys are stuck with just me for a few days,' Charles told his mother's pets. 'But I'm going out now for an hour or so. OK?'

He grinned ruefully to himself. I must be going daft, he thought — talking to a cat and a bird as if they understood; and they damn well look as if they do.

He went out to the car and drove back down the gravel-surfaced private road to the main road and stopped for a moment. To go to the part of the river known to him as Hentys' pool he would have to drive out on the road towards his mother's winery and orchard. *His* winery and orchard. It would be only a very few minutes drive further, but he knew he would not go, and he wondered a little why it was so. If he was sentimental enough to want to go out and see the rocky pool where he had learned to swim, why on earth did he feel he didn't want to see the place that had been his home for more than half his life? Maybe there were too many memories there that he didn't want to waken.

He shrugged and drove on.

Another gravelled road led off the sealed one and past the Henty farm. He stopped at the house, intending to explain why he was there and ask permission to go down to the pool, but the open garage was empty and no one answered his knock, so presumably the younger-generation Hentys were out. He drove on another half-kilometre or so and parked by the side of the road, smiling in pleasure and amused at himself for being pleased: the wooden stile was still in existence.

He climbed it and walked down to the pool and stood looking at it, where the river widened out from its course among boulders to spread in a quiet pool before sliding gently away over a series of tiny cascades. Not so large as childhood memory would have it, nevertheless it was as familiar as if he had swum there a month ago. His mind could hear the shouts and laughter and splashing of children who had been his schoolfriends and neighbourhood playmates. He didn't know where any of them were now, except for Warren Henty who now owned this place, as John Farrell had told him.

The decayed granite at his feet was like coarse sand, and just here it made a miniature beach, with sheoaks by the water, and a weeping willow. He didn't remember the willow.

The crash of the rifle shot and the little explosion of a bullet hitting the sand a couple of metres from his feet came simultaneously.

He spun around, disbelieving, to stare instinctively at the hill to his right.

'Hey, you bloody fool!' he shouted. 'There's someone down here!'

A second shot whined murderously past, and a third, scattering sand and echoing viciously across the hills, as Charles threw himself down and in a fast somersault plunged behind a jumble of small boulders, and got to his knees, crouching in stunned silence for perhaps three minutes. He turned quickly at the sound of a fast-moving motor vehicle.

A Nissan Patrol four-wheel-drive came charging across the paddock and skidded to a stop twenty metres away, and a grey-haired man leapt out.

'You all right, mate?' he demanded.

'Get down!' Charles yelled, and another shot ploughed into the ground close by.

'Great jumping jumbucks!' the man said, doing a creditably athletic sprint and a diving tumble down behind the rocks beside Charles. 'Cut it out, you loon!' he shouted in the general direction of the hillside. 'There are *people* down here!'

'I tried that,' Charles told him. 'I think he knows. He fired three more shots after that.'

'Good Lord!' the older man said. He looked at Charles. 'What have you done to make yourself so unpopular?'

Charles laughed shakily, liking him at once. 'If I knew that, I might have a better idea which rock to hide behind. Welcome to my war.'

'Sounds like a bloody dangerous one. I was doing a bit of fence-mending when I heard the shots and came to see what was going on. Any ideas?'

Charles shook his head. 'I came in off the road to look at the pool. I used to swim here when I was a kid. Then that clown up there

27

loosed off a few rounds at me.'

The grey-haired man looked at him keenly. 'Are you Charles Waring?'

'Sorry. Yes. I forgot the introductions.' Charles held out his hand and the other man shook it.

'Jack Henty. I used to own this place when you were a youngster. My son has it now.'

They fell silent, crouched and listening.

There were no unusual sounds. After a few moments Jack Henty said, 'Well, it's an old trick but we may as well try it.'

He took off his slightly battered felt hat and Charles, guessing what he had in mind, handed him a short piece of broken branch that lay near his feet. Jack put the hat on the end of it and carefully raised it so that it would show the top of the hat above the boulders. There was no response from the gunman.

'Whoever it is would know it wasn't my hat, and so presumably not my head,' Charles said. 'So maybe he wants me specifically. Feel like trying your luck to get back to your vehicle? I guess we should tell the police. Otherwise we could be here a long time.'

'Or we could be dead.'

'Or we could be dead. What do you think?'

'Sure, I'll have a go for the Nissan. But

what about you? Whoever it is could be manoeuvring for another sighting.'

Charles nodded. 'I know. But I got to know this place pretty well, the way kids do, and I remember it even now. I can work my way up that gully under pretty good cover, can't I?'

Jack Henty nodded agreement.

'If I remember rightly, there's a good chance I can get fairly high up on the hill without being spotted, so I'd like to try a bit of manoeuvring myself. I confess to a certain degree of curiosity about the identity of that sod up there.'

Jack grunted. 'I dare say. Wish I had the twelve-gauge in the Nissan. If I did, I could cover you a bit. Sure you don't want to head for the wagon with me and get the hell out of here?'

Charles shook his head. 'My guess is that, whoever it is, it's me he's after. If we go together he can cut us both down. If you go alone, there's a fair chance he'll let you go so he can concentrate on me. That way, there's a chance we might both survive.'

'He'll know I'm going for help.'

'He'll also know he's got at least twenty minutes — maybe double that time — before the police can come. Time to stalk his prey and still get out.'

'I guess you're right.' Jack sounded reluctant. 'Good luck.'

'Thanks. You too. We'll make a bolt for it together, going opposite ways. Might confuse our friend.'

The two men looked at each other for a moment, and a good deal that was unspoken was in that glance — the bond of comradeship created by a common danger, the silent but certain knowledge that each would risk his life for the other, notwithstanding that a few minutes ago they were strangers. 'Right,' Charles said quietly. 'Go.'

Bent low and weaving, Jack Henty ran towards the Nissan Patrol. At the same moment Charles made off in a crouching run in the opposite direction, jumping up a small riverside embankment to throw himself down behind a clump of low bushes growing around an alarmingly small rock.

No shot.

But was it only because the gunman, presented with two moving targets, had hesitated over which to choose?

The shallow gully up which Charles intended to try to work his way was still ten metres away, but at least it afforded better shelter than where he was now. He got up in the manner of a sprint runner in the starting-blocks, and launched himself in

30

a dash across fairly open ground and tumbled like a trained combat soldier into the shallow depression that was filled with rocks and small bushes.

He heard the four-wheel-drive vehicle start up and drive off fast, lurching over the rough ground of the open paddock.

No shot.

He let out a thankful breath: Jack Henty had made it. But now he was on his own, and he had no intention of staying passively where he was and waiting for the police, because the gunman could very well be trying to work his way around for another shot, and the cover in the gully was far from total. Charles was angry as well as scared — the sort of blazing anger which fear itself can generate as its own antidote — and the combination worked to sharpen his survival instincts.

Raising his head cautiously to peer through a screen of branches, he scanned the hillside above. He was pretty sure he knew where the shots had come from: a cluster of rocks up on the hillside where he and other neighbourhood children had played at being bushrangers lying in wait for imaginary stage-coaches.

They had also played, he recalled now with a flicker of rueful amusement, at being

31

troopers circling around to get above the hide and ambush the ambushers. And that was the role he must play now in deadly earnest. If he was spotted this time the penalty would not be just a childish voice shouting: 'Bang! You're dead, Charles!'

This gully didn't lead directly to the ambush site, but to another jumble of rocks some forty or fifty metres to its left and overlooking it. He was relieved to find the gully was almost exactly as he remembered it, even to the vegetation, though in places that was a shade more dense. He moved through it slowly, crouching and cautious, trying to be as quiet as possible and disturb the bushes in his path only marginally. He didn't wish to signal his movements to any watching eyes.

The day was pleasantly cool and crisp, but he could feel his shirt damp with sweat that had nothing to do with temperature or exertion. At every step he was acutely aware that if this gully provided cover for him to work his way *up* the hillside, it equally provided cover for a homicidal maniac working his way *down*, and the prospect of meeting him suddenly face to face around a shrubby bush was not one to relish.

At the head of the gully he stopped and

crouched, dismayed.

The great log of a fallen eucalypt which used to give cover to small stalkers over the last twenty metres and would still have given protection to his adult form if he had gone on hands and knees, was gone — burned long ago in a bushfire, it appeared. All that looked like cover now between where he was and the point where he could overlook the ambush site was a scatter of small bushes that wouldn't hide anything bigger than a rabbit.

Charles stayed crouched, trying to think carefully, to sort out the facts as he knew them, as distinct from the emotions they aroused.

Fact one: the gunman had a powerful rifle. Bad news. Fact two: he was a rotten shot, Charles thought grimly, or I wouldn't be here wondering about him now. Slightly better news. Third fact: he hadn't worried about Jack Henty getting away, because even if for some reason he hadn't wanted to harm Jack, or had failed to make a decision over which running man to shoot at, he'd had adequate time and firepower to disable the Nissan. He must have known Jack would raise the alarm and fetch the police, but for some reason that didn't matter. Why?

Because he was confident he could finish

Charles off and make his escape before help arrived?

That seemed the most probable answer. But *why*, damn you, Charles thought bitterly: what have I done that you want me dead?

He swallowed hard. Very well. He had to assume that homicide was the objective, never mind the reason. So what would the thinking gunman do in the circumstances? Either manoeuvre across the hillside to get a view of the rocks where Charles had originally taken shelter, or stay and wait in ambush in expectation of Charles trying to get to his car still parked out on the road.

In either of those cases, the chances were his attention would still be focused on the area by the river. A quick dash from where Charles was now, up and across the slope to the rocks above the hide, may well go unnoticed. Crouching, he broke cover and ran, feeling this would be the longest twenty metres he had ever run in his life — and probably the fastest, though it seemed to take minutes, and at every step he half-expected the smashing impact of a high-calibre bullet, his flesh cringing in anticipation. Then he was flinging himself down in a heap behind the rocks, the hammering of his heart pulsing in his ears. And there had been no shot.

He waited a moment, forcing himself to

take slow, deep, steadying breaths. Then, very cautiously, he raised his head just far enough to be able to peer over the rim of one of the lower boulders.

The ambush site was empty. He sank back to his knees; then instinctively whirled around to look behind him. There was no one in sight. No tricks, no traps. The gunman was gone.

Gone where?

Charles swore under his breath in fierce frustration that was sharpened by the chilling edge of fear. He couldn't be certain that in fact the gunman had ever been in that childhood hideaway below him. He had assumed it because it seemed the logical place, but the shots could have come from slightly higher up the hill, and in any case the shooter could now be anywhere on the hillside. Or, guessing Jack Henty had gone to call the police, he could have bolted.

Charles huddled, unmoving, for what seemed like half a day but was just over five minutes by his watch. Head raised again just enough for seeing over the rocks, he scanned the gully, the hillside, the river-banks, the area around the pool. No sign of movement, no sound of birds disturbed into sudden flight by a human intruder in their domain.

Charles looked down into the incomplete

circle of rocks again. If the shots had been fired from there, as he still believed, there should be spent shells, and he began to have a growing conviction that the police were likely to look on the whole thing with a good deal of scepticism unless there was some actual evidence. If the shots had been fired at him, which he also still believed, the shooter either didn't know where he was now, or he had left the area. Either way, it should be safe to go down to the ambush site.

He ran and scrambled down to the partial shelter of the lower rocks. A cheerful-sounding butcher-bird was the only sound. The butcher-bird continued his warbling, uninterested in human peculiarities, and gradually other birds began to resume their normal daily activities, restoring the river and hillside to the normal pattern of sound which had been shattered into alarmed silence by the rifle-shots. Funny, Charles thought: I was so busy with thoughts of my own survival I hadn't missed the bird-calls till they began again.

He looked at the ground around him — rocky ground with sparse grass; not ground which would reveal footprints. Not possible to tell if the grass had been flattened by someone sitting in wait there. There were no spent shells. If the shots had been fired from there, a careful gunman had picked them up. He hadn't been thoughtful enough to leave cigarette butts or chocolate wrappers, either.

The only thing to suggest human presence was a crumpled paper tissue the wind had blown half-under one of the boulders, and apparently the gunman hadn't noticed, or it wasn't his. Carefully Charles picked it up by one corner. It looked freshly dropped, but there hadn't been rain, for days and it could have blown from somewhere else.

Why, he wondered bitterly, wasn't it a handkerchief with the sod's initials on it instead of a one-of-millions anonymous paper tissue? He frowned, lifting it closer to his face. There *was* something about the tissue: a faint but definite scent of something.

Aftershave, most likely. The fact the scent still lingered suggested the tissue had been dropped by the hunter, but it could be a very commonly used aftershave, of no use in narrowing down suspects. He carefully pushed the tissue back where he had found it and settled down to wait.

And at once his imagination threatened him with mental pictures of a madman coolly walking up to shoot him at point-blank range; with imagined sounds of stealthy footsteps.

But the minutes passed. The birds went about their affairs unperturbed. Ten minutes, twelve. No one came. No one, Charles finally allowed himself to believe, was going to come.

Hard on the heels of that realization came the growing wail of police sirens and two police cars stopped beside Charles's car on the road, followed closely by Jack Henty's Nissan. Five policemen, all wearing flak-jackets and three of them carrying shotguns, jumped from the cars and began scanning the terrain while they kept the cars between themselves and the river, one of them motioning to Jack Henty to take the same cover.

'Mr Waring!' one called through a loud-hailer. 'Are you all right?'

'I'm fine,' Charles shouted, waving an arm. 'I'm up here on the hill. I'll come down. I think he's gone.'

'Stay where you are!' The officer sounded alarmed. 'We'll come up to you.'

Two policemen, one with a shotgun and the other with his revolver drawn, leapt over the stile and ran along the river-bank to scramble up to the rocks while the others crouched in firing positions behind the cars, ready to lay covering fire. Nothing happened.

As the two watchful young officers escorted him back to the cars, Charles began to feel swamped by an acutely embarrassing sense of anti-climax which was intensified by finding the senior officer was a detective inspector who gave every appearance of regarding the whole thing as a very minor incident which had been wildly over-dramatized.

'Are you quite unhurt, Mr Waring?'

'Yes, thank you.'

'Were any further shots fired after Mr Henty left?'

'No.'

'And you didn't at any time see the person who fired the shots?'

'No.'

'Mmm.' Inspector Rogerson was a tall, lean man with greying black hair and the look of a man who has seen too much rottenness to retain much faith in the human race. 'It seems most unlikely that whoever it was intended you any harm, Mr Waring, but we'll certainly do a search of the area. Careless hunters or target shooters can kill, as you would well know, and they have to be made aware that dangerous negligence can't be tolerated.'

He turned to Jack Henty and asked a few questions about the nature of the terrain, then deployed his men to search, with instructions they were to radio back to him if a suspect was sighted.

Charles said with a touch of anger, 'You think I'm overreacting to the whole thing.'

Inspector Rogerson shook his head. 'I assure you I'd feel exactly the same as you do. After all, if you're shot by accident you're just as dead as if you're shot deliberately. But the overwhelming odds are that this *was* an accident, and the shooter decided to scarper when he realized he'd nearly shot someone. Or maybe he just went off, never knowing what he'd almost done. Though,' he added drily as another car with media identification logos arrived, 'he'll no doubt read about it tomorrow.'

A reporter and a photographer, looking cheated at not being able to report a bullet-riddled body, interviewed Charles with a clear desire to extract all possible drama from the incident.

Inspector Rogerson stopped short of expressing his opinion it was all an accident, saying only that a thorough search of the area was being carried out and investigations would continue.

After half-an-hour's search it was called off, and the limited media attendance went home.

'One thing bothers me, Inspector,' Charles

said. 'If the whole thing was an accident, why didn't the fool stop shooting when I yelled at him that I was here? He'd have to have been deaf not to have heard me.'

'If in fact he was in those rocks where you thought he was,' Rogerson countered. 'With a big rifle, echoing off the hills, he might have been much further away than you thought. And we didn't find any evidence of anyone having hidden in those rocks.' He smiled. 'Except the tissue. I know. But it could have been blown there, or left there days ago by someone on a much less sinister errand.'

'But there was a scent on it — aftershave, I imagine, as I told you. That wouldn't last for long in the open air.'

The inspector shook his head. 'You may be right, sir, but none of us could detect anything like that on it.'

'Do you,' Charles said, *believe* it was a careless fool, or is that just something convenient to think?'

Rogerson's eyes narrowed for a second, but his tone remained unruffled. 'I've been a policeman long enough not to jump to easy conclusions, Mr Waring. There is something I haven't asked you: do you have any idea who might want to kill you, or why?'

'As to the 'who',' Charles said slowly, 'no, I have no idea. For the question of why — '

He hesitated. 'Yesterday, at a gathering of people who had just attended my mother's funeral, I almost unthinkingly said I couldn't believe her death was an accident. Probably a dozen people heard me say it, and no doubt spoke of it to others, so I have no idea of how many people know it was said. At the time I scarcely literally meant it. This makes me wonder whether I frightened someone.'

The inspector was watching him alertly, his demeanour suddenly changed. For a moment he was silent, and then he said quietly, 'Your mother was the lady who drove off Erskines' Road, wasn't she, Mr Waring?'

Charles nodded, and then looked at him sharply. 'How did you know she was my mother?'

'Oh, I know a good deal of what goes on in my district. I just like to know. And of course, accident assessment is a regular part of police work.'

'Did you view my mother's death with suspicion?'

'Not at all. It was a tragic accident, but unfortunately tragic single-vehicle accidents on roads entirely familiar to the driver are not all that uncommon. It's fully routine for us to check out a vehicle involved, to assess whether there was any mechanical failure contributing to the cause of the accident.'

42

'Was my mother's car — the wreckage of it — checked?'

'Certainly.'

'And nothing was found to be wrong?'

'No.'

'Is it possible to be certain, when a vehicle has been severely damaged?'

'It's unlikely any deliberate tampering would be overlooked, if that's what you're wondering. Things like accidental failure of brakes or steering, or a blown tyre, can be more difficult to detect. In view of your concern, I'll have our fellows go over the vehicle again.' He looked at Charles steadily. 'With special emphasis on making absolutely sure it hadn't been tampered with.'

Charles nodded. 'Thank you. I'd appreciate that, for my own peace of mind.'

Inspector Rogerson smiled, with a sudden very human twinkle in his eyes. 'And now I think it might be a good idea if you went home and had a stiff drink.'

Charles smiled ruefully in return. 'That might be a good idea. And — thanks, Inspector.'

The policeman waited until Charles turned to leave. 'You know,' he said mildly, 'there is one other point worth considering.'

Charles turned quickly. 'Yes?'

'How far is it from those rocks where you

think the shots were fired, to where you were standing beside the pool? In a direct line?'

Charles considered. 'Sixty metres, maybe seventy.'

'And the shooter used a heavy-calibre rifle like a Ruger. Dead-flat trajectory over a considerable distance. Awfully bad shot, wasn't he? And you weren't armed. If he'd wanted to kill you, he didn't even have to stay in hiding. He could have walked up and shot you at close range. I don't really think anyone tried to kill you, Mr Waring.' He nodded. 'We'll be in touch.'

3

Half an hour later, Charles sat in a comfortable chair in Jack Henty's sitting-room, having gratefully accepted his invitation for a drink before going back to the Erskine house. Jack's house was set in an attractive garden on the outskirts of Stanthorpe, and the room was a pleasant one with a much-lived-in look, with bookshelves, a fireplace, rugs scattered on a polished timber floor. Jack had been busy in the kitchen, but had just come back to settle into one of the other chairs, a glass in his hand.

He looked keenly at Charles and made the first reference to the thing which clearly was uppermost in both their minds. 'Do you think the police will do anything more to try to find who shot at you?'

'I don't think they believe anyone shot at me,' Charles said. 'I think it will be put down to a near-miss and a near-accident resulting from carelessness on the part of a person unknown.'

'Does that make you angry?'

'It did at first, because I was so angry with the shooter — angry because I was

45

dead scared there for a while, and nobody likes being frightened. But what else can the police do? They gave it their best shot in the search of the area, and turned up nothing. But for the fact that you were there when the last shot was fired, I couldn't blame them if they thought I'd made the whole thing up.'

'You weren't imagining it, I promise you,' Jack said drily.

Charles grinned. 'Quite. But I have to agree that the way the police see it has a lot going for it. I had to think that myself, when I stood in our old childhood hide among the rocks and looked down. He should never have missed with the first shot, not from there. I was standing still, in full view.'

He took a sip of the whisky. 'And even when he fired the second shot I was still standing there not believing it. He didn't even come perilously close, really. And when you came, why didn't he put a few shots into the Nissan and disable it? Then he could have come down and finished us off at his leisure; unless of course he genuinely didn't want to harm anyone except me.'

Jack Henty looked at the whisky in his glass. 'You go along with the careless-hunter theory?'

Charles hesitated. 'I don't know. It seems

the most logical explanation. But — I'm still sure those shots came from up among those rocks. If they did, he had to be angling the gun deliberately down the hill. To do that, and clear the rocks, I simply can't imagine that he wouldn't see me. Even if he didn't, why didn't he hear me shout a warning? And why did he carefully gather up the spent shells?'

'Maybe because he realized afterwards he'd nearly shot someone, and he was a bit anxious not to be identified by having those shells checked against locally-owned rifles,' Jack suggested.

'Maybe. But if it *was* deliberate, I'd have to agree with Inspector Rogerson that whoever it was didn't want to kill me. I think someone wanted to frighten me by making me think I was a target for murder. Someone wants me to leave town quite soon.'

There was a little silence, and then he went on, 'Well, he was right on two counts out of three.'

Jack raised a questioning eyebrow.

'He frightened me. He made me think I was a target for murder. But he failed on the third count: I'm not leaving just yet. I'm curious. I'm very curious indeed. Why *does* someone want me to leave? Why am I such a nuisance?'

The older man said slowly, 'Did you tell the police you dropped something of a bombshell yesterday by querying whether your mother's death was an accident?'

'Yes, I did. Apparently they'd already checked over the car for any sign of mechanical faults, albeit naturally-occurring ones. The inspector promised they'd check again — for sabotage, this time. But I'm sure he doesn't expect to find anything.'

He looked at Jack sharply. 'How did you know about that remark of mine? Were you there? Forgive me, I don't remember.'

'No, I wasn't there. I'd been visiting my brother in Sydney and only got back last night. But Pip was there — Philipa, my daughter. She told me.' He smiled and added, 'I believe you and she didn't get off to a very good relationship. She was the one who braked her car suddenly to avoid a cat, and made you run your car off the road.'

'Oh.' Charles nodded, embarrassed. 'I dare say she didn't have anything complimentary to say about me. I wasn't very nice to her about scratching the hired car. I'm afraid I was really the one to blame: I must have been travelling too close, and I suppose I had my mind on other things — perhaps especially that stupid remark I'd just made,

48

not intending it to be overheard. I felt a complete fool the moment I'd said it.'

'So you didn't believe a word you were saying?' a girl's voice said from the doorway. 'From what I hear, *someone* thought you meant it.'

Philipa — slim, auburn-haired, eyes disconcertingly brown instead of the blue her colouring would suggest — came briskly into the room.

'Pip,' Jack said, 'this is — oh, but of course, you've met.'

'Certainly have,' she agreed. 'Mr Waring believes I have either defective eyesight or a vivid imagination. And whichever it is, I'm a lousy driver. Are you all right, Dad?' she asked anxiously. 'There's a story circulating around town that you and Mr Waring were being *shot* at. Is that right?'

'I'm perfectly all right, and I'm sure I wasn't really being shot at. I just happened to come along when *Charles* was being shot at.' He chuckled suddenly. 'And I'm not so old and feeble that I can't take a bit of excitement now and then. So stop worrying.'

She had perched herself on the arm of her father's chair, a hand on his arm, looking slightly pale.

Pip. Watching her, Charles was struck by

an air of something about her which he could only define as strength — a strength that had nothing to do with her small, slight frame.

'Pip looks after me,' Jack was saying with an affectionate grin, and added as a flicker of a shadow fell across his face, 'I looked after her — and her brother, though he was older — when my wife died. One way and another, we helped each other survive, I guess. Dinner's ready to put on to cook,' he added to Pip — quickly, as if to shut off any comment on a past agony that was never far enough past. 'I prepared a bit extra for Charles, if he'll stay. Hope you don't mind.'

Pip smiled. 'Fine. I'll go get things cooking. You will stay for dinner, won't you?' she asked Charles. 'Then I'll feel better about your car.'

'I'd like to. Thank you. And I must apologize for my bad temper yesterday. The whole thing was my fault.'

She looked at him for a moment. 'You were under a lot of stress,' she said gently. She held out her hand. 'Friends?'

He took the outstretched hand. 'Friends.'

'And after dinner I want a first-hand account of everything that happened down by the river today. In detail.' She paused in the doorway and looked back at Charles, eyes twinkling. 'There really was a cat, you know.'

'I never doubted it for a moment,' Charles said.

'Liar,' she said cheerfully, and they both laughed as she disappeared in the direction of the kitchen.

★ ★ ★

The television newsreader had got down to the minor news items before the sports segment. 'Police in the Granite Belt area were called out this afternoon to what was initially believed to be a siege. Charles Waring told police he had gone for a walk beside the Severn River on the property of an old friend when a hail of bullets from a high-powered rifle forced him to take cover behind rocks. A neighbour called police, after he too was fired on. However, a thorough search of the area where the shooting took place failed to reveal any trace of the gunman, and while police say it appeared to be a deliberate attempt on Mr Waring's life, it is possible the shooter was either hunting or target-shooting, and say this afternoon's near-tragedy is a further confirmation of the wisdom of the government's tough anti-gun laws.

51

'And now here's Cal Fellows with today's round-up of sport.'

The person standing near the television set had stretched out a hand as if to shut it off halfway through the last news item, but had paused, staring as if fascinated.

A second person came into the room. 'What was that last item? Did I hear it right? Didn't it say Charles Waring had been *shot* at?'

'Charles? I wasn't really listening. Some sort of hoax or something, I think it was. Do you really think it said Charles?'

'I thought so, but I was in the bathroom and I didn't hear properly. It would be pretty hard on him if it *was* Charles — I mean, bad enough at any time, but after just losing his mother it would be especially nasty.'

'Yes, it would. Extraordinary.'

★ ★ ★

At the Henty house the conversation over dinner had remained around general topics, but when Pip had served coffee she said, 'Now tell me exactly what happened today.'

Charles and her father told their stories and she listened intently, her eyes concerned. 'It must have been pretty frightening,' she said finally.

'I've been happier,' Charles agreed. 'I think the worst moment was when I looked down into the hide and saw it was empty and realized I had no idea where the gunman was. It didn't occur to me that he'd bolted and left the job unfinished. I thought he was still there somewhere, stalking me. I suppose he must have left while I was working my way up the hill.'

'He could have left at any time, really,' Pip said. 'It's perfectly easy to get from that pile of rocks you call 'the hide' and over the shoulder and down to the road on the other side without being seen.'

She laughed when he flung her a startled glance. 'Don't forget my brother and I played over those hills when we were kids, too, and so did half of the neighbourhood kids. But if you look at it, you'll see there's quite enough cover on that side of the hill, on the opposite side to the rocks to where you went up. Anyone looking for the best spot for an ambush, leaving a vehicle out of sight, would have realized it was easy to come and go there without being seen. Whoever it was needn't ever have been there before.'

'Pip's right,' Jack Henty nodded. 'There is fair cover there.'

'Which strengthens the police theory of the careless shooter,' Charles said. 'If the shots were only fired from somewhere near those rocks instead of actually from behind them, then I couldn't see the gunman because he was behind bushes, and he wouldn't necessarily have seen me, either. That's certainly the logical explanation.'

'You can't believe it was an accident,' Philipa said sharply. 'You can't!'

Charles and Jack looked at her, taken aback by her vehemence. 'I didn't say I believed it,' Charles said slowly. 'But there are two alternatives: first, it was an accident, and the shooter hightailed it out of there when he realized what he'd almost done; or else he just left without ever knowing, which I doubt. The other alternative is that it was a deliberate ambush. And, as the inspector pointed out, the goon couldn't have been trying to kill me.'

'You *agree*?'

He nodded. 'I told your father before you came home. To my thinking, there are many things against the accident theory. There was surely nothing there to be hunted with that kind of firepower. And if he was doing some target practice, why there? There are plenty of more logical places. But if it was an ambush, no one who is any kind of reasonable shot should have missed me at all. My gut feeling is that someone wanted

54

to frighten hell out of me. At the time, of course, I thought he meant to kill me. But since I've had time to consider, I don't think that any more. I think he just wants to ensure my early departure for Canada — or anywhere else, for that matter.'

'So in fact,' Pip said carefully, 'someone is afraid of *you*.'

Charles hesitated. 'If my theory is right — yes, I guess so.'

'And,' Pip went on, 'if someone is afraid of you, it would have to be because you said you couldn't believe your mother's death was an accident. It would have to be because of that, wouldn't it?'

Charles was holding his coffee mug as if he had forgotten its existence, staring blankly at the far wall, his face taut. 'I guess you're right,' he said. 'I guess you're right.'

Philipa said softly, 'I'm sorry, Charles.'

He shook his head. 'It isn't easy to come to terms with the fact that your mother may have been murdered.'

There was a long silence as the last word seemed to lie in the room like something tangible, something as cold and bleak as a blast of the blackness of an Arctic night. Something that belonged only in news stories about total strangers.

Presently Jack said matter-of-factly, 'Look,

I don't want to pry into your affairs, but I should guess that your mother's estate would amount to something fairly substantial. Does anyone benefit financially by your absence?'

Charles shook his head. 'Not at all. Neither dead, nor alive and departed for foreign shores. I have a will which left everything to my mother, or in the event she predeceased me, leaves all my earthly possessions to a couple of charities. And all it amounted to anyway was a bit of money in a bank account and a battered four-wheel-drive station-wagon currently residing in a friend's yard in British Columbia. Any money my mother had left to her by Anthony goes to his children. So — '

He stopped as a sudden thought hit him. His earthly possessions now included a vineyard and winery. So he had learned this morning. This morning? It seemed a year ago. Ursula had left him Glenlodge.

'What is it, Charles?' Pip was watching him curiously, and he realized he must have looked as startled as he had momentarily felt.

'Sorry if I looked to be woolgathering. I just remembered the solicitor told me this morning that Mother had left me the winery. I can't get used to the idea. Anyway, that makes no difference to whether or not anyone among my stepfamily, or anyone else, benefits by my departure. They don't.'

'But they do benefit from your mother's death,' Jack said steadily, the inflection of his voice letting the words hover between query and statement.

'Considerably,' Charles agreed. 'Yes. But I can't see one of them committing murder, damn it!' He thumped one fist into the palm of his other hand. 'They're just — just ordinary people!'

There was another silence. Then he sighed. 'Yes, I know. Most murderers seem to be just ordinary people. Until.'

Pip looked at him silently for several seconds, as if she were trying to assess something. 'Ursula mightn't have been killed for gain,' she said. 'It needn't have been family. We don't know what the motive was.'

'We don't know that it was murder,' Charles countered.

'Why else was someone shooting at you? Even if it was only to frighten you into leaving? You say we can rule out good old-fashioned gain as a motive for getting rid of you. And it needn't have been a family member you frightened. It could have been anyone who was within earshot when you made that remark yesterday.'

'Or anyone who was told about it later,' Charles agreed ruefully. 'It seems a lot easier to put it down to a careless hunter.'

'Don't talk like that!' Pip said sharply. 'You know you don't believe it.'

'No,' Charles nodded wearily, 'I don't. I wish I did, that's all. It would make everything so much simpler.' He looked at her with a frown. 'But just a minute: why are you so sure Mother's death wasn't an accident? You *are* sure, aren't you?'

Pip's hands were clenched tightly in her lap, and she looked down at them for a moment. 'Yes,' she said quietly. 'I'm sure. I've been terribly certain of it from the beginning — from the moment I heard about it. But I had nothing, really, to go on, and if I'd gone around blurting out suspicions like that everyone would have thought I was just being hysterical.'

Jack stared at her. 'You didn't say anything to me. I know I only got home last night, but — '

'I know, Dad. I didn't say anything to anyone. I didn't see how I could. Until the shooting this afternoon there wasn't anything to make anyone believe a word I'd say.'

'But you must have had a reason to think of foul play.'

'Nothing concrete.' She sighed. 'That's

been the problem. You can't go around saying you think something's happened when you haven't a shred of evidence of it. You'll probably both think I'm dramatizing even now.'

No one spoke and after a moment she went on, 'Your mother and I were very good friends, Charles, in spite of the difference in our ages. For the past couple of months, Mrs Erskine — Ursula — seemed absent-minded and under some kind of stress. She was a very good chess player who could run rings around me as a rule, and she was also a whiz at Scrabble, and clever at cards. I enjoy games, too, and often at the weekends or in the evenings I'd go out to her place for a games session, as Dad can tell you. Sometimes Jill would go out also — she often spent a weekend out there with Ursula. They got on very well.'

She flicked a glance at Charles. 'I'll miss your mother. Very much.'

Her voice caught for a second and then she said, 'Suddenly, as I say, a couple of months ago, I could beat her at chess most of the time. She'd make mistakes or foolish moves. At first I thought she was doing it deliberately to let me win so I wouldn't get discouraged, and I confess I grew a bit annoyed at being treated like a small child.'

She shook her head. 'But it happened in other games as well, and I realized something was wrong. She seemed unable to concentrate, and I became concerned, because of the way she looked, as well. She was pale and looked as if she wasn't sleeping, and she was losing weight. Eventually I asked her if she was ill, and she looked at me for a minute as if she was trying to decide whether to tell me something or not. Then she said: 'I'm well enough, Pip'. She got up and went to the window as if she was looking out, but I don't think she was seeing anything. 'I'm afraid, Pip. There's something I have to find out, something I hope I'm wrong about. I hope I'm wrong, but I'm so terribly afraid I'm not'. Then she turned and smiled and said to forgive her silly talk, and she came back to the table and finished the game.'

The men were watching Phillipa in silence.

'That was about three weeks ago,' she went on. 'Ursula continued looking ill and distracted. I was concerned and I think Jill was, also, but I didn't like to mention it again. Then one evening when we'd been playing Canasta — just Ursula and me — she put down the cards as if she didn't know why she had them in her hand, and said: 'Pip, do you think people change?' I said cheerfully, 'Sure, all the time'. And she said: 'I mean

60

evil people, cruel people'.

'I was a bit stunned, but I said no, I didn't believe so. 'No,' she said, 'neither do I. I have to decide something, Pip, and I don't know what's best to do. I just don't know'. 'She was speaking quietly, but there was — oh, I don't know — a kind of desperation in her voice. I was rather shocked, and I just sat there feeling useless because I didn't know what to say. She seemed to have forgotten for a minute that I was there, and then suddenly remembered and looked up at me. 'I'm sorry', she said. 'I shouldn't have said anything. I'd no right to unload my worries on you. And please, I must ask you not to say a word of this nonsense to anyone. *Not anyone*. Please promise'.

'I promised, of course, and she said, 'I'm exaggerating things'. But that wasn't what she'd thought a moment before. And three days later her car went over a cliff.'

4

Charles drove into the town next day to visit the police station. Beyond that, he wasn't sure what he was going to do. He had spent a night when sleep had been hard to come by, his mind too active to shut down. But the mental activity had been frustrating and unproductive, leaving him with nothing but a tight, cold anger.

If Ursula, his brightly intelligent mother, with her kindness and her ready laugh, had been callously murdered, he wanted that murderer caught. He wanted that very much.

More, even, than that. He wanted that person dead.

He was faintly shocked that the intensity of his anger should make him want the total revenge. He would never have regarded himself as a vindictive person. Civilization, he reflected, was only a very thin veneer that was all too ready to peel away under pressure.

And he knew, also, that even now his anger might not be justified. The shadow of an unknown killer might be no more than that — a shadow in his mind, a subconscious wish to turn his grief into anger against a real foe instead of against nothing more substantial than cruel chance. Perhaps Ursula Erskine had simply met with an accident; perhaps the worries she had spoken of to Pip — perhaps those and the trigger-happy gunman by the river had been simply coincidental.

He had had an early phone call from Sandford, sounding concerned. 'Charles! I've just seen the newspaper. It says — is it right?'

'If it says I had someone put a few slugs uncomfortably close to me yesterday, then yes, it's right.'

'Good God! Do you go along with the theory that it was some goon who didn't know you were there?'

'I'm convinced no one was trying to shoot me.' Sandford didn't seem to notice it wasn't quite the same thing.

Sandford had barely hung up when there was a similar call from Jill, who did note that 'no one trying to kill' did not necessarily mean accident.

'What are you saying?' she demanded.

'It may have been an accident,' Charles said carefully. 'It may have been a warning.'

'A *warning*? Why?'

'The only thing I can think of is my unwillingness to accept that my mother's death was accidental. It may have been a warning to me to leave well — or ill — alone.'

There was a silence. 'That,' Jill said very quietly, 'raises something quite horrible.'

'Yes,' Charles answered.

'For God's sake, Charles, what are you going to do?'

'Wait a while, I guess. And see.'

To his surprise she said, 'Yes. Yes, I suppose you must. But, Charles, be careful, won't you?'

'I shall indeed.'

★ ★ ★

He was shown into Inspector Rogerson's office almost at once. The inspector smiled and waved Charles to a chair. 'I'm afraid we've nothing further on the gunman, Mr Waring, and equally never likely to have, I regret to say, unless he decides to come forward when he reads this morning's paper, and admit he was responsible. But I honestly feel it was not an attempt on your life.'

Charles nodded. 'I agree with that. With hindsight.'

The inspector looked at him with one

eyebrow raised quizzically, but merely said, 'Ah.'

He picked up a folder from his desk. 'I had our vehicle expert go over Mrs Erskine's car again, in detail. Specifically examining it for any indications of tampering of any kind, mechanical or otherwise. He reports there is no evidence whatever. No tampering with brakes, steering, gears. Tyres in good condition, though of course a sudden flat — coming off a wheel rim or some such — can't be ruled out after the damage the tyres have since sustained. In the accident, that is. Overall, there is no damage which is not entirely consistent with a vehicle crashing over those boulders.'

'I see.' Charles thought for a moment. Then he reached into his jacket pocket and produced a sheet of notepaper. 'Just one more thing, Inspector. My mother, it seems, expressed grave concerns to a friend about not knowing what to do in connection with someone she described as 'evil'. That may not sound important to you, but evil is a very strong word which Mother would not have used lightly.'

He handed the sheet of paper across the desk. 'I would very much appreciate it if you could tell me whether any of these people have a criminal record.'

The inspector took the sheet of paper, but his eyes remained fixed on Charles. 'You're persistent, aren't you, Mr Waring? Would you tell me something? A minute ago you said you didn't think yesterday's gunman was trying to kill you. Yet you persist in your belief your mother was the victim of foul play. Yesterday, you thought the two were inextricably linked. Why have you changed your mind?'

Charles shook his head. 'I don't necessarily *believe* my mother met with foul play. I suspect it is a possibility. I don't have any answers. Only questions. My mother referred to someone she knew as being evil. A few days later, she died. I made a remark — easily overheard, unfortunately — that I didn't believe her death was an accident. Next day someone loosed a fistful of bullets very close to me. I wouldn't be human if that didn't raise a few questions in my mind. But I agree that the gunman didn't try to kill me. Either he didn't know I was there, or he was trying to frighten me off. I don't know which, Inspector. That's not a very comfortable feeling.'

Inspector Rogerson went on studying him for a string of seconds, then without comment he read the paper Charles had given him, and looked up again.

'These are your stepbrother and sisters.'

'And, in two cases, their spouses, yes. Jill Erskine isn't married.' He looked at the inspector keenly. 'You, of course, can get that information readily enough, can't you? Surely you can give it to me?'

Rogerson frowned. 'Mmm. Very well, I can tell you this: none of the people on your list have any criminal record.'

He smiled at the startled expression on Charles's face. 'Does that surprise you?'

Charles shook his head. 'Well, no. I simply wondered, that's all. What surprises me is that you checked the Erskine family backgrounds. You don't do that after every fatal accident.'

'It was a slightly unusual accident, given the circumstances, and some people stood to gain quite a lot of money in consequence. Certainly there were — and are — no suspicious circumstances. I was curious, that's all.'

Charles stood up. 'Thank you, Inspector. I don't want to waste any more of your time. And — I really appreciate what you've done.'

He held out his hand and the inspector shook it. 'You're returning to Canada, Mr Waring?'

'Not just yet,' Charles said. 'There are

some things I have to tie up first.'

'Of course. Your mother's estate details. Goodbye, Mr Waring. You've been through a very stressful time,' he added unexpectedly. 'I'm sorry.'

He went on sitting motionless behind his desk for several minutes after Charles had gone. 'It was an accident, Mr Waring,' he said very softly. 'There is not the faintest evidence of anything else. It must have been an accident. If you would just believe that, I might be able to believe it also.'

* * *

Charles walked down the street, almost oblivious to his surroundings, asking himself the same question that had haunted the dark hours when he should have been sleeping. What had his mother learned about someone?

Ursula Erskine was not given to dramatic overstatements. Evil was not a word she would use without good reason. If the person were part of the family, that evil was not on record. Yet Pip had seen her profoundly disturbed by her knowledge, and that seemed to suggest that the person concerned was someone close to her, someone important to her.

Someone close, and the evil not known, apparently, to anyone but Ursula.

'Are your thoughts worth the proverbial penny?' asked the girl who, unnoticed, had fallen into step beside him.

He stopped short and looked down at Philipa Henty. 'I doubt it,' he smiled. He looked at his watch. 'Have you had lunch, or can you tear yourself away from work long enough?'

'No to the first, you betcha to the second. If you'll share the worthless thoughts over a sandwich.'

They found a quiet corner of a coffee shop and he told her about his visit to Inspector Rogerson. 'So where do you go from here?' she asked, her face intent with interest.

'I think,' he said thoughtfully, 'I shall pay a few friendly visits to my various stepsiblings and their spouses, and gently try to winkle a little information from them. About what, I'm not entirely sure. Past nastiness, perhaps.'

'Are they going to tell you things like that?'

'Probably not — at least not about themselves. But they may drop a hint or two about other members of the family. And sometimes it's surprising what people tell you about themselves without actually telling you anything at all.'

She laughed. 'You sound more like a detective than a geologist.'

He sighed. 'I'm more at home with igneous rocks, I assure you.' His jaw muscles tightened. 'But if there's any chance some bastard killed my mother, I'll play detective to the hilt.'

Pip reached across the table and put her hand on his arm wordlessly. After a moment she said, 'When are you going out to the winery?'

'Glenlodge? Oh, I don't know. I hadn't intended to go at all — just let John Farrell handle the sale of it. But now that I might be around for a while, I suppose I must go out and talk to the people who work there. They need to know what's happening. If I'd been leaving as soon as I intended, I'd have left John to deal with all that, but now I guess I'd better do the decent thing and at least go out and talk with the people who staff the place.'

'Aren't you interested in it? You grew up there, didn't you?'

'I left when I was barely eighteen and didn't see much of it after that. And I don't know the first thing about wine-making.'

'You wouldn't need to. Ursula always

70

said she didn't have a sufficiently delicate palate to be a wine-maker. That's why she employed Rob Carlyle. And he is very good. Ursula managed the place and he made it worth managing. That's what she used to say.'

Charles was looking at her in wry amusement. 'You can't think I'd want to stay and run Glenlodge Wines?'

Her brown eyes studied him earnestly. Then she shook her head. 'I don't know enough about you to know what sort of person you are. But I think running Glenlodge would be a most exciting challenge.'

'More exciting than igneous rocks?'

'All right, you're laughing at me. But at least go out and see the place. Ursula left it to you. You owe her that much.'

'I owe it to her,' he said, with an edge of anger in his voice, 'to find out whether someone killed her.'

She looked away and fiddled with her coffee cup. 'I'm sorry. I didn't mean to lecture.'

He shrugged and stood up. 'And I didn't mean to snap. Look, I'm going to Toowoomba this afternoon. I'll stay overnight and pay a friendly call to Miriam and Douglas. The day after tomorrow is Saturday. I'll go out to the winery then.' He paused.

71

'Will you go with me, out to Glenlodge?'

'I'd like that. What about Marmaduke and Aristotle if you're going to be away tonight and tomorrow? Would you like me to go out and feed them?'

He shook his head. 'I'll feed Marmaduke and leave some dried food and plenty of water before I go. Aristotle has automatic seed and water dispensers, but I'll make sure they're topped up. And I'll tell Jill I'm going. But thank you for offering.'

She nodded approval of his concern for Ursula's pets. 'I'll see you on Saturday.' She hesitated. 'Will you tell me if you learn anything significant at the Wentworth place? I haven't any right to ask that,' she added quickly.

'I'll tell you,' he said, his face serious. 'Though I don't have the faintest idea of how to go about learning anything. I'm not even sure what reason I'm going to produce to account for my sudden visit. After all, I know even less about horse-studs than I do about wine-making, if that's possible. I certainly don't expect to come up with any dramatic solutions. I don't even know if there's anything to solve.'

On the street, they turned to go their separate ways, and then Pip turned back. 'Charles.'

He stopped and looked at her questioningly. 'You will . . . be careful, won't you?'

He raised an eyebrow. 'You mean in case someone takes another pot-shot at me?'

'I mean Ursula knew something she didn't really want to know. That knowledge may have cost her her life.'

She turned and walked away quickly.

Charles stood staring after her as she disappeared among other pedestrians, startled not so much by her concern as by his reaction.

'Charles, my boy,' he said to himself, 'you could become addicted to that girl.'

It was only when two or three passers-by glanced at him curiously that he realized he had spoken aloud.

★ ★ ★

He returned the hired car to the company's local office, dealt with the matter of the scraped mudguard, and took a taxi back to the house. The solicitor had assured him there was no reason he shouldn't take possession of his mother's car, since it was his under the 'rest and residue' clause of her estate, and the necessary paperwork had been dealt with accordingly. The little Suzuki in which Ursula had been killed was her runabout work car. A white BMW, a gift to her from Anthony, was in the garage of the house.

When he arrived back at the Erskine house, to be greeted by the customary gritty, 'Hello, larrikin' from Aristotle, he walked slowly through, from room to room, really looking at it for the first time, trying to learn something more of Ursula through the furnishings and general decor of the rooms. The house Anthony Erskine had built for her, and which now doubtless would be sold by his children, was large and tended towards formality, almost ostentation, with slate-tiled veranda and marble-floored entrance hall. But it was furnished simply and tastefully and achieved a comfortably lived-in look. Some pieces of furniture Charles remembered: a silky-oak bookcase, a cedar desk in the study, a wing-backed chair of tan leather.

Trailed by a cautiously friendly Marmaduke, he went into Ursula's room for the first time, knowing he had been deliberately avoiding it, and knowing he could not go on doing so. It was just as she had left it when she went out of the house for the last time — a jacket tossed across the foot of the bed, a couple of letters on the dressing-table, apparently waiting to be posted, an alarm-clock set for

74

5.30. Everything with an air of waiting for her to walk in.

He opened the wardrobe door and flicked a glance over her clothes, then shut it again quickly. He would have to get someone — Jill, probably — to help him sort out Ursula's personal things. He hadn't stopped to think, previously, that it would have to be done. Some organization which helped the needy would doubtless accept things like clothes. He turned away, feeling depressed, feeling frustrated anger at a life so needlessly extinguished. Feeling the shaking, gut-wrenching empty grief for someone loved.

He was left with the odd feeling that this was a stranger's house and he was an intruder — a feeling that was only partly due to the knowledge that it belonged to his stepfamily and he was there only because it suited them to have him there, and soon he would have to move out so that it could be placed on the market. Then he would have to decide whether to go back to Canada when his leave ran out, or — if he felt his investigations were unfinished but had a chance of resolution — he would have to find somewhere else to stay.

But his feeling of not-belonging was naturally mostly due to the fact that he had never spent much time here, coming only to stay during holidays. And he felt, almost frustratingly, that the house hadn't taken on much of his mother's personality, in the sense that he couldn't feel that she had been particularly fond of it — not in the way he knew she had been attached to the house at Glenlodge.

He told himself he was being fanciful. He fed Marmaduke and left the laundry door open for him to sleep there, checked that Aristotle had adequate food and water, and told them, 'Sorry, fellers, but I won't be back till tomorrow evening. You'll be all right till then, though, won't you?'

He called in to the veterinary surgery on his way through town and told Jill he'd be away overnight, but had made provision for the cat and bird. She nodded and said, 'Thanks, Charles. If you find you're going to be away longer, let me know so I can check up on them. I have a key, because I always looked after them when Ursula was away.'

She seemed to accept that it was perfectly natural that he was going to visit Miriam and Douglas, and he supposed that it was, in fact.

He drove northwards, the orchard and vineyard country presently giving way to lightly timbered grazing land, and then, almost abruptly, the harsher land was left behind, yielding to the rich, dark soil of the great Darling Downs, with its fields of grain and sunflower and various other crops, some of the fields ploughed and not yet under crop — a huge, scarcely rumpled patchwork quilt of splendid farmland.

In the city with its reddish soil of a fertility that made it famous for the private gardens its citizens took such pride in, he booked into a pleasant motel, and next morning enquired the way to Top Bend horse stud. It was quite a distance out of the city, and by the time he drove up the drive with its cypress avenue, the sharp frostiness of the early spring morning was fading to pleasant mildness in the sun. The timber house was long, low-set and painted white, and there were flower-beds and trim lawns and hedges. An off-shoot of the gravelled drive ran past the house and beyond white-painted gates and curved around in a direction which suggested that it led to the stables and yards. A double garage stood open and empty, which indicated that Douglas had gone to his surgery and Miriam was probably with the horses.

Charles walked along the drive past the house, the gate opening with a well-oiled click and swinging with silent ease on its hinges. Everything, Charles thought, spoke quietly but firmly of prosperity. Not wealth, perhaps, but certainly prosperity. There was nothing at Top Bend, outwardly at least, to suggest an urgent need for Ursula Erskine's money.

The general atmosphere of a well-cared-for property was continued at the business end of the place — the stables and yards. The stables held a number of stalls in two rows facing a courtyard. Beyond was a large shed which Charles assumed was a barn or machinery shed; and extensive yards with white-painted timber post and rail fences. He caught a glimpse of sweeping pastures beyond the buildings, with horses grazing, brood mares with foals at foot.

A dark-haired woman of medium height, dressed in jeans and gumboots and sweater was deep in conversation with a fair, lean man similarly dressed. They were standing at a gate, looking down across the paddocks, their backs to Charles, and turned when he spoke. 'Hello, Miriam.'

'Charles! Is there something wrong?' She seemed neither pleased nor displeased to see him, merely surprised. There had been, Charles had noted, no concerned or curious phone call from her or Douglas following reports of the shooting. 'Oh.' She bit her lip. 'Did you want help with sorting out Ursula's things? I'm sorry. I simply didn't think of that. I guess it's extra hard for a man.'

He shook his head. 'That's all right. I can manage, though I'll probably ask Jill to help, since she's closer to the house. If there's anything you'd like — books, music, jewellery or anything, please just tell me. I'd be very happy for you to have her personal things shared among you. I've no idea what jewellery she had, but as I recall she didn't care for it much.'

'She had very little, I think,' Miriam agreed. 'But thank you for the thought, Charles — it's very nice of you. I should like something — a couple of books, perhaps — as a keepsake.' She glanced at the man who stood watchfully beside her.

'Charles, this is Garth Williams, my right hand when it comes to the horses. My stepbrother, Charles Waring, Garth.'

As the men shook hands, Garth Williams looked at Charles with interest. 'That's the name of the bloke who was shot at, day before yesterday,' he commented, making it half a question.

Charles nodded. 'I'm afraid that's the name and that's the bloke.'

Miriam stared at him. '*Shot* at? Charles! What — ?'

'Well, shot at isn't strictly correct, I'm sure,' Charles said easily. 'The police believe it was an accident.'

'Good grief!' Miriam looked shocked. 'How did you know about it?' she asked Garth Williams.

'Read about it in the paper,' he said. 'Didn't know he was related to you.'

'We only came home yesterday, early,' Miriam told Charles. 'We met friends who asked us to stay on an extra night and have dinner with them. So, with rushing back to work yesterday we didn't read the papers. I'm sorry, Charles. You must have thought us rather off-hand not even to enquire if you were all right. Do — did the police find out who did it?'

'No. He'd left the area before the police arrived.'

So Miriam and Douglas had stayed in town. They had *all* been in the vicinity — all his stepfamily. If that had any significance.

Miriam, looking slightly rattled, which was unlike Miriam as far as he knew her, said, 'Look, Charles, I've absolutely got to make a quick dash into town — I shouldn't be more than an hour. One of my teeth has lost a filling and I have a dental appointment. Can

80

you wait till I get back? And stay for lunch? I've got to hear more about this shooting thing. And by then my tooth will be feeling much happier.'

'Sure. I can wait, if you don't mind me wandering around the stables and things. What I don't know about horse studs fills all the books on the subject.'

She gave him a quick smile. 'Fine. If there's anything special you want to know, Garth will help, I'm sure. And I'll leave the house unlocked — make yourself a cup of tea or anything you fancy.' She hurried off.

If there's anything special you want to know, Garth will help. Oh, yes, Charles thought, there are things I want to know; but somehow I'm not sure Garth will help me find out. Not if he knows he's helping.

There was that air of watchfulness about Garth Williams — an intensity in the blue eyes which suggested very little would escape Garth's notice. Maybe that came from being responsible for valuable animals, or maybe it was a necessary qualification for anyone who was caring for such animals. Garth was a man about Miriam's age, Charles guessed. In the few minutes of seeing them together, he had gained the impression that they were very good friends, and he wondered fleetingly if it went beyond friendship on Garth's part.

'Do you and Miriam run the place on your own, or are there other employees?' Charles made it a casual question, wanting to at least begin a conversation.

'Top Bend is a relatively small stud,' Garth answered pleasantly, rather as if he was accustomed to answering questions from people who hadn't the least idea about horse studs, 'but it certainly needs more than two people to run it. It's especially busy when the mares are dropping their foals, particularly as they have to go to the stallion soon after foaling. Most of the mares you see here aren't Miriam's. They've come here to be mated with one of her stallions — she has one exceptional stallion. But she does own some mares of her own, of course. We put on extra hands for the busiest times. Otherwise there's myself — I have a cottage on the property — and two young lads and Liz Fitzgibbon as permanents.'

Charles reflected a moment. 'There must be rather a lot of valuable horse-flesh walking around at times.'

Garth looked faintly amused at the understatement. 'Rather a lot,' he answered laconically.

Charles glanced at what he could see of heads poked inquisitively over stable doors. Then he recalled very roughly how many mares with foals he had seen out grazing, and did an even rougher mental assessment of the possible value of the merchandise currently walking around Top Bend, and whistled softly.

Garth, clearly aware of Charles's line of thinking, allowed himself a small smile. 'Quite,' he said.

'I think horses are truly beautiful creatures,' Charles said, sensing Garth's contempt for the unoriginal comment, 'but I don't know the first practical thing about them. I don't want to get in your way — I know you're busy — but is it all right if I just wander around? I promise not to harm the merchandise.'

'Sure. Anywhere you like. I'll be around the stables for a while if you want me for anything.' He swept a quick glance over Charles, approving, Charles thought, of his dress of boots and jeans and jacket, all of them obviously well-worn. 'You might like to go down the paddock a bit and look at the brood mares that have foals.'

'Thanks,' Charles said.

He made his way down to the pastures where mares, with their foals frisking all around, grazed contentedly. In one paddock several youngsters which, he guessed, would probably be put up for auction at the next yearling sales, were gleefully showing their race-track potential with spontaneous gallops, heads high, manes flying, muscles rippling under glossy coats. He watched them, smiling in real pleasure at their grace and beauty, wondering how on earth anyone could look at them and decide which, among such splendid creatures, would be a potential winner of The Oaks or The Melbourne Cup.

He said as much to Garth Williams when he returned to find him cleaning out a stable.

Garth studied him for a moment as if trying to decide whether it was an idle I-had-to-say-something question or whether it deserved a serious answer. He opted for the second.

'There are a great many factors to take into consideration,' he said quietly. 'You have to know the physiology of horses, naturally. You have to know the animal's blood-line — who its parents and grandparents were and what they did — aunts and uncles and brothers and sisters, too, for that matter. And, of course, you're looking for different attributes for different purposes. I mean, whether you want a sprinter or a stayer, or a hurdler, for that matter; and what a youngster will mature into. And — ' He paused, and for a moment his face took on an almost

84

dreamy quality, as if he had forgotten Charles was there.

'There are other things,' he said slowly. 'Things you can't define and can't teach. Maybe something in the way an animal moves, or holds its head. Maybe something about its eyes. Something you can feel. It only comes with experience and it comes to very few.'

He gave a quick, almost embarrassed laugh. 'And the best judges in the world can fall for a dud. And mugs can accidentally choose a champion.' He shrugged. 'Not that *that* happens very often.'

'My stepsister is a good judge?' Charles asked.

'Very. Of course, as you probably realize, much of the income of a stud farm comes from its stallions. Owners of highly rated mares will pay a handsome service fee to breed their mares to a top stallion. All three stallions here have excellent blood-lines and one had an outstanding track record before he was retired to stud, and that automatically puts him in demand as a sire.'

Charles considered asking what sort of fee such a stallion might command, but looked at Garth's wary eyes and thought better of it, asking instead, 'How would Top Bend's horses rate — say, yearling sales?'

He saw Garth stiffen slightly and withdraw into himself. 'They're well respected,' he said coolly, in a manner which clearly said he was not going to discuss Miriam's business affairs.

'Sorry,' Charles said at once. 'I wasn't meaning to pry. I simply don't know my stepfamily very well, and I'm just interested in them and the things they do. I gather Miriam is very proud of this place, as well she might be. She must be very fond of the horses, I should imagine. She strikes me as a kind person.'

He didn't know her well enough, in fact, to form an opinion. But Ursula had called someone evil, cruel, and Charles wanted to throw out a feeler.

The blue eyes were cool and unresponsive. 'An unkind person can't run a successful horse stud,' Garth said flatly.

Charles saw his glance shift and heard a movement behind him. He turned. A slight, wiry, dark-haired young woman had emerged from one of the stables. 'Miriam cares about her horses,' she said. 'But she never lets sentiment stand in the way of business.'

'You can't, if you're going to be successful,' Garth said. 'This is Charles Waring, Miriam's stepbrother. Liz Fitzgibbon.'

Liz Fitzgibbon nodded. 'Hello. I suppose

86

you're right, Garth, but I can't ever forget the Echelon colt. Rambo's fine,' she added. 'He enjoyed a bit of a workout. I think he still misses the track. Beau Rameses,' she added to Charles. 'We call him Rambo for short. Did you ever see him race?'

Charles shook his head, smiling. 'I don't know the first thing about horses or racing, except that I've heard a lot of people enthusing about how much you can win by backing horses, but rarely about how much they actually *have* won.'

'But you've heard of him, of course.'

'Sorry. I've been overseas for several years.'

'Really? What a pity. Not to have seen him run, I mean.'

'He was good, then?'

'He was brilliant. Come and see him.' Liz Fitzgibbon's eyes shone with pride as if Beau Rameses was a personal achievement. 'Back in ten minutes, Garth. Do you want to check that mare for yourself?'

'Maybe later,' Garth said easily, and went on with his shovelling.

'Why was this stallion retired?' Charles asked as they walked down past the stables to where a proud black stallion was in the act of rolling gleefully in the sand in a special sand-pit.

'He tore tendons and cracked bones and

87

did all sorts of nasty things to himself in a bad fall. It ended his racing career much too early and he was retired to stud. In fact, at first it was feared he might have to be put down.'

Beau Rameses, hearing Liz's voice, came swiftly to his feet, almost as if embarrassed at being caught so joyously enjoying a simple roll in the sand. Not really the behaviour of an aristocrat, he seemed to say apologetically. And even Charles could see that this was indeed an aristocrat.

'He's magnificent,' he said quietly.

'Isn't he, though?' The black horse came to the wooden rail and nibbled at Liz's shoulder. 'That is one hunk of valuable horse-flesh. By the end of his last racing season, if he'd been able to go on, he looked a certainty to top the million-dollar mark in earnings. For that season alone.'

Charles was startled. 'He must have been a gold-mine for Miriam and Douglas.'

'Oh, Miriam didn't own him then. She only bought him after he'd been retired. He should prove to be a small gold-mine at stud, of course, because his success naturally lifts the prospective value of his progeny. He cost a small gold-mine to buy, I assure you, even though Miriam bought him when it wasn't certain he wouldn't be too crippled even for stud. I was a bit surprised Miriam went that far in debt for him, but of course he'll be well and truly worth it in time.'

'You speak of Miriam,' Charles said. 'Doesn't Douglas have an interest in the horses?'

Liz laughed shortly, rubbing Beau Rameses' nose affectionately. 'It depends what you mean by an interest,' she said drily. 'But the stud is Miriam's. He doesn't have a partnership in it.'

Charles looked at her curiously, aware of something cynical underlying her tone. 'But he's interested in the horses,' he said neutrally.

'Horses, dogs, football, two flies crawling up a wall — anything you can put a bet on. Oh,' she said quickly, 'don't misunderstand me. I'm very fond of Douglas. He's a very nice man, and he's a good doctor, and I owe him and Miriam a lot. But he's a compulsive gambler. That's why he doesn't have a partnership in Top Bend stud — he'd ruin it. Miriam's had to bail him out of debt more than once, I know, so she knows better than to let him lose Top Bend money as well as his medical practice income.'

Liz looked up at Charles suddenly, concern in her face. 'I sound like a rat, telling you this, though it's pretty common knowledge anywhere around the race tracks. Only — I think Douglas gambles in a good deal heavier way than Miriam knows. She believes he's reformed.'

'I see,' Charles said cautiously. 'Do you think he still might be in debt?'

'I don't know. I've heard that he quite often bets in thousands, and often loses, naturally. It seems he spreads his bets around by getting other people to put his money on for him, even on different courses. That way, it looks as if he's keeping his bets at a reasonable level, when all the time he's being quite reckless. But how much of that is only rumour I'm not sure. Possibly not much. It's a terrible curse,' she added rather grimly. 'My father was a compulsive gambler and I know what it did to our household. I'd hate to see this place ruined because of gambling, too.'

'But if Top Bend is entirely in Miriam's name, that can't happen, surely,' Charles suggested, feeling oddly touched by the genuine distress in the girl's eyes, and her willingness to confide her worries to him, because he had the distinct feeling that she was not a gossipy person who chattered about her employers' affairs to all and sundry.

'He can't spend Top Bend money,' she agreed. 'But if he got into real debt — and I mean *big* debt — well, I guess Miriam would stick by him, whatever it cost.'

'Even her horses?'

'Could be. Look,' she added quickly, as if confirming his thoughts. 'I don't go around talking about the Wentworths' affairs. But it scares me, sometimes. Because of my own family, I guess. I'm not quite sure why I've been telling you, but I suppose I just feel someone ought to *know*, and when Garth said you were family — ' She hesitated, then smiled wryly. 'You got elected as my confessor. Sorry. I don't see what you or anyone else can do about the situation, anyway.'

'Thank you for telling me, Liz. I guess there isn't anything I can do about it, but sometimes it's helpful to know these things. At least it can stop me from putting my foot in it sometime.'

He rubbed the stallion's neck. 'What was that about the Echelon colt?'

'Oh, that.' She shrugged. 'I was just annoyed with Garth doing his nothing-out-of-place-ever-happens-here act. It was just before the yearling sales two years ago. There was this top-notch bay colt by Echelon out of a good mare and he was expected to bring a very good price at the sales. Someone failed to latch a gate properly and it blew open, or

91

the colt pushed against it accidentally and it opened — no one saw what happened. He got out on to the road, and the first thing anyone knew he was running races with the traffic. It was all-hands-on-deck stuff, of course, and there we were, trying to hold up traffic and catch the wretched colt. He was perfectly used to being handled, but by that time he was so excited and half-scared he wasn't about to let anyone get near him. Finally a truck spooked him — not the driver's fault — and he took off like a rocket, decided he could clear a neighbour's barbed-wire fence, and didn't. He was all right, but his legs were very badly gashed and it was pretty obvious no one was going to outlay much of their bankroll on him. Miriam was furious and told Garth to shoot him.'

'You didn't feel it was necessary?'

'Well, he wasn't going to be a top racehorse, but he wasn't going to be a cripple, either. Garth says she was just being practical, and maybe that's right. But she wasn't even willing to wait and see how he healed up — didn't even wait to find out what the vet might say. She was just blindly angry because the colt wouldn't let anyone catch him, and she hated him for it. He'd damaged himself unnecessarily and he was — had been — valuable property.'

Liz's voice shook with close tears, even after two years. 'He was beautiful,' she said.

Charles said quietly, 'I'm sorry.'

She glanced up at him. 'Yes,' she said. 'I think you are.' She took a quick breath. 'Heavens, Rambo, if I don't get back to work Garth will have my head.' She gave the black horse another pat and smiled ruefully at Charles. 'I've poured out more woes to you in ten minutes than I would to most people in a lifetime. I guess I sound as if I hate my employers, one way and another. But I don't. Not at all. Quite the contrary, believe it or not. They're family to me.'

Charles nodded. 'I believe it.'

He did believe it. This girl cared about Miriam and Douglas, cared rather a lot. That was why their failings hurt her.

Liz hurried off to attend to the demands of more of her equine charges, and Charles walked back toward the stables where he had left Garth, and found that Miriam had returned. She smiled at him.

'How do you like Top Bend?' she asked.

'Looks great to an ignoramous and I'm sure it would look even better to an expert. Tooth better?'

'Yes, thank heaven. It was still repairable. Come up to the house and have coffee. Out

93

of respect for my damaged fang I didn't have breakfast, and I'm famished.'

'Liz introduced me to Rambo,' he said as they walked. 'She loves the horses, doesn't she?' It was more statement than question.

Miriam nodded. 'Almost too much, sometimes.'

'She strikes me as being a very nice person.'

'Yes.' They went into the big kitchen and Miriam waved him to a chair while she busied herself with coffee mugs and a plate of biscuits. 'Her mother was a cousin of Douglas's. Her father was a charming, happy-go-lucky man who was a compulsive gambler — or that was the excuse. You know the sort of thing: poor fellow, he can't help it. Maybe he couldn't; maybe he could. He had a good job, but the family was always desperate for money, because he lost it faster than he could make it. His wife had to work to keep them fed, but she wasn't well and could only work part-time. Liz was their only child. White coffee or black?'

'White, please. No sugar.'

Miriam handed him a steaming mug and sat down opposite him at the pine table.

'Finally,' she said, 'when Liz was fifteen, a notice came from the bank to say they were foreclosing on the mortgage on the house.

Liz came home from school on the bus that afternoon — her mother was still at work — to find her father had blown his brains out with a shotgun in their back yard.'

'My God,' Charles breathed.

'Yes. Her mother collapsed on being told the news and never came out of hospital. Liz came here to live with us, so she's almost like a daughter, though she's years older than our children. Almost automatically she became part of the work-force here — never wanted to do anything else, though we urged her to go on to university after she finished high school. She's always been an independent type of person, and when she turned eighteen she rented a cottage for herself and used to ride back and forth to work here on a push-bike until she could afford an old car.'

Charles was silent for a moment. No wonder Liz had seemed to care about Miriam and Douglas. No wonder that she was distressed that Douglas was a compulsive gambler.

'You've been very kind to her,' Charles said.

'She's been an asset to Top Bend in return.' Miriam looked at him intently. 'Charles, why are you here? And what is this thing about being shot at?' She made an impatient gesture. 'Asking why you're here doesn't sound very welcoming. I didn't mean it to be like that. But, well, you said goodbye, and you were going back to Canada.'

'Yes. Well, now I'm not. Not yet. And to answer your questions, I guess I'm here because I was shot at. At least, as I've said, I don't believe I was actually shot at.'

He told her briefly what had happened, while she watched him with faintly disconcerting intensity.

'So,' she said slowly, 'you think Ursula was murdered. You really think that?'

'I have to believe it's likely. Why else would someone want to frighten me away?'

'If anyone did. It still could have been an accident.'

'Yes.'

'And you've come to ask if I know any reason she might have been murdered?'

'Partly that, I admit. And partly because I simply don't know what to do next. I'm not exactly well up in the detective business. In one sense, I have to play a waiting game.'

'Waiting to see if someone takes some more pot-shots at you?'

'Mmm. Well, something like that. *Do* you know any reason someone may have wanted my mother dead?'

The light brown eyes were suddenly hard. 'You're thinking that all the Erskine clan made money out of her death, so we're all prime suspects. Well, I didn't kill her and if you like I can produce witnesses to the fact I was here all day. And Douglas was busy in his surgery. So you can take your amateur sleuthing elsewhere.'

There was tight fury in her voice.

He held up a hand. 'Hold on a second, Miriam. I'm not accusing anyone of anything. I'm not suspecting anyone. But I've been away a long time. A great many things could have happened. All I'm asking is whether you know of any way Mother might have made an enemy. It's the question I'm going to have to ask a lot of people. I'm not suggesting anyone in the family killed her. I find that impossible to contemplate. But at the same time I have to try to look at the whole thing quite impartially, ruling no one in and no one out. I'm not suggesting she was killed for money. I don't know that she was murdered at all, but I desperately want to find out, if finding out is possible, and it seems to me the first thing to look for is whether there was a motive. Surely you can understand that?'

The anger slowly faded from her face. 'Yes, I can understand that. But I can't think of any reason. Enemies? Enemies and Ursula don't seem to go together at all.'

She seemed to think carefully for a

moment, and then shook her head. 'No.'

'You don't happen to know of some kind of *crime* that's been committed recently, where Mum could have been a possible witness?'

Miriam shook her head, then asked curiously, 'What makes you think of that?'

He shrugged. 'It's just a matter of looking at possibilities. You see, you assumed that I thought that if she was killed, it was for gain. But there are many reasons why people are murdered.' He was not about to make what Ursula had told Pip public knowledge. Not yet, at least. 'And I don't know of any other possibility in this case.'

Miriam nodded. If she was still angry with him it didn't show, and he thought it had evaporated. 'If it's what you want to know, I can't think of anyone, inside or outside the family, who could be capable of cold-blooded murder. And having said that, I accept that it isn't always possible to know. Are you staying for lunch? I'd quite like to show you a bit more of Top Bend, actually.'

He was touched. 'And I'd quite like to see it. Thanks.' He thought of Liz Fitzgibbon's concern over Douglas's gambling. 'I guess, as a breeder, you often go to the races,' he suggested.

Miriam was picking up their coffee mugs.

'It's part of the business,' she said. Then she turned suddenly with an unexpectedly disarming smile. 'Plus which,' she said, 'for me there is nothing on earth more exciting than watching good horses run. I can't explain it. But those splendid creatures, so beautiful, so perfect, all with that instinctive desire to be out in front — to *win* — it's — it's magic.'

She said the last word softly, looking beyond him to something that she was seeing inside her own mind. He thought in some awe that just for a second he had seen a glimpse of Miriam few people ever saw. Then she laughed and said, 'An awful lot of punters wouldn't agree that every horse wants to be in front.'

Charles smiled. 'Being an expert must give you a distinct edge when it comes to betting on a race.'

'I've never bet a cent since the day Liz's father shot himself,' she said quietly.

After a moment he asked easily, 'Does Douglas get your expert advice before he has a flutter?'

Her face went blank and closed. 'No,' she said. 'Will toasted sandwiches do you for lunch?'

Subject of gambling closed. 'That sounds fine to me,' he said.

After lunch he went with her as she made the rounds of the horses. He learned considerably more about the complexities of running a horse stud, but very little more about his stepsister, and Douglas still had not returned home when Charles left. As he drove, he kept remembering something Miriam had said about the racing thoroughbreds: ' . . . those splendid creatures, so beautiful, so perfect . . . '

Perfect. He thought about the way the place was kept, from gleaming white-painted fences to well-oiled gate hinges to neatly clipped hedges. He thought about the Echelon colt whose headlong recklessness had ruined his perfection. He thought of Douglas Wentworth's terrible imperfection of compulsive gambling which could, if Liz was right, ruin Miriam as well. Perfection was important to Miriam.

It was almost dark when he arrived back at the house. He had questioned Miriam about his continued occupancy, pointing out that he assumed the family would want to put the house on the market, and now that he planned to extend his stay he would be fully prepared to find himself other accommodation. Miriam had brushed aside the idea, assuring him it was much more satisfactory to have the place occupied, and they had all been a little concerned about the best thing to do about it when he left, so they were delighted to have him stay on.

Aristotle was drowsy and merely greeted him with an uninterested 'Hello, larrikin' when he unlocked the door. But Marmaduke was huddled in a wary, wide-eyed crouch in the laundry, plainly disturbed, and though seeming pleased and relieved to see Charles, was unwilling to follow him into the rest of the house.

'Come on, fella,' Charles told him cheerfully, 'it's dinner-time and I'll bet you're ravenous.' He picked up the black-and-white cat to carry him in, but as he stepped into the kitchen Marmaduke growled and leapt from his arms.

Charles stood still, listening, apprehension prickling his scalp. There was no sound, and he strode rapidly through the house, snapping on lights and telling himself he was being absurd to react to a cat's uneasiness. He stopped feeling absurd when he went into his mother's bedroom.

When he had been in the room the day before, a camel-coloured wool jacket had been lying where she had tossed it, across the foot of the bed. Now it was lying across the chair by the window.

5

He hadn't moved the jacket, surely? He stood frowning, trying to be certain. He *was* certain. He had been much affected, at the time, by the atmosphere the room had: that Ursula had walked out of it without the slightest thought that she would never come back. He had not moved anything.

Someone had been in the house.

Jill? Sandford? Come to check on things because he was away overnight and they wanted to make sure all was well? After all, it was the Erskines' house.

No. Marmaduke knew them both, knew them well. He wouldn't be upset that either of them — or Netty, Sandford's wife — had been in the house.

Charles swiftly checked through the rooms again, but could detect nothing unusual, nothing disturbed. He went around the doors and windows. Everything, except the door he had just used to come in, seemed locked. There was no sign of a forced entry.

He hesitated by the phone, wondering whether to call the police. But for what? No damage, nothing missing as far as he could tell, only a jacket not where it had been twenty-four hours earlier. And who was going to believe he hadn't simply made a mistake about that? And the whole house would be full of assorted fingerprints from the gathering after the funeral.

He opened the telephone directory and ran his finger down the 'H' columns until he found Henty, J & P, and dialled the number. Pip answered.

'Hi,' he said. 'The sleuth has returned from sleuthing Part One. While I was away, someone paid the house a visit.'

'*What?*' There was shock in her voice. 'Charles! Is there damage? What about Marmaduke and Aristotle?'

'They're fine, except Marmaduke apparently didn't approve of the company and I would dearly love to know why. And there is no damage whatever and as far as I can tell nothing is missing. But I don't know my mother's personal possessions well enough to know about them. Would it be asking a great deal too much to ask you to come over later and check through things?'

'Of course I'll come. Have you called the police?'

'No. There doesn't seem much point, unless something is missing; I can't even prove anyone's been here, except I know that a jacket is not now where it was when I left. But I don't see the police taking that piece of evidence too seriously. And Pip?'

'Yes?'

'Ask your father to come with you. If he can't come, I'll come and get you. I don't want you driving on this road alone, not at night.'

'Charles!' She was amused. 'You're not serious!'

'I am absolutely serious. Ask your father.'

He heard her voice, muffled as she covered the telephone mouthpiece. After a few seconds she said, 'Dad's going to ride shot-gun for me. I still think it's a fuss about nothing. Who's going to want to harm me?'

'No one, I sincerely hope. I just want to be sure, that's all. Have your dinner first. Sleuthing can wait that long.'

They came about an hour later, both looking serious. 'You're quite sure someone's been in the house?' Jack asked.

'Unless a jacket of Mother's managed to transfer itself from the foot of her bed to a chair by the window about six feet away. I particularly recall seeing it on the bed just before I left yesterday. I can't notice anything else out of place or missing. I thought Pip would have a better chance of picking up something like that.'

Pip looked around the living-room. 'Those two antique chairs would be worth some hundreds of dollars, and there's some solid silver in that glass-fronted cabinet, so it wasn't a burglary — or not that sort of burglary. Did you have any money in the house?'

Charles shook his head. 'What about jewellery? I don't recall that Mum wore jewellery, really — not expensive stuff, anyway. Miriam gave me her watch — the police had given it to Miriam — it's a gold one, but it had been broken in the crash. I put it in a drawer in the room I'm using. Oh!' he added as a memory jolted him. 'Someone — someone from the undertakers gave me her rings. I put them in the drawer, too. I haven't thought to see if they're missing.'

The rings — an engraved gold wedding-ring and a sapphire and diamond engagement ring which looked expensive — were where Charles had almost absent-mindedly pushed them into a drawer along with the watch and some clean socks. No burglar worth *his* clean socks would have missed them.

Charles frowned, his uneasiness growing rather than decreasing. 'The rings are there, the watch is there, all the electrical goods thieves love are there. There simply doesn't seem to be anything missing. Maybe I *was* wrong about the jacket. Looks as if I've cried wolf. Sorry.'

Jack said, 'Maybe one of the family — Jill or Sandford — came in for something.'

Pip was looking carefully through Ursula's wardrobe. 'I think someone's been looking for something,' she said quietly. 'Only a week ago — two, perhaps — Ursula asked me to come in here, into her room, because she wanted to show me a new suit she'd bought. This one, actually.' She held up teal-blue linen. 'I noticed then how she had all her clothes arranged so methodically, with winter things at one end of the wardrobe and summer things at the other — not at all like mine. Now they *are* like mine: all mixed up. And unless it's at the winery, her brief-case is missing. It was always on that bedside table.'

They were silent for a few moments. Then Charles said, 'Not one of the family. Or not on any ordinary mission. The house is theirs, but not any of Mother's personal effects or business things. No one in the Erskine clan had any occasion to rummage. Not any lawful reason. And Marmaduke was afraid. He wouldn't have been afraid of them; he knows them.'

'But can you be *certain*?' Jack half-protested. 'That someone was here, I mean.

For one thing, we don't know for sure that the brief-case is missing. It may very well be in the office at the winery. If she'd had it with her when the car crashed, the police would have returned it to you. They didn't?'

Charles shook his head. 'They'd given everything to Miriam, and she gave them to me. Mother's watch, a small purse with a few dollars in it, and her house-keys. Apart from that, only stuff that would have been in the glove-box, I guess: log-book for the Suzuki, registration papers, a Brisbane street-directory. No brief-case.' He looked at Pip. 'Do you know if she always took it to the winery?'

'I shouldn't think so. But Miriam may have it — may have forgotten to give it to you.'

'I'll check.' He looked up Miriam's phone number and used the phone beside Ursula's bed. No; Miriam, sounding puzzled, had not been given a brief-case.

'It's still fully possible,' Jack pointed out, 'that it's at the winery. And it's also possible that Ursula may have rearranged her summer and winter clothes herself. Have you checked for any sign of forced entry? Doors and windows?'

Charles looked at him. 'I'm an idiot. I didn't think to check the windows in the lounge. I made a quick check and thought they were all fastened before I left, but I could have missed one.'

He began to turn toward the door, and then stopped and turned back sharply.

'What is it?' Jack asked.

'Someone was here, all right,' Charles said. 'Yesterday there were a couple of letters lying on the dressing-table, stamped, waiting to be posted. Now they're gone.'

Pip walked across to the dressing-table, then stooped and picked something up from the floor. 'And whoever took them didn't take them away to post them. Whoever it was opened them.' She held out a raggedly torn fragment of an envelope with a corner of an unfranked postage-stamp adhering to it.

'Did you see who the letters were addressed to?' Jack asked.

Charles shook his head. 'I didn't take any notice. I just saw them and they — well, they got at me a bit, I suppose, emphasizing how unexpectedly her life was cut off. I remember thinking I'd have to check who they were meant for and whether those people needed to be contacted. But it was something I was glad enough to postpone.' He turned away. 'Let's look in the other rooms for the brief-case.'

It was not in the room Ursula had used

as a combined office and library. It was not to be found, after half an hour of diligent searching.

'It isn't here,' Charles said finally. 'But that may not be significant. Let's check to see if I left a window unlatched.'

They found one lounge window unfastened. Closed, but the latch hadn't gripped. Anyone could have entered that way and simply closed it behind him. Or her. Unless they used a key.

'Are you going to tell the police?' Jack asked.

Charles hesitated, then shrugged. 'I can't see any point in it. There's no damage; apart from a couple of letters and possibly a brief-case there's nothing missing; and we've touched window-latches, drawers, cupboard doors. Our fingerprints — or mostly mine — will be on everything an intruder is likely to have touched, and, in any case, somehow I doubt if this intruder would have been so stupid as to not wear gloves.'

'Except maybe he or she wouldn't have expected you to notice anything was wrong,' Pip said. 'And I suppose in fact we don't know that nothing was stolen. It's simply that neither you nor I can miss anything. What about money? Do you know if there was cash in Ursula's room? Some thieves don't want anything they have to sell — only cash.'

'If there was any — and I guess most people have *some* in the house — I suppose it would be in a handbag, wouldn't it? Did you notice any handbags in the wardrobe?'

'Yes, I looked especially. There are three, I think — different colours — and a clutch purse which was probably for evening wear.'

They went back into Ursula's room and Pip took the handbags out and laid them on the bed. Careful, this time, not to touch anything where he might destroy fingerprints, Charles opened them. Evidently Ursula had transferred money from one handbag to another as she used them, because only a tan leather shoulder-bag contained a wallet, with driver's licence, automobile club card, a couple of plastic credit cards, some small change, and $240 in banknotes.

'No ordinary burglar,' Jack Henty said quietly.

'No,' Charles agreed, putting his mother's purses away again. 'I wish it had been. The question is, what the hell was he looking for?'

'Some sort of incriminating evidence,' Philipa suggested. 'From what Ursula told me, she knew something awful about someone. Perhaps that person was aware of what she knew. Perhaps whoever it was believed she

110

had actual evidence of that awfulness. Perhaps she did. Perhaps he found it.'

Charles frowned. 'It's all speculation, isn't it? But maybe I was wrong. Maybe I should tell the police. But it can wait till morning, I imagine. I can't think they'll find anything. There's nothing but my word that anything was disturbed. I said I'd go out to Glenlodge tomorrow.' He smiled at Pip. 'We'll find out then if the brief-case is missing.'

They went into the living-room and Charles made coffee. 'Did you discover anything of interest at the stud?' Pip asked.

Charles had lit a fire in the grate against an evening chill, and he put more wood on it. 'Ah,' he said. 'The place appears to be distinctly prosperous and running on well-oiled hinges. I met a second-in-command who is uninformative when it comes to anything remotely concerning the Wentworths or their affairs. No doubt this is due to loyalty and a natural aversion to getting too chatty with nosy outsiders even if they do happen to be stepbrothers. Perhaps especially if they're stepbrothers. I also met a lively young woman employee who's some sort of relation of Douglas's. She is, I believe, no less loyal, and probably very much more so, but she was much more informative.'

111

He told them what he had learned of the Wentworths.

'So,' he said eventually, 'there it is. So much for the Wentworths. Douglas is a compulsive gambler who is very anxious his wife shouldn't know. Miriam has an explosive temper — apparently seldom roused, but which makes her unreasoning and unreasonable, maybe vindictive. Liz felt she had ordered the colt shot because he'd refused to be caught, not because his injuries were so severe. Not perhaps the most relaxed of households, but what is there to suggest a reason to kill? Certainly neither of them killed my mother, if Miriam was telling the truth about their whereabouts that day, and I'm sure she wouldn't be so foolish as to lie, because it's something easily checked out. Of course the hired killer is always possible but, damn it, I can't see either of them getting involved in cold-blooded murder.'

He took a sip of coffee. 'It also seems a safe bet that there's only one person involved. Not any kind of conspiracy. Given that, the person Mum described as evil must have been the person who was in the house while I was away, whether that person had anything to do with her death or was simply taking advantage of it to look for whatever evidence she may have had, and remove it.'

'That still points toward someone in the family, doesn't it?' Pip suggested. 'You told Jill. She's hardly likely to have mentioned it to anyone except one of the family — not deliberately, but just as the sort of thing you might say in the course of conversation. And whoever came in seems to have known you were away, and had time to go through things carefully.'

'Yet I can't feel it *was* a family member. Marmaduke was frightened. Really frightened. He's not an especially nervous cat, and he wouldn't be afraid of anyone in the family. He'd know them.' He sighed. 'There's nothing simple about the whole foul thing, is there?'

'And yet,' Jack said slowly, 'when it's all unravelled, you'll probably find it was perfectly simple. I guess the crimes that are most difficult to solve often are the simplest: the killer who strikes without apparent motive and simply walks away to carry on living as if nothing had happened.'

They fell silent for a bit, and then Jack said gently, 'Charles, how do you think it would have been done? How do you think your mother's car was made to crash? If it was.'

Charles raised his head from staring at the fire to look at the older man. 'I don't really have a theory. I know the police say they couldn't find any evidence of tampering with brakes or steering, but I guess it was something like that, and it doesn't show up because of the overall damage to the car. If, as you say, there was any tampering.'

'Maybe. But if you think about the road up here, as it climbs the ridge, there are only two places where running off the edge could be confidently expected to be fatal. I'm sorry, Charles. Maybe I shouldn't be saying this.'

Charles watched him steadily. 'Go on.'

'Well, brakes or steering could fail at any point. Brakes are virtually ruled out, because Ursula was coming home, *up* the ridge. Steering failure could have simply run the car into the embankment with no more harm than a few dents and scratches. Tampering with the car is too hit-and-miss, at any rate on this particular road. And she'd been at the winery all day. Whoever did any monkey business would have had to do it there, and the risk of being observed would be awfully high.'

'Are you suggesting she may have been killed first, and *then* someone ran the car over the edge? I suppose it could happen that way.'

'That would be possible, but there's another possibility,' Jack said. 'You know exactly where it happened?'

Charles nodded.

'It's on top of the ridge. The road levels out, and is straight for eight metres or so, then it comes to a sharp bend. A vehicle travelling toward that bend, with a totally unsuspecting driver, could easily be catapaulted straight over the edge if hit from behind by a following vehicle. There was rain, I believe, and it would have been dusk by the time Ursula was getting home. The other driver could have simply followed her up the road, then turned around and gone back to the main road and left the rain to blot out any tyre tracks.'

Charles was staring at him, seeing in his mind the crumpled wreckage of a car, the shattered wreckage of a body.

'Sorry, Charles,' Jack Henty said again.

Charles shook his head. 'It's very feasible,' he said, keeping his voice steady. 'But surely there would have been damage to the other vehicle — damage that would have to be accounted for. Although I suppose as long as there was no reason to link that driver with the accident, the damage would be easily explained.' He paused. 'I'll mention it to the police when I phone them in the morning. And thanks — thank you both.'

He and Pip arranged a time to go to the

115

winery the following day, and she and Jack left. Charles sat for a long time looking at the fire.

The next morning the detective sergeant and the uniformed constable who came to the house assured him that yes, they had considered the possibility of another vehicle coming into contact with Mrs Erskine's vehicle, but because of the state of the wreckage and the absence of any detectable abnormal paint flakes, it was not possible to determine whether this had occurred. They also told him, sadly, that it was most unfortunate he and Miss Henty had touched things in the house last night, as they had probably destroyed any fingerprints which may have been evidence of an intruder. But they dusted possible surfaces carefully, and said they would need to check Miss Henty's fingerprints, took Charles's statement and his fingerprints, and assured him they would let him know if anything useful turned up.

They left Charles feeling frustrated and foolish.

* * *

Joe Franklin came to the driveway of the little service station as the vehicle pulled up at the fuel pump. 'Hi,' he said cheerfully to

116

the driver. 'Fill her up?'

'Thanks.' The driver unlocked the fuel cap.

'Nice day,' Joe commented He was nineteen, and his overalls hung with easy looseness on his lean, long-limbed frame. He was eager to please, delighted to have secured an apprenticeship as a motor-mechanic. He ran his eye over the vehicle. 'Hello,' he said, looking surprised. 'You've had the bull-bar taken off.'

There was a moment's silence. 'Bull-bar? Why do you think I had a bull-bar on it?'

'Guess I noticed because it was a very heavy one. New, too. Thought you must be really worried about hitting a kangaroo. Mind you, they sure can make a mess of a car if you hit one fair and square.'

Then Joe laughed. 'Oh, I see. You wonder why I remember it was your car? Because of the number plate. It's a kind of game I play with myself — making up words beginning with the letters on registration plates. Yours was tricky, but I came up with a funny one.'

'Really?' The driver smiled. 'Where did you see the car? You seem to have a remarkable memory.'

'It was parked on the side of the road, just along from here a bit. I guess,' he added, suddenly serious, 'I remember specially because it was the day that lady, Mrs Erskine, was killed. I remember she waved to me as she drove past on her way home, and next morning I heard she'd been killed in an accident. She often used to get petrol here, because it was on her way to and from the winery. She was a real nice lady.'

He replaced the petrol cap carefully, said, 'That's eighteen dollars, thanks. Everything else OK? Oil? Tyres? Right. I'll just get your change.'

He ducked into the tiny office and came back with the change. 'So why'd you have the bull-bar taken off?'

The driver shrugged. 'I decided it spoiled the look of the vehicle. As you say, it was a heavy one. Do you work this place on your own?'

Joe smiled. 'Not likely. The boss'd have a fit. His wife hasn't been real well, and he just nicked off home to check she's OK. He shouldn't be more than ten minutes or so.'

The driver nodded and then said as an afterthought, 'Maybe I should have the tyres checked after all, if you wouldn't mind.'

'Sure. No problem.' Joe ran out the air-hose and dropped down on one knee to check a front tyre, whistling cheerfully, totally unsuspecting of the driver standing behind him.

6

Charles phoned Tom Rushton, the foreman of Glenlodge orchard, to ask if he would be at home later. 'I'm sorry I haven't been out to see you before, to talk about the future of the winery and orchard,' Charles told him. 'And now it's Saturday and you're entitled to the day off, of course, so if it's inconvenient we'll arrange another day.'

Tom Rushton assured him he would be at home, and was anxious to discuss the situation. 'We don't worry too much about sticking rigidly to days off,' he said. 'It's always worked out well.'

Charles drove to the Henty house via the police station, where the sergeant told him gloomily that the only significant finger-prints recovered from the house were his and Miss Henty's. 'I'm afraid you'd have eliminated any others by touching wardrobe doors and drawers and such, Mr Waring.'

'Or the intruder wore gloves,' Charles suggested.

'Or the intruder wore gloves. If there was an intruder, of course. You will let us know whether or not you find Mrs

Erskine's brief-case, won't you?'

Charles assured him he would check through his mother's office at the winery immediately.

There seemed, he thought, an unusual amount of activity around the police station, and the sergeant seemed to have most of his mind focused on something else. He learned why when he arrived to pick up Pip.

Looking distressed, she said at once, 'It's awful about Joe Franklin, isn't it?'

She saw his blank expression and added quickly, 'You haven't heard. The young fellow at that little service station just past the Erskine Road turn-off. Someone killed him this morning in broad daylight. His boss had only left the place for twenty minutes, and when he came back, Joe was lying just inside the office. Someone had hit him with a heavy spanner or wrench and simply left it on the ground beside the petrol pumps. Apparently that's' — she gave a little shudder — 'that's where he was killed, and then dragged inside, so passing motorists wouldn't see him, I suppose.'

She gulped. 'I've known Joe since he was a little boy. His family live a few doors up the street from here. I was walking home from doing some shopping, and I'd stopped and was talking to his mother in their garden when the police came to tell her.'

Charles put an arm around Pip's shoulders. 'I'm sorry,' he said. 'It was rotten for you.'

No wonder there had seemed to be more important things on everyone's mind at the police station. A break-and-enter with nothing, apparently, stolen, must have seemed trifling indeed.

'It must have been a pretty brazen — or pretty desperate — thief to do that in broad daylight,' he said.

Pip shook her head. 'That's what somehow makes it more awful. His mother said, 'There wouldn't even be much in the till at this hour. They killed my son for a few dollars. A few miserable dollars, and they killed him!' And the detective said the till wasn't touched. Nothing was missing at all.' Her voice shook. 'It was worse, even than his mother said. They didn't even kill him for a few dollars. They killed him for *nothing*!'

Charles stood very still, almost feeling the shock and grief which was crushing the unknown boy's mother. But there was something else — something hovering just below conscious thought in his brain. Something — some thought, some memory — but it eluded him.

He said slowly, 'He wasn't killed for

nothing. There was a reason, if we only knew what it was.'

Pip was staring at him.

'The night before last — or sometime yesterday — my mother's house was entered by someone who took only a couple of letters and possibly a brief-case. No money, no valuables. Today a boy is killed at a service station in what looks like a hold-up. But nothing is taken, except a life.'

Pip shivered. 'What's going *on*, Charles?'

He shook his head. 'I wish I knew. I wish I knew.'

Jack Henty had come in. 'You think the two things may be connected, Charles?'

'I don't know. There's a kind of similarity, though it may be nothing but coincidence. I think I'm beginning to see significance where there is none.'

'I've just been to see young Joe's parents,' Jack said. 'I hope the police get the mongrel who did this, and I hope he gets put away for keeps.'

Charles and Pip said little on the drive out to Glenlodge.

The clear, bright beauty of the spring day, the early blossoms appearing on some of the fruit trees in the orchards they passed, the air of peace it all presented, seemed grossly at odds with the vicious death of a bright young man and the anguish of his family. Seemed grossly at odds with Charles's own dark suspicions.

There was a hastily painted 'Closed' sign outside the service station as they passed, and a police car still stood in the driveway. Ursula would have passed that service station every day on her way to and from the winery, Charles reflected. She no doubt bought petrol there. She no doubt knew the boy who had been killed. Charles frowned. Was it possible that, for some reason Charles couldn't even guess at, that was *why* that boy had been killed? Because he knew Ursula Erskine? Or knew something about her that was dangerous to someone?

Charles shook his head. He was seeing criminals behind every door. He had to stop wild speculation and stick to facts.

Pip said, 'Stop around the next bend.'

He stopped, knowing why. Glenlodge, with its orchard, its vineyards and its winery, lay on the gently rising hill to the left of the road, and from here one could see most of it. The stone-fruit trees were frothing into a marvel of blossom, the vines with their pale-green new leaves striped the grey-white soil. The winery, he noted, still had the vines trailing above the entrance arches, and the soft grey roof of the white-painted house showed above the trees that surrounded it, deep-green conifers, the grey-green of a couple of eucalypts, two big old Liquidambers whose limbs were softening from winter bareness into green brightness.

Three years since he had seen it, much longer since he had lived there. But as he sat silent, looking at it, he knew why he had wanted to avoid coming here. It persisted in his mind as home, and he didn't want it to be so.

He didn't belong here. The work that was done here was alien to him. Once he had settled the question that hung over his mother's death — even if the final answer was that there never could *be* an answer — he would go back to Canada and shut the door firmly on the past. There was nothing for him here.

Neither Pip nor he spoke, and he restarted the car and drove up to the house.

Tom Rushton was a stocky man of fifty-plus, with a weathered face and shrewd eyes; a man Ursula had trusted implicitly in the day-to-day running of the orchard. He came out of the house and shook hands with Charles and smiled a greeting to Pip, whom he obviously knew. If he wondered about seeing them together he gave no sign of it.

'Will you come into the house?' he asked.

'Or would you like to look around first?'

'I'd like to look through the office at the winery,' Charles told him, and explained briefly about the missing brief-case.

Tom Rushton shook his head. 'I doubt if it's there. I've had to do a few things in the office and I haven't noticed it. I don't think she ever left it here. I think she always took it home when she used it, but she didn't always have it with her.'

Behind the vine-draped arches of the winery, a flagstoned veranda opened, via heavy wooden doors, to the cellar-door sales area, with its polished timber counter and racks of wine bottles on the wall, where visitors to the winery could taste samples of the products and purchase anything from single bottles to carton lots. It was a relatively small but important part of the whole enterprise, and running it had been part of Ursula's work.

Tom led them through the area to a small, entirely functional office. A search of cupboards and filing cabinets revealed no brief-case. They went carefully through the sales area, but apart from the cupboards under the counter for glasses and cartons, there was nowhere Ursula could have left a brief-case.

Charles frowned. 'What would have been

in it?' he asked. 'Would there have been money — cash from the retail sales at the front counter?'

Tom Rushton looked doubtful. 'I shouldn't think she'd have been carrying much, if any. She banked the cash a couple of times a week, never on a regular timetable, and in the meantime the money was kept here in the office safe. There'd have been a key to that in the brief-case, probably. But I'm sure she'd banked the cash just a day or two before, and I wouldn't think there'd have been many visitors here buying over the counter in that space of time, though I'm mostly out in the orchard, so I really don't know. Rob Carlyle would have a better idea — he's the winemaker, so he's around the place most of the time — but he's off for the weekend. He'd have a key to the safe, perhaps. I don't ever have any cause to use it.'

'The police returned Mother's keys,' Charles said, taking a small leather folder of keys from his pocket. 'Maybe one is for the safe. I'm very surprised it's not a combination-type lock.'

Tom Rushton smiled. 'Mrs Erskine always called it The Thieves' Delight because it had such a simple lock, and said it had practically come out of the Ark. But she said there was never enough of consequence in it to tempt a thief. Your mother was a real nice lady, Mr Waring,' he added quietly.

Charles glanced at him quickly, touched by the edge of genuine grief in the foreman's tone. 'Yes,' he nodded. 'Yes, she was. Thank you.'

There was a silence while he sorted the keys and found one which fitted and opened the safe door without fuss. The safe was large enough to hold a brief-case, but it did not. There was an address book with what obviously were business places listed in Ursula's handwriting, an unlocked cash-box containing just over $200, and a worn-leather folder designed to hold two photographs. Charles opened it and stood still, partly because he was moved by it and partly because he was surprised.

Moved, because one side held an enlargement of a snapshot Ursula had taken of him the day he left to return to Canada after his last visit home three years ago. The last day they had seen each other.

Surprised, because the other side held a photograph of his father. All those years after the marriage ended, after half-a-dozen affairs he had wandered in and out of with other women, Ursula had kept Geoffrey Waring's photograph — not displayed like the silver-framed one of Anthony Erskine which stood on the mantelpiece in the fine home he had built for her, but hidden quietly away where she could look at it in private. He wondered whether she had done so, or whether she somehow simply felt the photographs of father and son should be together.

Pip and Tom were looking at the photographs Charles held. 'Hello,' Tom said, 'who's the other fellow? A brother of Mrs Erskine's?'

Charles shook his head. 'Geoffrey Waring — her first husband. My father. I don't expect you've ever seen him.'

'Oh, but I have,' Tom Rushton said emphatically. 'He was here only a couple of weeks ago.'

'Here?' Charles looked at him in surprise. 'Did he often come here?'

'I'd never seen him before. But that's him, all right. Not a real happy man the day he was here, though. Not smiling like in that photo. Not when he left, anyway.'

'In what way was he unhappy?' Charles asked. 'Sad? Angry?'

'Angry is nearest, I guess.' He shot an uneasy glance at Charles. 'Look, I wasn't eavesdropping and I don't want to go gossiping.'

'I appreciate that. But it could be important. Did you hear anything that was said?'

'Well,' Tom said slowly, 'I'd just come in from the orchard. It was lunch-time, and I'd been seeing to the trickle irrigation on the nectarines, I remember, so I hadn't had the tractor. I'd walked in, so I guess they didn't know I was about, and Rob Carlyle was away. I was coming in to see Mrs Erskine and I heard voices. I thought there must have been customers at the front counter, so I just waited near the cellar. Then I realized the voices were in here, and I heard the man — he was shouting by then — say: 'But damn it, you must be able to help me out'. I didn't hear what she said because she was speaking more quietly. Then he said, 'For God's sake Ursula! You and your damned principles!' Then he barged out — nearly bumped into me, actually, but I don't think he even saw me.'

'That's the only time you ever saw him?'

'The only time I saw him here. I saw him at your mother's funeral. I remember thinking that whatever the argument was about, they couldn't have been really bad friends — he looked really quite upset, I noticed. Not like the day he was here, of course. Sad. Not desperate like that day.'

Charles nodded with a matter-of-fact manner his thoughts didn't match.

'Well, I'll have to call the police and tell them the brief-case is missing and so it seems to be the thing the person who got into the house was looking for, though we can't imagine why.'

Pip and Tom went out of the office while Charles made his call. After he hung up he sat for a minute, thinking.

Desperate. That's what Tom had said. Why had Geoffrey been desperate? Presumably for money. Only desperation would drive him to ask his ex-wife for money. It was Charles's understanding that Rhelma, the present Mrs Waring, was a highly successful businesswoman in her own right, so if Geoffrey had got himself into some financial hole, apparently he was extremely anxious to hide the fact from her. But not from Ursula.

There was some kind of wry humour in that. Geoffrey Waring still felt more comfortable in his first wife's knowledge of his failings than in the second wife's awareness of them. Maybe because Ursula knew them all already.

So, assuming he had come to Ursula for money, she had refused him. Well, from what the solicitor had told Charles of his mother's finances, she had borrowed in order to expand her business by buying the adjoining orchard — a sound deal in the solicitor's eyes, but which meant that Ursula had no substantial cash reserves without dipping into the money which Anthony Erskine had left her. Geoffrey would not have known of her strong feeling that that money belonged, not to her, but to Anthony's children. The BMW, the house, had been Anthony's gifts to her, and those she would keep and use. But she had been determined that her vineyard, her winery, her orchard, would be her sole source of income, and she would succeed or fail in her own right.

Given the depth of her commitment to those ideas, she could not have helped Geoffrey even if she had wanted to. 'You and your damned principles.' No doubt Tom had recalled that remark accurately. Whether or not she had wanted to help, no one would ever know.

The more he thought about it, the further the initial sick fear receded in Charles's mind. His father could not possibly have expected to gain by Ursula's death. Besides, Charles had never known Geoffrey Waring to do a violent thing in his life. A weak man in many ways — even a bit of a rogue — but a cheerful, easy-going man.

Irresponsible, never vicious; never in any way, let alone to the point of murder.

Charles took a handkerchief and wiped his face, discovering that he was sweating in the crisp spring air, and felt ashamed of the hideous suspicion he had momentarily felt. Then his jaw set grimly. He couldn't afford *not* to be suspicious of anyone and everyone. Reason, not sentiment, had to be his only guide.

He went out and found Tom Rushton and Pip. 'Come into the office, will you? Tom, you need to know about my intentions as far as Glenlodge is concerned.'

'Shall I go for a discreet walk?' Pip asked.

'No, of course not. There's nothing private about the business.'

They all sat down, Charles in the swivel chair behind the desk, where his mother must have spent many hundreds of hours; Tom and Pip in two comfortable armchairs.

'I've taken it for granted that you'll be selling the place,' Tom said.

Charles nodded. 'Yes. The point is, it's quite a fair-sized concern, so, of course, it's quite probable that whoever buys it will want you to stay on, and I'd certainly recommend that to a buyer, but naturally I can't guarantee it.'

'Thanks, Charles,' Tom said. 'But I'm leaving anyway. I've a brother who wants me to go into partnership with him to buy an orchard in Victoria, and I've agreed to do that. I guess I wouldn't have if Mrs Erskine had still been here, but — well, anyway, it seems the best idea now. Cliff Barber, in the other house, is quite a capable bloke with enough experience to do the day-to-day work around the place till the new owner takes over. You'd only need to look after the business side of it.'

Charles passed over the last sentence with a faint smile. 'Well, it sounds like an opportunity you shouldn't let slip, and I'm sure my mother would have been pleased for you, too. This fellow — Cliff, is it? — in the other house: where's that? I mean, there used to be a couple of cabins for seasonal workers, and a cottage for the fellow who was orchard foreman before you — while my parents still lived in this house — but that cottage is gone, pulled down years ago.'

'That's right. But when your mother bought the next-door orchard and added it to this one, the purchase included the house and sheds and everything on it. Cliff Barber lives in that house. He's a young bloke with a wife and a couple of kids, and he's a good worker and knows what he's doing. But, of

133

course, like I said, you'd have to handle all the actual business.'

Charles nodded. 'Well, I don't expect to be here, but I'm sure I can arrange for my solicitor to handle it.'

Tom stared. 'Oh, no, it's not the sort of thing you can handle from an office in town. It's *everything*, like ordering spray, or parts for the equipment, or fruit-boxes; it's taking orders from wine-merchants and restaurants and bottle shops, and dealing with fruit-marketing agents — all that sort of thing. You've got to be on the spot, and anyway a solicitor wouldn't know the first thing about it.'

'Neither do I,' Charles smiled, but with a growing sense of apprehension. 'I'd simply have to leave it to Cliff Barber and Rob Carlyle, the winemaker. You assure me they're both capable, and they're certainly more knowledgeable than I am.'

'Oh, they're capable in their own fields, and they can certainly *advise* you. But — well, it's your show. Someone has to take the overall responsibility. Just until the place is sold, of course.'

Then he gave a quick shake of the head. 'Sorry. I shouldn't be telling you what to do with your own property. But I stand by what I've said, just the same.'

'And you're right, of course,' Pip said quietly. 'Someone has to manage the marketing side of the business, and make the decisions of management, day by day. You do see that, don't you, Charles?'

He sat silently for a full minute. 'I see the point, yes. I'll have to see what arrangements I can make for Cliff Barber and Rob Carlyle to be given the authority to manage the place jointly, but until then, or until it's sold, whichever comes first, I'll have to take responsibility for it. Heaven knows what sort of mess I'll make of it.'

He looked at Tom. 'A crash course in what-happens-at-Glenlodge is what I'm going to need, so let's begin. I don't even know how many people work here full-time, nor what's grown here, apart from grapes — and you mentioned nectarines.'

Over the next few hours he learned a good deal of the broad outline of the orchard's operation as Tom and Cliff Barber unhesitatingly gave up their spare time to show him around. There were five men permanently employed — Tom, Cliff, Rob, and two general hands who didn't live on the property: brothers named Riccardo and Giovanni Petroni.

The stone-fruit orchard specialized in nectarines and peaches and, according to

135

Tom, had been very progressive in introducing improved varieties and modern techniques — an initiative of the orchard's previous owner, and it had been the main reason Ursula had been ready to go into debt to secure it, because she regarded it as a sound investment.

Charles and Pip were introduced to Cliff Barber, a lean, tall young man with blue eyes and cropped sandy hair and an obvious enthusiasm for his work, especially the fruit trees.

'Giovanni knows more about the vines than I do,' he said. 'I mean, I know all the basic stuff, but he's got a special flair for the vines — always seems to know just when and how much to water, for instance, to give Rob the kind of grapes he wants. And he's about as good as Rob at knowing when the grapes are exactly right to pick for whatever wine they're meant for — though Rob does all the lab. stuff — testing for pH and sugar and all that. You'd probably remember Giovanni, though? And Rob? Giovanni's been here seven or eight years, I think, and Rob's been here a long while, too.'

Charles nodded. 'I'm sure I've met them. I seem to remember Rob as a slightly built fellow with fair hair going a bit thin. A rather serious sort of fellow.'

Cliff nodded. 'That's him. Mrs Erskine took him and Giovanni with her a couple of times when she went south to look at top vineyards and what varieties of grapes they were growing, in the Hunter Valley and in Victoria and around Barossa in South Australia. Giovanni helped her decide the best varieties to *grow* here, and Rob concentrated on types for special wines. It's a bit of a different ball-game, growing wine-grapes in this area, so much further north. But, of course, we're around seven hundred metres above sea-level, so that gives some of the cold weather the vines need.'

Charles grinned. 'I do remember some humdingers of frosts.'

'Nothing nearly so cold as you've been used to in Canadian winters,' Pip suggested.

'No, but distinctly nippy. Did my mother introduce new types of vines here?'

'Oh, yes.' It was Tom who answered. 'Like a lot of other growers here, she started going all-out for specialized wine-producing varieties a good many years ago. Most of the grapes grown right throughout the Granite Belt now are destined for wine-making rather than as table grapes.'

He glanced at his watch. 'Look, before we start going through the vines to see what's what there, come to the house and have a bite of lunch.'

'Might be better if we go to my place,' Cliff suggested. 'Tom's wife has started to pack things away for when they leave, so unexpected visitors might be awkward. Angie, my wife, won't mind you coming. On the contrary, she enjoys company.'

Charles accepted almost hastily, and Pip threw a curious glance at him. Angela Barber proved to be a smilingly imperturbable young woman who produced a lunch of thick soup with toast, followed by apple pie. 'I always seem to make too much food for a meal,' she said cheerfully, 'so there's lots to go around.'

Afterwards Charles and Pip were introduced to the vineyard, though Charles realized Pip was already familiar with it, because her questions to Cliff and Tom were clearly born of knowledge, while his had their roots almost entirely in ignorance.

The vines were planted principally on a gentle north to northwest slope, in blocks according to variety.

'Of course,' Tom explained, 'the earlier wine-makers here used table grapes, and there are still some used — white Waltham Cross, for example. But Glenlodge has used Shiraz and Pinot Noir for a long time, and Cabernet

138

Sauvignon. Then your mother introduced Semillon and Rhine Riesling. Across here,' he pointed as they walked between the newly leafed vines where the bunches of tiny immature grapes were beginning to show, 'there are Malbec and Merlot, and the Sauvignon Blanc that have been very successful. And these are Chardonnay.'

'How on earth,' Charles asked, 'do you know which is which?'

The others smiled. 'You'll soon learn,' Cliff said cheerfully.

As he and Pip drove home Charles said almost irritably, 'Why the devil do they think I *want* to learn?'

Pip smiled. 'They love what they're doing. They can't imagine that you wouldn't become just as involved.'

Charles was silent, and presently Pip said gently, 'You didn't want to go near the house, did you?'

He raised an eyebrow. 'There wasn't any occasion to, and with Tom and his wife in the throes of packing up to leave, we'd have been an inconvenience.'

'I see.'

Something in her tone made him frown. 'What is that supposed to mean?'

She hesitated. 'Look, I'm sorry. What you do is none of my business. I simply wondered, that's all.'

'Wondered what?'

'Well, why going into the house is hurtful to you.'

'Hurtful?' He seemed to consider the idea, driving for a while without speaking. 'It isn't hurtful,' he said presently. 'But Glenlodge is gone out of my life. It's not relevant to me. I chose to leave it a long time ago, and that choice remains the same. I don't belong there.'

It was her turn to be silent for a time. 'I wonder,' she said seriously, 'whether you're a little afraid of it. As though it's making demands on you that would cause too massive a change in your life.'

He laughed shortly. 'You get some damned funny ideas.'

Neither of them spoke again until he stopped the car outside the house Pip shared with her father. Charles turned his head to look at her. 'You're right, of course, in a way. I do have the feeling of circumstances conspiring to entangle me in something I don't want. But I think I'm still in charge of my own life to a sufficient degree.'

He smiled. 'I was most ungracious. I'm sorry.' He slipped an arm around her shoulders and bent his head to kiss her lightly on the cheek.

As she turned her face toward him with a smile, his arm tightened and his mouth sought hers and felt her response as fire leapt through him.

Then abruptly, shocked, he pulled away, dropping his arm to his side, staring at her.

That morning, when almost in tears, she had told him of the young service-station attendant's apparently senseless murder, he had put an arm comfortingly around her shoulders. Something had stirred in his subconscious, something like a memory trying to surface, but it had eluded him. He knew now what it was.

Pip, he thought numbly, it was *Pip*.

She was staring at him in bewilderment. 'What is it?' she demanded. 'Charles! What — you look as if you've seen a ghost!'

His senses were reeling as if he had been struck a physical blow to the head. 'A ghost?' he said bitterly. 'Oh, no. Something horribly real.'

'What are you talking about?'

'I'm talking,' he said with icy deliberation, trying to sort out words from seething thoughts, 'about a charming, helpful girl who tried to kill me. Right now I daren't let myself think why, because I would have to know the answer.'

She lurched back against the door of the

car as if he had struck her across the face. 'What?' she whispered. '*What?*'

He didn't answer. The waves of shock, betrayal, fury, left him without words.

They went on staring at each other for a string of electrified seconds. Then in a shaken, very quiet voice she said, 'Charles, please. What in God's name are you talking about?'

He had to swallow against the tightness in his throat, and then he said with cold calmness: 'Perhaps I told you, perhaps I didn't. The day I was shot at beside the river in your brother's paddock, I picked up a paper tissue among the rocks above the river. I felt the shooter had dropped it, because I could detect a scent of something I assumed to be aftershave on it, which would mean it was freshly dropped. The police didn't think it had any significance because by the time they arrived the scent had faded, and even if it hadn't, how would it have helped them? But when you've just come close to being killed, things tend to be impressed on your mind. I haven't forgotten that scent, but it isn't aftershave: it's the perfume you use. It was you who tried to kill me.'

'I see.' Her voice was tightly controlled, like his own. 'I thought you'd decided the shooter was only trying to frighten you.'

'I did. But I rather think you failed only because you're not used to handling a gun.'

'Is that right?' She jerked open the car door. 'Very well, you stupid, blundering idiot. If you think I was trying to cover up a murder, perhaps you can explain why I've urged you, from the beginning, to believe there *was* a murder, to follow up that belief. Can you explain that?'

He didn't answer.

'You're right in one thing. Yes, I was the mystery gunman. And was I trying to kill you? My father will be away playing golf. Come into the house and get his rifle. Oh, don't be alarmed, you can get it out and carry it yourself. I'll show you where it is.'

With shaking hands she unlocked the front door and led the way into the house. He followed in silence. In the study she reached under the top of the desk and brought out a key that had been hanging there out of sight, and tossed it to him.

'Unlock that tall bookcase and get the rifle out.' She jerked open a drawer. 'Here's the loaded magazine. We don't leave it in the gun. I have a phone call to make.'

He took the magazine and unlocked the bookcase without speaking. A bolt-action Savage .222 rifle stood in a section of the bookcase. He took it out and flicked the breech open to make sure there wasn't a single bullet left in the chamber. He closed the bookcase and put the heavy magazine into his pocket.

Pip was speaking briefly on the phone. 'Warren? Hi, it's me. Listen, don't be alarmed if you hear a few shots down by the river. I want to run a little experiment with Charles. So don't think it's a homicidal maniac. OK? No, but I'm about to. See you.' She hung up and turned to Charles.

'Let's go. You can lock that thing in the boot.'

Neither spoke another word as they drove out past Warren Henty's house and stopped beside the wooden stile. 'Here, I presume?' Charles said tersely. Some of his outrage had been invaded by bewilderment.

'Yes.' She opened her handbag and took out a shorthand notebook and tore out a few pages. 'Get the rifle.'

She climbed the stile and strode off toward where the river widened out into the pool he had known so well in childhood. He followed.

At the pool she placed the notebook pages down on the little sandy beach, weighting each page with a small handful of the crumbled decayed granite, placing the pages

144

about a metre apart.

'Now we'll go up to the rocks,' she said briefly.

When they were behind the boulders some sixty metres from the river she turned and looked at him. 'Put the magazine in the rifle,' she said quietly, 'and hand it to me. Are you afraid to do that?'

The blazing anger that filled her earlier, almost matching his, appeared to have lessened, perhaps replaced by hurt.

He answered her by snapping the full magazine into place and handing her the rifle with the safety-catch on.

She turned away from him and knelt with the barrel of the rifle steadied in a cleft between two boulders. She flicked the bolt and brought the first live shell into the firing chamber, steadied herself again, and fired.

The notebook-page on the left of the row ripped apart in a little spurt of sand. She flicked the bolt again and fired at the next impromptu target. One by one, from left to right and unerringly, she blasted each of the tiny targets. Then she took the magazine from the rifle, ejected the last empty shell that was left in the breech, and handed the lot to Charles.

She met his eyes steadily. 'Was I unable to hit you, that day?'

He was staring at her, stunned all over again. 'My God,' he said shakily. 'What have I said? What have I thought? What have I done? Pip — But what? *What*?'

She took a long deep breath. 'It's all right,' she said. 'I would have told you. I should have told you sooner. It's my fault. I'm sorry. I wasn't sure how to tell you.'

He leaned against a boulder, feeling his legs might not support him. 'Pip, in heaven's name, why?'

'I couldn't think of any other way.' She was leaning against one of the great boulders also, her face dead pale, her fists clenched in a kind of desperation.

'I was so *certain*,' she went on after a moment, 'so certain Ursula had been murdered. After what she had told me — not the words so much as the way she spoke them — it was too much to believe that her death was an accident. But I hadn't a shred of evidence. I didn't feel it was an ounce of use to go to the police with a wild story like that. Then you came along — Ursula's son — and said you didn't believe it was an accident. And my heart leapt — I had an ally.'

She swallowed. 'Then as soon as you'd said it, you backed down and said you'd been talking nonsense. You were going back to Canada. And if you did that, it was finished. No one would ever do anything. I know finding her killer can't bring her back, but he — or she — mustn't go free, never paying any price at all for what was done.'

She sighed. 'I tried to think of some way to convince you to stay — to shock you to take your suspicions seriously, tried to push you to do some sleuthing for yourself, even if the police didn't think it was worth any further investigation. And I thought if it seemed someone had tried to kill you, or even just tried to frighten you off, you'd absolutely believe your mother's death was murder, and you'd stay and do everything you could to find who killed her, and why. And even the police would have to have second thoughts about it. Oh, Charles, please try to understand!' Her voice shook suddenly.

'What,' he said slowly, 'made you think you wouldn't simply succeed in frightening me off?'

She met his eyes. 'Because you're not that sort of man.'

'You didn't know me. You still don't.'

She shrugged. 'Call it intuition, then.'

'Do you realize the trouble you could have been in? With the law, I mean? There are probably about a dozen charges they could have brought against you!'

'The chance I'd ever be caught was pretty remote. I know my way around this locality awfully well. I got one heck of a fright when Dad turned up,' she added with a rueful smile. 'Because I guessed he'd make a dash for it and call the police from Warren's place. So I had to get out in more of a hurry than I'd planned.'

Charles shut his eyes. 'You are a bloody little fool,' he said faintly.

'Why?' She was much more comfortably in control of herself now — even faintly amused.

'You don't seem to understand the risks you took!'

'What were the risks? I'm a good shot, even if that sounds like bragging. I understand that gun. No one was going to get hurt.'

'What about the risks to yourself if your planning went wrong and you were caught? Didn't you *think*?'

The mild amusement went out of her eyes and her face went gravely still.

'Oh, yes,' she said quietly. 'I thought. I thought long and hard. I cared very much about your mother. Maybe there was a big gap in our ages, but that had nothing to do with it. She was the best friend I ever had. I believed some rotten piece of filth had killed her. I am still certain of it. On my own, I had not even the remotest chance of finding out who it was, but finding out was — is — terribly important to me. If I had to take a risk, if I had to frighten a couple of people, if I had to do something not lawful in order to make someone do some more investigating, then too bad. And I would do it again.'

The quiet conviction in her voice was more moving than any amount of dramatics. Charles found himself wanting urgently to go to her, to hold her, to go back to that moment of blazing promise in the car. But he went on leaning against the boulder, just looking at her.

'You're . . . quite a person, aren't you?' he said. 'Pip, I said — believed for a moment — awful things of you. I can hardly ask you to forgive that.'

She shook her head. 'It was my fault. I should have told you much sooner. It's not all that easy to tell someone you tried to terrorize him. It tends to put a damper on a friendship.'

Suddenly he laughed. 'My God, I hope you never *do* decide to take a shot at me!'

She smiled at him. 'I probably won't.'

'Does your father know who his near-assassin was?'

'Oh, yes. I told him that night. I think he

was a bit horrified, but in the end he went along with it happily enough. He thought very highly of Ursula, too. And, of course, I told Warren and his family. I didn't want them to think there was a nutcase gunman prowling around their farm.'

'I'm not sure there wasn't,' Charles said drily.

'Thanks,' she said, and the constraint between them was dissolved. 'It's getting late. We'd better get back.'

They walked back to the car in companionable ease, and Charles drove her home. At her front door she turned to look at him.

'Charles, you will please be careful, won't you?'

'Careful?' he queried cheerfully. 'With no phantom gunman lurking anywhere?'

'No phantom gunman who misses his target,' she said very gravely. 'But a very real killer who doesn't. Don't forget for a moment that a young man was bashed to death this morning — a young man who knew your mother, saw her often. Would have seen her drive past on her way to work every morning; would have seen her drive home every evening. Would have seen her drive home the evening she was killed. Maybe he saw too much.'

Charles nodded slowly. 'I know. I shan't

forget. And if the two deaths are linked, I want to find the killer for that boy's sake as well. But I can't think my mother's murderer' — he hesitated for a moment but didn't qualify it with 'if there was one' — 'could regard me as any kind of a threat. Certainly I've drawn a blank so far. The police will be a much bigger threat to him now, if he's responsible for both deaths. That could be his big mistake, that boy's murder.'

'I hope so,' Pip said bitterly. 'I hope so.'

Charles bent and kissed her gently on the cheek. 'Thank you for caring so much about my mother,' he said. 'And please try to forgive me.' Then he walked quickly out to the car and drove back to the Erskine house.

7

A restless and largely sleepless night, in which too many thoughts and emotions chased each other unproductively through his mind, left him with only two clear conclusions.

First, for what it was worth, he had to get on with the business of getting to know his stepfamily. It seemed to him that, somewhere there, the answer most probably lay. Perhaps none of them were directly involved, but they were the most likely people to know a reason, a motive, for someone to want Ursula dead — even if they didn't know the significance of their own knowledge. He must get to know them better, must talk to them, perhaps over and over, questioning without seeming to question. How, he had no clear idea. He would ask Jill to dinner. That seemed the logical way to get better acquainted with the only unattached member of the family.

The second and overwhelming conclusion was that Philipa Henty was an exceptional young woman and he would be both ends and the middle of a fool if he let her slip out of his life.

He fed Marmaduke and Aristotle and sat

in the kitchen over coffee and toast, with Marmalade stretched at his feet, accepting him now without reservations, though he would still alertly raise a black-and-white head at any sound that hope could possibly interpret as Ursula returning. It still hurt, but it endeared him to Charles, nevertheless. Even Aristotle had accepted Charles to the level where he now interspersed his gritting 'Hello, larrikin' with 'There you are, you funny old bird.'

After breakfast he telephoned Jill. 'Dinner? That would be nice, Charles, but I'm on call for emergencies at the surgery all this week. Look, Rex will be here most evenings this week, so why don't you come here for dinner one evening, if you'll take pot-luck with my cooking? You've met Rex, my fiancé, haven't you?'

Charles had a hazy recollection of a young man with more than a fair share of good looks, who had hovered attentively but fairly unobtrusively around Jill at Ursula's funeral. He wasn't sure whether getting to make an assessment of Jill Erskine would be easier or harder with Rex Bartlett in attendance, but since he wanted the occasion to appear no more than a casual stepbrotherly visit he couldn't sound reluctant.

'I remember him. But I don't want to horn

in on your time together. I think someone told me his job keeps him moving from place to place.'

'Well, yes, he's an area representative for an agricultural chemical film, which means he has a fairly big territory to cover. But he'll be in town nearly all week and I'd like you to meet him properly. Make it dinner on Wednesday?'

'Sounds good. What's your favourite style of wine? I'll see what I can do from the Glenlodge cellars.'

Those arrangements made, he drove back alone to the winery and sat in the office, at his mother's desk, carefully going over the books, checking what accounts, if any, needed to be paid, reading her correspondence — all of it business, both the incoming and the carbons of letters she had sent. There was correspondence with two wine-merchants, several hotels and liquorstores, and a few restaurants. Obviously Ursula had worked hard at promoting Glenlodge produce, and worked to some good effect.

Evidently one of the wine-merchants, or wholesalers, she dealt with was a long-standing associate, as letters addressed him as 'Dear Henry', and his to her were also on a first-name basis, though the letters were entirely business correspondence. The

154

most recent exchanges revealed that Henry, after a business trip to Japan to establish contacts, had sent a sample consignment of Glenlodge wines — along with some from various other wineries, naturally — and the Glenlodge product had met with favourable reception resulting in the placing of orders — small, but a foot in the door.

Ursula's delight at this spilled over into the correspondence and she clearly regarded it — with full justification, Charles realized — as a genuine compliment to Glenlodge wines, for only quality wine would reach into even this small niche in a highly competitive market.

In the blotter-folder on the desk he found a handwritten letter which stopped his hand in mid-movement. Dated the day she died, Ursula had begun writing a letter to him, and for some reason hadn't finished it. Sparkling with her enthusiasm, the words told him of the first overseas sale of Glenlodge wine, and how she was looking forward to seeing him on his visit home next month — *But don't be alarmed, I don't expect you to spend too much of your leave here. You'll find this far too dull after all the places you've seen and the experiences you've had. It'll be just grand to see you again, that's all, and I get excited whenever I think about it.*

There was a bit of news about the district. He read on, wondering if there was some kind of clue in it as to the worrying thing she had spoken of to Pip, but after two pages the letter ended, unfinished. Whether next day Ursula would have written something of her distress he would never know. There had been no next day for her.

After a long, aching stillness he folded the letter and put it into his shirt-pocket and tried to put it out of his mind, with its unfulfilled promise of meeting in a few weeks.

With a sigh of resignation he began sorting out which of the business correspondence he would have to deal with first, realizing that all the people with whom Ursula did business had to be informed of her death, and of the fact that the orchard and winery were temporarily under his management, pending a decision on their future.

He was a reasonably competent typist and had finished three letters before it struck him that he had indeed written 'pending a decision', not 'pending their sale'.

He sat frowning at the wall for a long run of minutes. Pip illogically wanted him to stay and run the orchard, the vineyard, the winery. Things he knew nothing about, beyond the inescapable childhood memories.

When his mother had left Glenlodge to him in her will, never guessing that it would so soon, so shatteringly soon, be his, had she cherished any secret hope he might make it his home and his career? She would not have *expected* it, but hope is sometimes divorced from practical realities. Ursula would never have wished him to feel bound to Glenlodge by duty; would never have wished it to be a burden to him, he knew. Right from the start, from when he had been a high-school student considering career options, she had encouraged him to make his own choice absolutely. She would still want him to make that choice freely and without pressure.

She had always had the firm opinion that as far as possible people should do the work they most wanted to do. Charles had never had any doubts. Until yesterday, when he had walked Glenlodge earth, stood in its cellars, seen the burgeoning of spring and the promise of eventual harvest on its vines and trees, felt the ancient, primordial cycles of nature that human hands may guide and share and reap benefit from, but never instigate, never create, never control.

And catching him totally by surprise, something in him had responded with rising excitement.

It was only, he concluded, because his

emotions were raw with grief and uncertain anger against the possibility of evil involved in his mother's death, stirred freshly by the certain knowledge that there was unquestionably evil involved in the death of the young apprentice mechanic he hadn't even known. Nerves strung tight could produce all sorts of emotional reactions.

He went back to typing letters, but he still typed the phrase 'pending a decision' on the future of Glenlodge. He assured everyone they would be advised of that decision at the earliest possible time. He decided he would go to Brisbane in the coming week to interview some of the clients personally, especially Henry, the wine wholesaler. He would telephone some of them in the morning and make appointments. He would also take the opportunity to see his father, partly because it would be rather unnatural not to visit him, even though he'd seen little of him for many years, and partly because he was curious to know why Geoffrey Waring had come in some kind of desperation to beg help from his ex-wife.

The necessary letters finished, he stood up and stretched and noted with surprise that the sun had already set and daylight was fading into dusk. There were no lights in the house, he noted, then remembered that when he had called there to tell the Rushtons he was going to spend the day in the office, Tom Rushton had said they were to visit friends and probably would be staying on to have dinner with them.

He walked slowly through the winery, finding light switches as he went, looking at things half-remembered and things totally unfamiliar: the crusher-destemmer through which the grapes first passed; the fermenter and drainer into which the must — the mixture of crushed fruit and juice — was pumped. Was it called must before or after it fermented? Then there was the press, and the series of pumps and tanks whose precise purpose he'd forgotten. He stood looking at the array of equipment for a while, and shook his head. Dear heaven, he thought, how on earth could I run a winery? The one thing which came clearly to memory was the sour, dank smell of fermenting must. It seemed to linger, even now, when crushing and fermenting were months behind — and months ahead — but he suspected it was lingering only in his memory. All here was spotless and sterile-looking.

The cellar with its barrels, some of oak and a few of softly gleaming stainless steel, had intrigued him even in childhood, and he stood a while, looking at the dark oak, surprised at remembering some of the terms, from the barriques of 150 litres through the hogsheads to the 500 litre puncheons and some great barrels much bigger again. So much work, so much skill, had gone into the wines that came to maturity here, some ageing for year after year after year in the oak; so much fine judgement was still required to decide when the contents had taken just the right degree of flavour from the oak itself and were best ready for bottling — the cellar represented, to Charles, the very heart of the winery. And he knew that perhaps that was a foolish notion, because there were so many factors involved, from the choosing of the best varieties to grow in a given situation, right through the care of the vines, the timing of the harvest, the blending of varieties, plus a host of other factors, to the actual marketing of the product. A winery, like any business, had many hearts.

He turned out the lights and went out to his car. Tomorrow Rob Carlyle, the winemaker, would be here to begin to fill him in on some of the basics he had forgotten or had never known. And so would Giovanni Petroni who, according to Tom Rushton and Cliff Barber, had a special feel for the vines. They must all look at Charles askance and wonder where Glenlodge would go under his ignorant direction. Wonder what sort of man Ursula Erskine's son was.

He drove away, back toward the Erskine house, his mind busy sorting out the things he must do in the coming week. It was clearly going to be rather hectic, and he reflected with some surprise that prior to the news of his mother's death he had been looking forward to his delayed leave with visions of spending a slice of it loafing on a beach in the Whitsunday Islands off the north-central Queensland coast, doing some reading, some snorkelling among the magical coral reefs, just relaxing and unwinding. Until this moment he hadn't even thought of gleaming white beaches and the lapping blue sea and the wonders which lay beneath it.

As he passed, the service station where young Joe Franklin had been killed the previous morning was in silent darkness, and Charles stopped the car and just sat looking at the darkened building, and thinking. Whoever had killed Joe hadn't robbed the service station. Whoever it was had struck the young man down, apparently, without premeditation, since a tool belonging to the service station had been the weapon. Charles sat in frowning concentration.

If Joe's killer had not come intending to steal, and had not come intending to kill,

161

why had he — or she — killed? Because he was a madman who struck randomly, at whim? It was possible. Or because Joe was for some reason a danger and the killer had not known it until that moment? The more he thought about it, the more Charles became convinced that one or other of those explanations must be right. But if it were the second one, was it in any way connected with Ursula's death, and if so, how?

Presently he started the car and drove on. He had never felt less like relaxing in the sun. Sometime, yes. But not now, not yet. Too much darkness lay over this peaceful district.

Peaceful. He thought about that for a moment, feeling that was a cynically smug assumption, to think of a town or district with a small population as being a tranquil, even rather dull, place. But in essentials, a small community was no different from a teeming city: people were born here; died here. They fell in love here; perhaps, sometimes, they hated.

He got out of the car at the Erskine house and felt in his pocket for the keys, and swore in exasperation. He remembered he'd put them in the pocket of his jacket, hung the jacket on the back of the chair in the Glenlodge office, and walked out without

162

it. Nothing to do but get back in the car and drive the several kilometres back to the orchard, thoroughly cross with himself for his absent-mindedness.

Unlocking the door to the office with the separate key he always carried in the glovebox of the car, he strode in, snapping the light on as he did so. He had a fleeting glimpse of the room he had left not much more than half an hour before, now a total shambles, with drawers pulled out and papers flung everywhere. Then he heard or sensed a movement behind him, and as he began to turn around, flinging up one arm instinctively in front of his face, something hit the side of his head and vision and awareness splintered into black nothingness.

He half-woke painfully to Tom Rushton's voice saying urgently, 'Charles. Charles! Are you all right?' Then, to someone else, 'Get an ambulance. And the police. My God, it's just as well we didn't stay to dinner like we intended.'

Charles struggled to sit up, and found a violent headache and a fuzzy lack of co-ordination made it all seem unwise. Also, it seemed to alarm Tom, who put his hands on Charles's shoulders and pushed him gently but firmly back to the floor.

'Take it easy, man. We're getting an ambulance.'

'No.' His voice seemed to be a long way off, but his head was clearing. 'I don't need an ambulance. Don't need a hospital.'

'Don't be daft. You must've stopped a hefty crack on the head. It might have done some damage.'

Charles ran a cautious hand over his head and found a sizeable swelling whose stickiness told him before he looked at his fingers that the blow had cut his scalp just above his left ear.

'Some lousy sod hit me when I opened the door,' he said.

'But it's hours since you came,' Tom said doubtfully.

'I came back,' Charles said, gradually getting his thoughts and his vision into focus. 'Left the house-keys in my jacket. Left the jacket. Forgot.'

He had another try at sitting up, and this time the room didn't somersault so often, and Tom didn't try to stop him, evidently satisfied it wouldn't do any major damage.

Charles squinted against the ache in his head and looked slowly around the office. Every drawer, in desk and filing cabinet, was pulled out and the contents emptied on the floor, the safe Ursula had called The Thieves'

164

Delight stood open. Everything suggested a search in frantic haste. There didn't seem to be any actual attempt at deliberate damage, except for a heavy crystal flower-vase which had stood on the filing cabinet. It was lying broken on the floor.

Following Charles's glance, Tom said, 'Reckon that's probably what he hit you with.'

'Mmm. What time is it?'

'Not quite seven. Our friends got word to say their daughter had just had a baby, and we knew they'd be really anxious to go and see her, so we said we wouldn't stay to dinner. Just as we were nearly at the house, on the farm-road here, we met a car going out, going fast, lights blinding on full beam, so we've no idea even what sort of a car it was, but it made us very uneasy, the way it was going — like the driver had been up to no good. We had to pull right over to avoid it. We expected you'd be gone, of course, and there were no lights on down here, so we raced straight into the house, afraid we'd been burgled. But everything was just as we'd left it, so we thought we'd come down here and check things out. Gave us a nasty shock to see you spread out on the floor — thought for a second you were dead.'

Tom's wife appeared in the doorway, a

quietly spoken woman with concern in her blue eyes. 'The police and ambulance are on their way,' she said. 'How is he?'

Charles managed what he hoped was a reassuring smile. 'I'm afraid the ambulance fellows will think I'm a fraud. I'll be fine in a minute.'

Lois Rushton shook her head. 'After being hit as hard as you were, you need to be checked out by a doctor, just to be on the safe side. Have you any idea what time it was when you were hit?'

Charles began to shake his head, but the pain made him think better of it. 'Not really. It was pretty well dark when I left. I went home without the house-keys and had to come back for them. I opened the door to the office and put the light on and saw everything was a mess, just for a second. Someone must have stood back against the wall, behind the door. I think I must have heard a movement or something. I started to turn around, and he hit me.'

Lois Rushton nodded in some satisfaction. 'Good. I mean, you're thinking straight. That's a good sign.' She glanced at the broken vase and looked at her husband. 'Do you think Charles was hit with that?'

Tom nodded. 'I'd guess so.'

'It's lucky the injury wasn't worse, then.

That vase would be heavy.'

'I think I might have spoiled his swing,' Charles said. 'I remember putting up one arm in front of my face — I think with some idea of protecting my eyes. I may have deflected his arm a fraction.'

The room was beginning to waver around him again with the effort of concentrating his thoughts, and he shut his eyes.

'Just sit still and don't try to talk anymore for a while,' Lois said gently.

'Thank God we came home when we did,' Tom said again. 'The bastard might have finished him off, just like poor Joe Franklin.'

Just like poor Joe Franklin.

The words seemed to tumble around in Charles's brain, and finally his head cleared enough for him to make the connection.

'The money that was in the safe yesterday — in a cash-box. Is it still there? Oh, hell, no — don't touch anything. Fingerprints.'

The Rushtons had already been scrupulously careful to avoid touching things.

'I won't touch it,' Tom said, 'but the cash-box is still in the safe, I can see. Whether the money's there I can't tell. It wasn't all that much, was it? A couple of hundred dollars?'

'Yes. It's just — I think I'll feel a lot better if it's been taken.'

The Rushtons exchanged puzzled glances and urged him to rest until the ambulance came. To his surprise, he was content to do so, but he had only a few minutes more to wait. Two ambulance officers, after a quick but professional check, wheeled in a stretcher and ignored Charles's protests that he needed neither stretcher nor hospital. 'It's OK, mate,' one assured him cheerfully. 'If they decide you're fit to go home after a doctor's seen you, we'll take you home again. But we'll let a doctor check you over first.'

'I've got to wait for the police to come,' Charles objected. 'They'll want to talk to me.'

The ambulance officer grinned. 'Matey, in my experience, if the cops want to talk to you, they're real good at finding you. Stop worrying.'

'I'll tell them what happened,' Tom Rushton said. 'And we'll deliver your car wherever you want it, when you're ready.'

'Marmaduke,' Charles said. 'I haven't fed the cat.'

'I'll go out and feed him,' Lois said. 'I promise.'

'Keys,' Charles said. 'In my jacket — are they still there?' They were. 'Take them,' he said.

To Charles's mild disgust the doctor who

examined him and sent him for X-rays then had him admitted to hospital overnight for observation, but although he tried to argue, some part of him acknowledged that it probably wasn't an unreasonably bad idea.

In the morning he was told he was fit to go home provided he rested for the day. Tom Rushton, smiling and looking relieved, arrived with the car and took him out to the Erskine house, Lois collecting Tom in their own car from there.

Charles was scarcely inside the door before the police arrived. When he had waved Inspector Rogerson and the accompanying detective to chairs in the lounge the inspector looked at him with steady eyes which showed no hint of what he might be thinking.

'Well, Mr Waring, you do seem to have an unfortunate habit of running into trouble. I gather you didn't see who hit you?'

'No. The place was in darkness, ostensibly just as I'd left it a half-hour or so before. I'd left my house-keys and had to go back. I simply walked in and switched on the light, saw the room was a shambles and sensed — heard, probably — a movement behind me. I began to turn around, I think, and I put my arm up — expecting an attack, I suppose. But I wasn't quick enough.'

'You didn't see, for example, any part of

your attacker's clothing? Trousers, shoes? Or a strange vehicle parked outside when you drove up?'

'I've tried to remember, but no, I'm certain I simply didn't see anything — certainly no vehicle, but it could easily have been parked out of sight.'

'Any impression of the person at all? A big person, a small person?'

'Big enough to hit pretty hard,' Charles said ruefully, 'otherwise, no, I've no idea. It was all too quick.'

'We assume,' Inspector Rogerson said, 'that you were struck with a heavy crystal vase, which was lying on the floor, broken. Quite a small person could have done you damage with it. Including a woman.'

'No fingerprints, I suppose?'

'Oh, a variety of them, but not on any relevant surfaces. Not a doubt that the intruder wore gloves.' He paused. 'Would anything of value have been kept in the office?'

'There was a bit over two hundred dollars in the safe. Was it taken? I know the safe was open, but there never was a serious attempt to keep it locked, apparently.'

'The safe was open, the cash-box was open, but there was the sum of two hundred and sixty-four dollars in it.'

Charles put his head in his hands. 'Oh, God,' he said.

Rogerson watched him curiously. 'You sound disappointed, Mr Waring. Did you *want* to be robbed?'

'I'd have preferred it,' Charles said grimly. 'A nice, simple robbery sounds preferable.'

'Might I ask why?'

Charles met his eyes. 'I think,' he said, 'you know why. I think that's why a fairly run-of-the-mill mugging has attracted the attention of an inspector when a lower-ranked officer would normally deal with it. First my mother's house is carefully searched while I'm out, and nothing is taken. Then the office at the winery is ransacked and the money is found but not touched. At the house, it seems, the intruder knew he wouldn't be disturbed. He had a whole lot of hours to go carefully and try to leave no evidence that there'd *been* any intruder. He made a mistake by not remembering where my mother's jacket had been — presumably he'd been through the pockets. I had no way of knowing what he'd been searching for, so I had no idea whether he'd found it. Obviously, he hadn't. So he came here; but this time he had to hurry, because although the Rushtons were out, he couldn't know when they'd be back, and he didn't want to be here then. The question is, what the hell was he looking for?'

'And,' the inspector added quietly, 'did he find it?' He paused. 'Tell me, do you have some idea of why this intruder — if it is the same person in both cases — might have been searching for something?'

'I think,' Charles said, 'it might have been some sort of incriminating evidence.'

Inspector Rogerson frowned. 'Incriminating evidence against whom?'

'Against him — or her — whoever the intruder is. You may remember I told you that my mother had confided in a friend that she had to make some kind of decision about someone she described as being evil. I'm now forced to believe that she had some actual evidence of that person's evil, and the person knew it was so.'

'And so you asked me whether any of Mrs Erskine's stepfamily had a criminal record. They haven't. But of course, the person need not have been a family member.'

'Which opens up the field by several million people, yes. And my mother's death may have been an accident, and the intrusion at her house and the incident in the winery last night may not be connected. I know that, too. But aren't there just too many coincidences? If the Rushtons hadn't arrived

172

home last night when they did, whoever hit me mightn't have been content to leave me alive just in case I *had* seen something. Apparently he saw their car-lights turn on to the winery road, and bolted. And in addition to the house and office being entered and not robbed, a young service-station attendant — who would have known my mother at least slightly and would have seen her pass the service station twice a day — is killed, evidently without premeditation, in what also looked like a robbery but wasn't.'

Inspector Rogerson was silent for a moment, his face as unreadable as ever. 'We're not blind to the possibilities, Mr Waring,' he said, 'but we can only work on evidence.'

'And you haven't any, even on Joe Franklin?'

'Our enquiries are proceeding.'

'In other words, you haven't a clue.'

'It's early days yet.' The inspector's voice was suddenly hard. 'I don't like murder, Mr Waring, and I don't like murderers to go free. I have a son just Joe Franklin's age. You are right: I haven't a clue — yet.'

Charles looked at him long and thoughtfully, seeing for the first time the man behind the carefully built mask of official calm detachment.

Inspector Rogerson raised an eyebrow quizzically. 'May I ask what you are thinking?'

'I was thinking,' Charles said, 'that if I were Joe Franklin's killer, I wouldn't like to have you on the case.'

The inspector smiled suddenly with a warmth that lit his eyes. 'Thank you. That's the nicest thing that's likely to be said to me today.'

He stood up and held out his hand. 'Just one thing: I said no member of your stepfamily has a criminal past. Remember, all that means is that none of them has committed a crime we *know* about. I can't prevent you from doing your own sleuthing if you wish. There may be nothing for you to discover. But a once-quiet backwater has been stirred, and there may be something very nasty lurking in the depths. Go carefully.'

He shook Charles's hand in what was more a gesture of comradeship than an official courtesy. Then he turned and walked out.

8

After the police left, Charles drove down to Glenlodge to keep his appointment with Rob Carlyle.

Tall, slim, quietly spoken, with thinning fair hair, and alert eyes behind rimless glasses, Rob expressed what seemed genuine distress at what had happened the previous night, and seemed concerned that Charles wasn't home resting.

Charles smiled. 'I admit to a stinking headache earlier, but a couple of codeine tablets have quietened it quite a bit. And there's this mess' — he gestured at the paper-strewn floor — 'to clear up. The police said they were finished with everything here, and I could pick everything up now.'

'I'll give you a hand, if you like. I'll gather up the papers and stuff and you can put it all away. Do you know if anything was taken? Tom Rushton said the cash-box wasn't touched.'

'I hardly know what was here, really,' Charles said. 'Maybe it was a case of sheer vandalism. Maybe whoever it was wanted something my mother had. If so, I don't know what it was.'

Rob Carlyle made no comment, and when the office was restored to order he sat down in one of the chairs and looked closely at Charles. 'What exactly did you want to talk about?'

'Basically, two things.' Charles sat on a corner of the desk and looked at him assessingly. 'The first, and I guess the basic one, is whether you want to stay on at Glenlodge.'

Rob rubbed his chin. 'Tom told me that you may sell the place. If that happens, it will depend on whether the new owner wants me.'

'From what I've heard of these wines, he'd be a fool not to want you to stay. Glenlodge's reputation is growing largely on your expertise, after all.'

'I'm only one of a team.' Rob shrugged. 'But I have to admit I'm proud of our wines. It's a fascinating business, wine-making, and I happen to have been given by nature a sensitive palate, so I can pick up all kinds of shadings of bouquet and flavour. That's the luck of the draw, that's all.'

Charles smiled. 'And I inherited my mother's *insensitive* palate, only worse, so I'd be useless. So, if whoever owns the

176

winery wants you to stay, you will?'

'I'd like to stay. There are wines maturing now, that I'd love to follow through. And there are new things I'd like to try. Oh, yes, all things being equal, I'd like to stay.'

'Good.' Charles nodded. 'Then the second thing I need to talk to you about — or rather need you to talk to me about — is the wine-making process itself, because for at least some time I'm going to be responsible for managing the place, and I know absolutely nothing.'

Rob looked startled. 'But . . . didn't you grow up here?'

'Until I was eighteen or so, yes. But although I used to help pick the grapes in the season, I was never interested in the processing of them. I used to help tip them into the crusher-destemmer and always thought it neat the way the stems were separated from the berries.' He grinned. 'But frankly I didn't like the smell of the fermenting must, and was quite happy to clear off and not get in anyone's way.'

He didn't add that he had always associated the winery with arguments between his parents, and had turned away.

'So,' he added, 'will you give me a run through the basics? I'll have to talk with people who *do* know rather a lot about wines and wine-making, so it would be nice to know a *little*. I realize,' he added, 'that it would take more than a lifetime to learn properly.'

Rob smiled. 'I'm certainly still learning. Right, let's take a quick tour of the place.' He stood up. 'The reds,' he said as they walked, 'are the most complex wines to make. That doesn't mean that it's easy to slap up a good white. Far from it. But the basic process is simpler and they require less maturing. Actually, we put out a couple of very good whites, especially one dessert wine I'm rather proud of.'

'I hear people talking about such-and-such a year being a vintage year for a certain area,' Charles said. 'What makes it so? Weather, I presume?'

Rod nodded. 'Rainfall at the right time, the right amount of sun, that sort of thing. Here we'd regard rainfall averaging around an inch a fortnight till January, then nice fine weather, as ideal. If the grapes ripen slowly, the sugar content is increased. If they ripen too quickly the flavour is impaired. They're tested, of course — acid level, PH balance and so on — to decide when each patch should be harvested.'

He smiled. 'Giovanni seems to know by instinct, but I have to run tests.'

They were at the back of the winery, where in the season the big doors would stand open for the trailerloads of grapes to be backed in and their loads tipped into the crusher-destemmer to be fed through the rollers which gently broke the berries from the stalks.

'Well, you know this,' Rob said, touching the next, elevated tank.

'That's where the must is pumped in to ferment,' Charles said, 'and that's about the limit of my recollection. I don't remember if it ferments naturally or has something added.'

Rob nodded. 'It has to have active yeast culture added immediately to speed fermentation and dominate the wild yeasts on the grape skins. Ethanol forms and extracts colour and flavour. When I feel it's right, the free-run juice is drained through the bottom of the tank, through the press, and is pumped up here to this tank for final fermentation. The screen in the first tank is raised and the skins, the pomace, drop into the press for squeezing the rest of the juice from them. Lighter 'pressings wine' goes in with the free-run, the heavier pressings can go to the distillery. The grape skins go back to the vineyard as fertilizer.'

'This is where the lees settle and the wine

is pumped off the top: racked off? Is that the right term?' Charles asked.

Rob grinned. 'You remember more than you thought. From here, through the racking pump, it goes into the fining tank. You see, there are still very fine particles in it which need some help to settle, so here we add things like egg white or gelatine, sometimes bentonite. When it's cleared enough it's racked off again into the oak barrels to mature.'

'For years, of course,' Charles said.

'Yes. As you see, there are various sizes of oak barrels. I like the smaller ones, up to the five-hundred litre puncheons, because they yield the oak flavour more quickly than the really big ones, up to four thousand litres, though they have their place, too. The time is governed by the style of wine you want. I have to sample it often.'

Charles ran his hand over one of the barrels. 'Do you get evaporation through the wood?'

'Yes, you do. We always have wine set aside specially for topping up the wine in the barrels. When I feel it's ready, it all goes into the blending tank.' He glanced at Charles with a wry smile. 'That's where I earn — or don't earn — my keep. In the blending. There again you might use fining agents for a special flavour. And if you get the wine the way you want it, I guess that's what you don't tell other winemakers: just how you did it. Then it simply remains to filter it once more and bottle it. Then it's up to you — or whoever — to sell.' He smiled. 'I guess it doesn't matter how good the wine is if it isn't sold.'

Charles looked thoughtful. 'You can't be a winemaker if you're impatient, that's certain. When you process this year's crop, you can't know for years whether it's really top stuff.'

'That's true of the reds. With the whites, it's quicker, because with them — '

Charles laughed and held up his hand. 'I've absorbed about fifty per cent of what you've told me. That's all I can handle for one day after being flattened last night.'

Then he was immediately serious. 'But I can understand why you find it such a challenge. I can understand why my mother found the whole business absorbing. Thank you, Rob. I'll never be a winemaker, but I understand a lot more than I did before.'

★ ★ ★

Charles was surprised, when he went to dinner with Jill and her fiancé Rex Bartlett as arranged, to find Miriam and Douglas there also.

'I found they were staying in town overnight, so I thought we could make a bit of a family gathering out of it,' Jill said.

They all made concerned enquiries about how he felt after being bashed, but he assured them that apart from an occasionally recurring headache he had completely recovered. 'I've been too busy over the past couple of days to think much about it. There have been heaps of people to contact about Mum's death and the fact the orchard will be under my management for the time being at least. And I've had to have a crash course in the basics of orchard and vineyard and winery management.'

Douglas looked at him thoughtfully. 'I shouldn't push it too hard for a few days yet. Not when you've had concussion.'

'I think it's best if I'm kept too busy for idle thoughts at the moment,' Charles said drily.

'So you don't have time to find yourself wondering, every time you open a door, whether someone on the other side of it is waiting to mug you,' Jill said with a slight shiver. 'I can understand that.'

'It was damned lucky you had time to put up your arm the way you said you did,' Rex said. 'It might have been worse than concussion if you hadn't. What did you see or hear that warned you someone was behind you?'

Charles shook his head. 'I must have heard something. After all, it'd be fairly hard to move silently, so I suppose just a rustle of clothing would have been enough, in the circumstances. I mean, I'd had a couple of seconds to see the place had been ransacked. All senses would have jumped to red alert. The unfortunate part is that I didn't *see* anything — anything of the intruder, I mean. As the police said, even the least thing — a shoe, a sleeve, anything — could have been helpful.'

'Did he get away with anything?' Miriam asked.

'Nothing that I know of. The money was still in the safe, so maybe I turned up in time to scare him off before he picked it up. Not that the money in the safe was going to put a down-payment on a new Mercedes for him.'

'You said just now,' Jill commented, 'that the winery would be under your management for the time being 'at least'. Do I detect a suggestion that you're considering *staying* here to run Glenlodge?'

Charles hesitated. 'I honestly don't know. A fortnight ago I'd have scoffed at the idea.

I'm a geologist. I don't know the first thing about orchards and wineries, beyond what is etched on my memory from childhood. I didn't know anything useful about it and I still don't. I didn't want to know. Now I'm not so certain that I don't want to know. It's very much too soon to make a decision. As politicians like to say, I'm keeping my options open.'

Rex Bartlett smiled. 'You've got more nerve than I have, if you're game to change your job in such a total way. Particularly if you have to contend with muggers lurking behind doors and people blazing away at you with high-powered rifles.'

Charles looked at him — a tall, powerfully built, good-looking fellow of around thirty, black-haired and blue-eyed, with an easy manner and a ready laugh that gave him an unstudied likeable quality. Jill, Charles reflected, would be the envy of her unmarried girl-friends — and possibly a few married ones as well. 'I'm sure,' Charles managed to say with an off-hand laugh, 'there's absolutely no connection between the two incidents. And no personal malice towards me in either.'

Douglas Wentworth raised an eyebrow. 'You really feel that? Someone bashed you without malice?'

184

Charles shrugged. 'Consider the facts. In the shooting incident, only a hopeless incompetent who had never picked up a gun in his life could have missed me, so I've no doubt whatever that it was some idiot target-shooting without thinking what else might be in his line of fire. But I wasn't the target. As for being mugged the other evening — well, I blundered into the wrong place at the wrong time, that's all. I panicked a thief.'

Rex nodded a shade dubiously. 'I guess when you put it like that it makes sense. I still think if it were me, it'd be a case of Canada, here I come. Preferably on the next plane.'

'Perhaps not if you suspected your mother had been murdered,' Miriam said. 'And her killer was still on the loose.'

There was a moment's silence while Douglas looked at the wall opposite, Jill toyed with her wine-glass, and Rex stared at Charles in unabashed astonishment.

'Do you?' he asked. 'Believe your mother was murdered? I mean, I know what you said, the day of the funeral — but I thought that was just the kind of thing you say when something is hard to accept.'

'I think,' Charles said, 'there are some unanswered questions.'

'And that's why you're staying? To do some investigating? Well, in that case I guess I can understand.'

'I'm no detective,' Charles said. 'Perhaps it's just a reluctance to go away and leave a doubt forever in my mind. Although, to be honest, how staying on can resolve that doubt, I can't really imagine.'

Jill said, 'You're probably being much too modest, Charles. You'll probably turn out to be a brilliant sleuth. If there's anything to ferret out, of course. But tell me, what sort of things are you learning at the winery?'

Charles laughed. 'The main thing I'm learning is that I have to learn everything. I'm tremendously fortunate to have a great team of fellows working there. They've all worked with my mother for years, and they're experts in their own fields. They run the place. I just answer the telephone.'

He stopped abruptly, struck suddenly — and, to his own amazement, for the first time — by the significance of what he had just said. What if it were one of her staff about whom Ursula had uncovered some horrible secret? That, almost as much as if it were a member of her stepfamily, would greatly distress her. Those men, he knew, were more than simply employees: they were trusted friends.

He rubbed his hand across his face, struck freshly by the enormity of trying to learn who, if anyone, had engineered Ursula Erskine's death. And with that thought came the realization that there was probably only one line of action that might work. And if it worked, he might very well perish in the attempt to resolve the problem.

There was something, somewhere, which someone was very anxious should never see the light of day; some knowledge which must remain unknown.

Very well, Charles thought grimly. If you, whoever you are, begin to believe I'm getting close to the truth, and if you *are* a murderer, you'll have to come out in the open and try to silence me. So I shall begin carefully dropping an occasional hint.

It was, he thought, rather like setting a large hook, with himself as bait, just to find out if there really was a shark in the water.

'Are you all right, Charles?' Douglas asked, and Charles realized they were all looking at him, and he wondered how many seconds he had let run in silence.

'Sorry. Yes, I'm fine. The brain went off on a sudden tangent, that's all. As a matter of fact, it occurred to me for the first time to wonder whether there could be someone on the orchard staff who wanted Mother dead.

Maybe I'm getting paranoid about the whole thing.'

'Why in the world,' Jill said, 'would someone on the orchard staff want Ursula dead? For that matter, why would anyone?'

'That's a good question,' Douglas agreed.

'A few days ago,' Charles reminded them quietly, 'a boy at a service station was killed by someone who drove in, killed him with one of the service-station tools, and drove away. Why did anyone want Joe Franklin dead?'

There was a moment of silence. Then Jill said incredulously, 'You can't think there's a *connection*?'

'I don't know,' Charles answered. But he had paused just long enough to allow a quality of doubt creep into his answer.

'The point I'm making,' he went on, 'is that the reason for murder isn't always apparent at first.'

'There is a glaringly obvious motive for Ursula to be murdered,' Miriam said drily, 'provided she was murdered by an Erskine, of course.'

Jill jerked her head around to stare at her older sister. 'Miriam! That's a hideous thing to suggest! What are you talking about?'

'Good old-fashioned greed. Or even need,' Miriam said calmly, though there was a

188

faint undertone of mockery. 'Look at it from Charles's perspective. How well does he know us? What does he know of our *real* financial situations as distinct from our apparent ones? Father's money was Ursula's for her lifetime. On her death it comes to us. Plenty of people have been killed for much less than we inherit.'

'But — I say, that's a bit rough,' Rex protested. 'From what I knew of Mrs Erskine, she was a very nice lady, on the best of terms with all of you. Charles, you can't think — I mean, bloody hell, man — '

'No.' Charles shook his head. 'I don't think that at all. At first, yes, I have to admit I wondered if such a thing was possible. Sickening, but possible. But now I believe there is an even more glaringly obvious motive. She knew something about someone, had perhaps some evidence about someone, knowledge she couldn't decide what to do with. And if she was murdered, I believe it was someone protecting a secret, not someone improving their financial situation.'

'What sort of secret?' Douglas demanded.

Charles shook his head. 'I wish I knew. Maybe she was witness to a crime of some kind, or had evidence of it. Whatever it was, it distressed her very greatly, apparently, which means it must have involved someone she knew very well, someone who was important to her.'

'Do you actually know that?' Jill asked. Her outrage at the suggestion of a family member murdering for money had subsided with Charles's assurance that he didn't suspect any such thing, and now a genuine curiosity seemed to have replaced the natural anger. 'I mean, do you *know* that Ursula had some damning knowledge of someone, or are you just speculating?'

'I know that she did have some damning knowledge of someone,' Charles said steadily. 'I don't know who the person was, I don't know what that knowledge was, and I don't know whether that person murdered her — or for certain whether anyone did. But I'd give you very long odds against a convenient accident.'

In the silence that followed he could almost feel the tension, the sense of shock, in the other four people at the table, the coffee Jill had served after the meal cold and forgotten in their cups.

He felt guilt and regret at what he was doing to these people who were, in a sense, his family. But in the same moment he knew he would go on.

'Charles,' Miriam said, 'may I ask how you know that Ursula had that information?'

He had anticipated the question, and had no intention of bringing Pip's name into the equation. A misleading half-truth would suffice. 'When I was going through papers and accounts in the winery office, I found a letter she had begun to write to me just before she died, and had never finished. She spoke of knowing something which she described as 'evil' about someone, and not knowing what she should do about it. But there were no names, no details, no hint of what it was that she knew. And, as I said, the letter was unfinished.'

'So,' Miriam said slowly, 'you think someone in the Erskine family has a terrible secret.' It was half-question, half-statement, and it was said without rancour, almost with a tinge of fear.

'No!' Charles said sharply. 'It doesn't mean it's anyone in the Erskine family. It has to be someone she cared about, that's all.' He paused. 'You would all know, better than I could, about her close friends — who they were; whether there was a special man in her life, for instance.'

'No one after Father,' Jill said positively. 'I mean, occasionally someone might take her to dinner, or something like that. Nothing more.'

'What about her own family?' Rex asked.

'Brothers and sisters and so on?'

Charles shook his head. 'She was an only child, like me. But she no doubt had close friends here — women friends? Sometimes a friend can be as much cared about as family.'

'Well,' Jill said, 'really Ursula's work was her life. She had friends, of course, numbers of them. But surprisingly few really close friends — close enough to be badly distressed about if she found they had some dark secret in their past. In spite of the age-difference, I guess Pip Henty was probably her closest friend, and I can't imagine Pip harbouring some fearful secret past. I've known her most of my life.'

She flicked a smile at Charles. 'And somehow, from the way she talks about you, I doubt if she's on your list of suspects.'

'No.' Charles smiled his response, then was instantly serious. 'Look, I don't have a list of suspects, and there isn't a family member I'd put on it if I did have such a list. If I'm sounding as if I expect to find my answers — or at worst, the guilty party — somewhere among you, please forgive me. It's not so.'

Miriam nodded and said simply, 'Thank you, Charles. But you'd be a fool not to keep an open mind, and we know that as well as you do.'

Charles swept a look quickly around the table at them all. 'There's one thing that's terribly important. You must not — must not — start looking at each other with suspicion. It wouldn't be possible, within a family, to hide the sort of thing my mother was talking about. She once said to me that the only evil was cruelty, though it can come in many forms. If one of you was that sort of person, the rest of you would know.'

Whether his words reassured them, he had no way of knowing, but the subject was dropped with relative ease, and the conversation became general again, and turned to a discussion on the prospects of a horse which Miriam had bred, and which was to run in an important race.

'Do you think it's really good?' Charles asked Miriam.

'I haven't seen him since he's been in training — I don't own him, of course. He was sold as a yearling. Certainly I liked the look of him then, but perhaps I'm biased. He has a likely blood-line. His owners called him Tuesday Turning, because they bought him on a Tuesday.'

Charles, going out to the kitchen with Jill to make fresh coffee, heard the animation in

Douglas's voice as he talked about the colt with an enthusiasm Charles had never heard in him before.

Jill glanced at Charles. 'Miriam breeds horses; Douglas gambles on them.'

She said it a shade wryly, but without the concern Liz Fitzgibbon, Miriam's stable-hand and close-to-adopted-daughter, had shown. But then, Jill might not have known the extent of Douglas's gambling the way Liz did.

'Does he follow Miriam's horses — Top Bend horses?'

'Only if he thinks they'll win.' She smiled. 'Do you like Rex, Charles?'

He smiled back at her, pleased and touched by the fact she seemed to care that he should. There was a quality of wanting an older brother to approve, and it made him feel she truly regarded him as part of the family, even though they had not seen much of each other over the years.

'He's a very pleasant, easy-going fellow, and certainly no-one's fool. He passes muster with me, for sure.'

She nodded, pleased in her turn. 'He has a good job, nothing spectacular, but solid. I think he's a bit embarrassed that I'll have more money than he has — money from the estate. I tell him that's an old-fashioned outlook, and anyway it's certainly not a fortune — just enough to let me buy a full share in the veterinary practice, years before I could have otherwise.'

Charles smiled. 'It does him credit, though, to mind.'

'I guess so.' She paused. 'One of the loveliest things about him is that he's so very kind. Not simply considerate towards me, but kind to everyone and everything. He found an injured dog the other day — it had lost half a leg, poor thing — on the roadside a few kilometres out of town, and he raced in to the surgery with it, blood spattered all over his suit and the dog trying to bite him because it was crazy with pain and shock, and Rex almost as distressed as the dog and saying he'd pay any bills if the owners couldn't be found. The leg had to be amputated, of course — or enough of it to tidy up the shattered bone-ends. But my partner knew the dog and contacted the owners and they were happy to pay.'

Charles was remembering the skinny kid Jill had been when her father and Ursula were married and she was still living at home — the kid who'd been besotted with animals, so that there had hardly been any question of the career she would choose.

'I think you and Rex will make a great couple. But you may need a large house.'

She looked puzzled. 'Why?'

'You'll probably fill it with stray animals.'

She laughed. 'Probably,' she agreed cheerfully.

★ ★ ★

Charles drove home from the dinner party in a thunderstorm. Rain hissed against the windscreen and lightning arrowed raggedly against the darkness, and as he drove up the road toward the Erskine house he remembered only too well that there had been an evening storm when his mother had died. It could so easily have happened as Jack Henty had suggested: Ursula watching the road ahead through the clear-and-blur of the windscreen-wipers, with no reason to be suspicious of the car behind her, even when it began to accelerate to close the gap. No reason to be suspicious until the last moment, when it was too late.

He passed the spot where her car had plunged down over the rocks, and swung around the last bend before the house — and felt icy, warning shock slam through him as the headlights swept across the front of the house.

A car was standing near the front door. A car he had never seen before.

Anger, outrage — a rush of emotions he would find difficult to analyse — charged through him with a kind of awareness of possible danger that had no time to turn into fear. He accelerated over the last little distance and braked savagely to a stop across the other car's path, so that the driver couldn't make a quick getaway, if getting away was high on the list of options. Charles leapt from his car and took two strides toward the house when the driver's door of the other car opened and a young woman stepped out, one hand in front of her face to shield her eyes from the headlights of Charles's car.

'Charles? It's me — Liz Fitzgibbon.'

He stopped short. 'Liz!' He laughed with relief. 'I thought I was about to go and punch up a housebreaker — or be punched up by one.' Then, in quick alarm: 'But what's wrong? Why are you here? Oh, come on, let's get inside. We're getting soaked.'

He snapped out the headlights and together they ran the few metres to the house. Even so, they were damp from the rain, and Liz's hair was clinging wetly.

'Whatever the problem is that brings you here, it can wait five minutes. The bathroom's through there — go find a towel and dry your hair. I'll make some coffee. Or would you prefer a Scotch?'

'Coffee would be great, thank you. And my hair will be all right.'

'Go and dry it,' Charles ordered. 'If for no other reason, it'll give me time to recover from the prospect of confronting someone lurking with intent.'

She smiled faintly and went. When she returned with her hair tousled but fairly dry, he had made coffee. He waved her to an easy chair and handed her a steaming mug.

'Now,' he said, 'tell me about it.'

She took a sip of coffee. 'I've been sitting out there in the car for the past two hours wondering exactly why I'd come. I'd just about decided to go home. I don't see what you can do.'

Charles had a recollection of her saying something like that the first day he had met her, at Top Bend. 'Douglas?' he asked.

Liz nodded. 'Dr Wellchamp — Ted Wellchamp, Douglas's partner — came around to my place a couple of nights ago because he was concerned. He asked if I knew whether Top Bend was in financial trouble. I was completely taken by surprise, because I rather think Dr Wellchamp is strongly given to minding his own business. Well, I know Miriam is in debt to the bank, fairly heavily, because she borrowed quite a lot to buy Beau Rameses and a couple of top-class mares at about the same time. But Top Bend is a solid business. I don't know all the financial details, but obviously the bank regarded it as a good investment, to lend against Top Bend as collateral. Miriam's prospects are excellent.'

Especially with the inheritance of her share of her father's money once Ursula Erskine died, Charles thought fleetingly, before pushing the thought away as unfair.

'So,' Liz was saying, 'I told Dr Wellchamp I was sure Top Bend wasn't in financial trouble and asked why he'd think it might be. He looked uncomfortable and said he didn't want to pry, but he was worried because Douglas had asked him for a loan, saying he needed money urgently and had most of his funds tied up in term investments where he could not get the money until the investments matured. That seemed odd, because it's almost always possible to withdraw funds from a term investment before maturity, even though it means a small drop in the profit. He assured Dr Wellchamp he could repay the loan in a couple of weeks. He apparently made it pretty clear he didn't want to talk about the reason for the urgent need for cash.'

Charles frowned. 'How much did he ask Dr Wellchamp for?'

'Twenty thousand dollars.'

Charles whistled.

Liz said, 'Exactly.'

'Did Dr Wellchamp lend him the money? Do you know?'

Liz nodded. 'Yes. He said Douglas seemed so up-tight about it he felt he should, and as luck — Douglas's luck, anyway — happened, he could produce the money.'

'Against what security?'

'Douglas's word, I gather. And the fact that their joint medical practice is comfortably successful.'

She hesitated, and Charles, sensing there was more to the story, said, 'And?'

'Dr Wellchamp began to get uneasy.'

'I can believe it,' Charles said drily.

'Yes. Well, he said he knows a private investigator, a very good one; he'd once been able to help in a medical emergency and the fellow had told Dr Wellchamp if ever he needed investigation done, to call him. Ted Wellchamp is what might be called a gentleman of the old school, and I gather he felt a total rat at checking on Douglas's affairs, but he asked this private eye if it was possible to learn the state of Douglas's finances. Piece of cake, he was told, and in

200

due course was presented with the details. In summary, Douglas is not only flat broke, he's in debt to the tune of nearly a hundred thousand dollars.'

'Bloody hell,' Charles said softly.

'His partner, not unreasonably, concluded Douglas had been borrowing to stave off a crushing crisis for Miriam. When I more or less picked up my addled wits and put them back together I waffled on a bit about Douglas apparently had been helping Miriam more than she really needed — wanting to impress her, I think I said. I hardly knew what I was saying, nor if it sounded any more convincing to Dr Wellchamp than it did to me. I-I remember saying that Miriam had come into a substantial inheritance, with your mother's death, so all would be well as soon as the estate was finalized. Sorry, Charles.'

He made a dismissive gesture. 'But I gather you don't believe that's what Douglas has done with his money?'

She shook her head. 'No. I know for a fact he hasn't been paying off any of Miriam's debt. It's a matter of fierce pride with her that Top Bend is *her* venture, and it prospers or fails solely at her hands.'

Charles gave a small wry smile, remembering his mother's refusal to let any of Anthony

201

Erskine's money be used to finance ventures at Glenlodge. Mother and stepsister not unlike. In that regard, at least.

'So,' he said, 'you think, in fact, Douglas has borrowed from his partner in order to pay off some of his gambling debts? The classic way to get in deeper? But if he's not been financing Miriam's debt, why is he in such debt himself?'

'Oh, Charles!' Liz said impatiently. 'Don't be deliberately obtuse. This is Douglas Wentworth we're talking about.'

'Are you saying he's run into *gambling* debts that size? He's borrowed now to pay off some bookmakers before they get too restive?'

'I'd say he's always paid his bookmakers. That's why he's in debt to his bank — or more likely assorted banks or maybe one or two other financial institutions.'

'Which are now snapping at his heels?'

'No. I think he's going gambling. In a big way.'

'When he's already in massive debt? He couldn't be such a fool. A hundred and twenty thousand in the red and he's going on a *gambling* spree? A twenty-thousand dollar gambling spree?'

'Not a spree exactly,' Liz said. 'I think just one single bet. Oh, I know all the symptoms.

I grew up with them, didn't I? It's all there, in Douglas, the past couple of weeks: the excitement he tries to keep hidden, the way he wants to talk about this horse, but wants it to seem like just a natural interest. But he talks about it a fraction too much, and his eyes get too bright and, if you watch, his hands shake just a little bit when he's talking about it. Those symptoms don't show up in all compulsive gamblers, I'm sure, but they did in my father. I learned to watch for all those signs before I was eight years old. I could recognize them, though my mother never could.'

'Tuesday Turning,' Charles murmured.

Liz raised her head quickly to look at him. 'How on earth did you know?'

'I had dinner at Jill's place tonight. Miriam and Douglas were there. Douglas talked about a horse Miriam had bred at Top Bend. He said it was racing on Saturday. The name amused me, and I remembered. I thought he was just interested because he'd like it to win for Miriam's sake. I didn't take much notice.'

'It's racing at Corbould Park — that's near Caloundra, on the Sunshine Coast — not one of the major racecourses, perhaps, but the scene on Saturday of a very special major race, the Feltington Cup, named for a big

203

development company which is putting up half a million dollars in prize-money for this one race, as well as sponsoring other races on the day, to promote provincial racing. Tuesday Turning is a youngster largely regarded as being a bit out of his class against some of the big names he'll be racing against, but Douglas knows the trainer, and he's good. He says T.T.'s a top chance and has had ideal preparation; and Miriam has always believed in that horse, too.'

Charles was silent for a moment. 'Douglas believes it will win. What sort of odds could he expect to get?'

'Probably about seven or eight to one on the day.'

'So if it wins it will more than wipe out his debts. But if it should happen to do what so many racehorses do and fails to come up to expectations, he'll have to ask Miriam to use most of the money she's inherited from her father to bail him out of disaster instead of paying off a sizeable slice of her own mortgage?'

Liz nodded bleakly. 'Instead of her being able to feel she's on a pretty secure footing, she'll not only be nearly back to where she is now, but it will happen with a vicious shock, because she doesn't know Douglas gambles more than a few dollars at a time. She'll have to face the fact that she never can be secure, because she can never depend on Douglas not to plunge just as deeply into debt time after time. It would leave her devastated. But she'd pay his debts because she cares about him. A great deal. Only . . . even that would suffer massive damage, too.'

She took a deep breath. 'And Douglas — well, he cares a great deal about her, too, even if it doesn't sound as if he does. I don't think he could cope with what he'd have done to Miriam. I don't believe he could face living with that. I don't believe he *would* face living with it.'

She stared silently at the floor, and Charles knew she was seeing again what she had seen in the backyard of her home one afternoon when she was fifteen and had come home from school to find her father hadn't been able to cope with what his gambling had done to his family.

'Can Douglas just take twenty thousand dollars on to a racecourse and put it on in a single bet?'

With a little shiver she raised her eyes from the floor, if not from the memory.

'Normally not at a smaller course like Corbould Park. But because this is a special day with big prize-money up for grabs and some big-name horses being sent there to get a piece of the action, there'll be some big-name city bookmakers there as well, and some big-spending punters. I should think that to avoid any chance Miriam will find out, Douglas will, in fact, literally carry twenty thousand dollars on to the track and put it on at the last possible moment. It will bring Tuesday Turning's price down with a thump. He's not among the most fancied starters at the moment — he's at about fifteen to one — but if his form is as impressive as his trainer says, he'll be at shorter odds on the day. You see, he hasn't started in a major event like this before. He's had enough good runs to be able to get into this race, but not enough is known about him to attract much attention, except from those few who really know him. He may be, and Miriam has always believed it, one of those almost freak horses who come from sound but fairly ordinary stock, but turn out to be anything but ordinary themselves. If he wins on Saturday he'll have suddenly emerged from obscurity.'

'So if he wins,' Charles said, 'at, say, ten to one, Douglas collects two hundred thousand dollars.'

'If he could get those odds, which he won't. But a very hefty sum of money, yes. And if he loses, God only knows what will

206

be lost besides a horse-race.' She looked at Charles. 'I'm frightened,' she said, and he heard the quiet anguish in her voice.

'Yes,' he said. 'I can understand that.'

'Charles.' She stood up and put a hand for a moment on his arm. 'That's really why I came, I guess. I'm frightened and I had to talk to someone. If Douglas is determined to risk everything, I don't see what you can do. Or even whether you should do anything. I shouldn't have dumped the problem on you. But thank you for listening.'

He stood also. 'Liz, it's after midnight. You can't drive all the way back to Top Bend tonight. Stay.' He smiled. 'Strictly spareroom stuff. I can lend you a clean pair of my pyjamas, even if they do hang a bit loose on you.'

'Thanks, but I'd better get back. I'll be all right. I'm so much on edge there's no risk I'll fall asleep at the wheel, and I have to be at work by six.'

'Whatever you want.' He walked out with her to the car. The storm had gone, lightning flickering off to the east marking its path. 'I've never been to the races in my life, but I'll go on Saturday and I'll stick like glue to Douglas Wentworth to try to stop him from throwing everything away — or risking it. Drive carefully, Liz. Miriam and Douglas don't know how lucky they are to have you caring about them.'

She reached up suddenly and kissed him lightly on the cheek. 'Don't go back to Canada, Charles. The Erskines need you in their family.' Then she slipped behind the wheel and drove away.

As he went back into the house Charles reflected that in fact it was more than probable that some member of the Erskine family needed him and his enquiring mind about as much as they needed a hole in the head. His assurances at Jill's dinner party that he didn't harbour suspicions of any of the Erskine family had been shamelessly untrue. Try as he might, he could not really believe that anyone but a family member had been the object of Ursula's fearsome knowledge, whatever it had been.

And some time between now and a horse-race on Saturday afternoon, he had to try to stop Douglas Wentworth from risking, as Liz had put it, God only knew what: his wife's respect, his professional standing, his marriage.

Quite possibly his life, if Liz was right.

Unstopped, he might win enough to clear his debts in one fling.

And Charles had no right on earth to try to

stop him, and certainly if Tuesday Turning won, Douglas was going to hate him. Charles was going to hate himself.

Dear God, he thought: what am I getting into?

9

When Charles phoned to say he'd like to go to Corbould Park on Saturday to watch Tuesday Turning run, Miriam seemed thoroughly delighted. 'Why, Charles, that's really nice of you! We'll be leaving after breakfast on Saturday morning, but it's a good deal further for you — about five hours driving. So why not come here and stay overnight and travel down with us? There'll be only the two of us going, so there'll be plenty of room in the car. We're staying at a motel in Caloundra overnight after the races, so we can book you into the same motel and bring you back on Sunday.'

Charles reflected grimly that by Saturday afternoon, whether or not he was successful in stopping Douglas from throwing borrowed money into a bottomless hole of debt, there was a fair chance Douglas would be more willing to murder him than be pleasantly sociable.

He thanked Miriam but made the excuse that he didn't want to be away for two nights because of Ursula's pets, and would leave very early on Saturday morning and return after the last race, brushing aside Miriam's protests that this made a very long day.

Saturday broke clear and mild, and in other circumstances Charles would have enjoyed the drive across the Downs, through Toowoomba, winding down the range, through the neat little township of Esk, then taking the road which snaked around the expanse of the Somerset Dam where remnants of fog drifted, being sucked up by the sun. At tiny Peachester, on top of the next range, he bought fruit for an impromptu snack at a roadside store, smiling to himself at a sign above the cash-register which warned: 'In God we trust. Everyone else pays cash'. He felt he would find little else that day to smile about.

True to promise, Miriam and Douglas were waiting for him at the entrance when he arrived at almost exactly the arranged time, and they ushered him in with what seemed, even on Douglas's part, genuine pleasure that he had taken the trouble to come all this way to see Miriam's horse run.

'Have you seen him race before?' Charles asked, as they walked under the great soaring roof which hung above the public area and covered not only the great expanse of flooring with its dozens of tables and chairs in the area which gave the best available view of the track, but also double-roofed the tote office, bar, eating-places and bookmakers' stands.

'No,' Miriam said. 'Of course, I don't own any share of him, but I always felt he had great potential, and I've kept track of what he's been doing.'

'What will he do today?' Charles asked lightly.

Miriam shook her head, smiling. 'He'll run,' she said. 'He'll give it everything, because that's the sort of thing he is. He has marvellous spirit and marvellous physique. But on the day and against the competition, no one can ever know.'

Douglas laughed. 'He'll win,' he said.

Charles found it hard not to constantly and obviously watch Douglas. For a man who was about to take a fearful gamble, he had himself under excellent control. There was certainly an air of excitement about him, but that was probably equally true of half of the casually dressed crowd who wandered about, watched television screens which monitored races at other Queensland courses and in other states, or pored over race-books, studying form.

The only discernible signs of tension in Douglas were a tendency to talk much more than usual, and, more tellingly, beads of perspiration which he kept brushing off his top lip.

'Let's go up to the members' stand,' Miriam said, indicating the adjoining glassed-in building.

'I'd really rather stay here,' Douglas said. 'Maybe it's silly, but I just like it better. Here's a vacant table with a good view of the straight and the post. But you and Charles go up to the members'.'

'Well, as a matter of fact, I like it here, too,' Charles said amiably. 'It's so light and airy under this tremendous roof, with all the palms and ferns growing.'

'Oh.' Miriam looked surprised, but clearly was in the mood to enjoy the day no matter what. 'All right. I don't mind staying here. It'd be rather fun, actually, because if I go up there, there'll be people who know I'm from Top Bend and they'll expect me to be an infallible judge of who's the best prospect for every race, not just the Feltington Cup. And here I can have a hamburger in a paper serviette for lunch and no one will raise an eyebrow. Sheer indulgence.'

It might have been cynicism, but it wasn't. Miriam's eyes danced with sheer happiness: she was with horses.

Charles felt ill. Miriam, Miriam, he thought: enjoy your day. You mightn't

213

enjoy another carefree day for a long time.

The first touch of uneasiness fell on Douglas: this was something he hadn't expected — Miriam at best not thirty metres away when he placed his bet. Charles saw the uneasiness and went and bought a race-book and began making selections with blithe disregard for the tips of the experts.

Miriam was amused, and Douglas seemed to relax a little, perhaps feeling that Miriam would become engrossed in explaining to Charles aspects of the various races listed, and not notice anything unusual in his actions or demeanour.

He was unconcerned when Charles went with him each time he went to put a maximum of five dollars on a race. 'I don't have a clue what to do,' Charles explained guilelessly. By the time they bought hamburgers for lunch, they had both bet on three races. Charles had lost four dollars and Douglas had won seven.

'Ruinously big spenders both of you,' Miriam laughed, displaying not the slightest interest in placing a bet herself. But each time the horses in the local races came out of the tunnel to the parade ring — which was anything but round, to Charles's mild surprise, but was brilliantly green with manicured turf — Miriam came intensely

214

alert, and when the horses, having swept around the far side of the course, came into the straight, she was on her feet, eyes shining, though none of the runners was a Top Bend product.

As the time for the Cup drew close, Charles could see the excitement growing almost unbearably in Douglas. The calm, detached professional man was on the verge of disintegration, hands shaking, face perspiring. Twice, Charles had let him go alone to place a bet, though he had sauntered through the crowd to watch without Douglas knowing. He had found his own face damp with sweat on both occasions, for fear Douglas would make his move on Tuesday Turning, but he didn't want Douglas to suspect what he was planning, and he had to trust to Liz's judgement that Douglas would leave his bet as late as possible.

Finally the fourteen starters in the Feltington Cup were led out to parade before the eager onlookers. 'There,' Douglas said, in a quietly conversational tone. 'With the number-four saddle-cloth.'

Tuesday Turning was a gleaming chestnut with a white blaze. To Charles's totally inexpert eye he looked magnificent, but so did the other thirteen, muscles rippling under coats that looked as if they had been polished. Certainly Tuesday Turning held his head up, ears pricked alertly, with an air of intelligence, and though he stepped out crisply he was not nervously restive like some of his rivals.

'He's beautiful,' Charles said, in honest admiration.

Miriam nodded. 'He has turned out well, hasn't he?'

Douglas said nothing, and made no move towards the book-makers' stands. Charles felt his stomach muscles knotting with tension, wondering in near-despair whether after all Douglas had managed to place his $20,000 bet unobserved and unrestrained, perhaps making an arrangement days before, for all Charles knew. Miriam and Douglas were both silent, just watching the horse.

'I think I'll be daring and put five dollars each way on him,' Charles said. 'What do you think, Douglas?'

'Each way?' Suddenly Douglas was laughing, almost as if all doubts and tensions had been resolved. 'No way. Back him to win.'

'Are you going to?' Please don't say you already have, Charles thought.

'I certainly will. I just want to see the jockeys mount, first. But you go along and put your bet on. I'll wait for you to come

216

back and keep Miriam company.'

'Don't be silly,' Miriam smiled at him. 'Go along with Charles. How much are you going to splurge on my baby?'

Douglas didn't hesitate. 'Twenty. To win.'

Close to the truth, Charles thought cynically: only one word missing from that answer.

Previously when he had gone with Douglas to place a bet, Douglas had always gone to the same bookmaker, and they went there now, Douglas motioning Charles to go first. Charles held out his ten dollars — and realized Douglas wasn't behind him. He snatched the note back from the astonished bookie with a mumbled: 'Sorry — changed my mind', and pushed desperately through the crowd, looking for Douglas and seeing him third in line at a different bookmaker's stand. Rudely pushing, Charles drew up beside him as the bookmaker, clearly recognizing him, said: 'Hello, Dr Wentworth.'

'Better odds here?' Charles asked brightly in Douglas's ear.

Douglas gave a violent start, turning to stare at Charles, his hand inside his navy reefer jacket frozen in mid-movement.

He recovered in a second. 'An old friend,' he said. 'Tuesday Turning in the next local,

Don,' he said, turning back to the book-maker. 'Twenty dollars to win.'

'Sorry,' the man said, 'how much did you say?'

'Twenty to win,' Douglas repeated, and Charles saw a muscle twitching in the side of the doctor's jaw. The ticket was written, the money paid, and before taking Charles's ten dollars the bookie adjusted his board to lengthen Tuesday Turning's price from eight-to-one to nine-to-one.

Douglas now was showing clear agitation. 'Go back and wait with Miriam,' he said. 'I have to go to the gents'. I'll be back in a couple of minutes.'

'I think I'll go with you,' Charles said, trying to sound casual.

'For God's sake, why can't you leave me alone?' Douglas snapped. 'Clear off and give me some peace, will you?'

Charles gave up pretence. 'Sorry, Douglas. I'm sticking to you like a limpet to a battleship. You've got a lot of money on you which you plan to gamble on that horse. It isn't even your money. If you lose that, a lot of things will be ruined, won't they? I can't let you do it.'

'Damn you, I don't know how you know all this, but *I won't lose it*. That horse can't lose.'

'He can,' Charles said, quietly reasonable. 'You can't risk it. If you're ruined, it's not just you who gets hurt. If I have to knock you out cold and get arrested for assault, I'll stop you from placing that bet.'

'It's none of your bloody business!'

'No. It isn't. Now come back with me and watch the race, or do you want me to tell Miriam you're massively in debt from gambling?'

Wondering what on earth he actually could do if Douglas ignored him, Charles saw hopelessness hit the doctor like a runaway bus. His shoulders slumped, his face turned grey and haunted and he turned and walked back silently with Charles to where Miriam was sitting. Across the great ellipse of the race-course, the jockeys' colours rainbowed, distant specks, as they took their mounts into the starting gate.

Miriam, watching the horses through binoculars, took little notice when Douglas muttered that he was going to walk down to the rails to watch the finish from close up. Charles followed, keeping a little distance from him, feeling achingly sorry for the man, but knowing he would still stop him from risking Ted Wellchamp's money, if he made another attempt.

Douglas was watching through binoculars

as the horses lined up at the barrier and the starter's light came on. Then the bell sounded as the horses leapt away, too distant for Charles to pick out Tuesday Turning's colours with the naked eye. Please, T.T., he begged silently as they circled the course, lose this one; win as many as you can after this, but lose this one. His hands were wet with perspiration, his stomach muscles ached. He dared not even wonder what Douglas was feeling.

Then, on a rising roar from the crowd, the horses were thundering up the straight toward the post, flanked with its neat flower-beds that no one was thinking about. Charles saw Tuesday Turning come into the straight a bit wide out on the track, but up with the leaders. Then he straightened and came in nearer the rail, and was past the post a clear length in front.

Charles closed his eyes. He could feel his heart hammering and he felt sick in the stomach, but beyond that he seemed frozenly numb. He forced himself to open his eyes and look at Douglas. Everyone else who had walked down to the rails for the closest look at the finish was now moving back to the stand, some laughing, some looking glum, most chatting to others with them.

Only Charles and Douglas remained

motionless, Douglas with binoculars clutched against his chest, staring fixedly at the winning-post as if still seeing the lovely young chestnut flash home a clear winner. Charles saw the numbers rolled up in the frame on the big indicator board beside the post: four, seven, nine, with number one in fourth place.

The horses slowed, circled and came back into the parade ring for unsaddling, and Douglas turned and walked slowly back. As he reached Charles he paused, his eyes dark in a dead-white face.

'You bloody *fool*,' he said, with the quiet intensity of pure hatred. 'I'll kill you.' And he walked past.

Charles turned to follow, wordlessly, because he had no words. A bell rang, and Douglas wheeled sharply to look at the winner's board, where a red light had blinked on beside the notice: Protest. A quick murmur ran through the crowd, and Douglas once more stood rigidly, as the voice on the public-address system announced dispassionately that there had been a protest lodged: second and third against first.

'How long,' Charles asked of a stranger who had stopped near him, 'will it take to decide on the protest?'

'Shouldn't take any time,' the man said. 'That jockey'll face suspension for careless riding, I'll bet. Brought that chestnut horse across too far and crowded the others out of a chance. Pity, really. Horse would probably have scraped home anyway, even though he was out wide.'

Charles felt the next couple of minutes were about the longest he had lived through. Then the voice of the public-address announced the protest had been upheld. Horse number four had been relegated to third, and the past-the-post second and third became first and second.

Feeling his knees would barely support him, Charles went to Douglas, who hadn't moved, but was simply standing looking stunned. 'Let's go and commiserate with Miriam,' Charles said quietly.

Douglas slowly turned his head to look at him. Then he took a very long, slow breath. 'Yes, of course,' he said.

Miriam seemed only mildly disappointed and smiled cheerfully when Charles said, 'What rotten luck,' and thought he had never said anything less sincere in his life.

'But didn't he run splendidly?' she said.

'He certainly did,' Douglas said, putting an arm around her. 'He's top stuff. It was only the jockey's fault — just grew too keen,

I guess, and let his enthusiasm wreck his judgment.'

He smiled affectionately at her and casually tore up his betting ticket with a show of indifference which Charles felt was of Oscar-winning quality.

Afterwards, Charles had only a blurred recollection of the rest of the afternoon. Douglas laid no more bets, and Miriam seemed not to notice the slowly-lessening shaking of his hands. Somehow both he and Charles managed to keep up a semblance of normality without directly speaking to each other until Miriam went off to speak to someone she recognized.

Douglas turned to Charles. 'I don't know how the hell you know what you do.'

'It doesn't matter how I know. Douglas, I can't stop you in the future from doing what you almost did today. But you have a secure medical practice. You can repay all your debts in time from that. Whether you do that, or destroy yourself and Miriam by gambling is up to you. You're a doctor. You know better than I do that you have an addiction as real as if you were hooked on alcohol or cocaine. You know you need help — professional help. Get it, before you finish up like Liz Fitzgibbon's father. Now, I've a long drive home. I'll just say goodbye

223

to Miriam and head off.'

He touched Douglas lightly on the shoulder and walked away, reflecting that in the end nothing he or anyone else could do or say could help Douglas Wentworth unless he would help himself.

10

Geoffrey and Rhelma Waring's home was attractively set on a well-kept tree-scattered block in a suburb where the houses generally suggested solidly comfortable financial circumstances rather than actual wealth. In fact, Charles thought, the Waring house had the same air of understated elegance that Rhelma herself had. He wondered whether, inside, the atmosphere would have the same lack of warmth.

He had been intending to visit here in any case, but it had been made easy by his father, who had phoned, urging him to come. 'Stay a couple of days — we'd both love to have you.'

Charles couldn't envisage Rhelma being remotely enthusiastic about any such thing. But he very much wanted to know why Geoffrey had visited Ursula just before her death, and quarrelled with her. Whether he would learn the reason remained to be seen.

He had wanted to talk in person with a couple of Ursula's business contacts in Brisbane, especially Henry the wine-merchant. He had done that today, and felt the interviews had been very worthwhile. Henry had proved to be about Charles's own age, short, stocky and full of enthusiasm for his work. He had assured Charles that Glenlodge wines were steadily making a name for themselves, and he had shown genuine sadness at Ursula's death. He had also assumed Charles would be taking over the running of Glenlodge, and Charles had not commented.

As he parked his car to one side of Geoffrey and Rhelma's driveway, Charles reflected that aside from anything else, he probably owed it to both of them, and to himself, to try to get to know his father's wife at least a little, if she would ever allow him to do so. So he had been glad to accept his father's invitation, and had arranged for Jill to feed Marmaduke and Aristotle while he stayed away one night.

The day was sliding down toward dusk, and both Geoffrey and Rhelma were home from work. Geoffrey welcomed him with an enthusiasm which Charles thought was probably designed to counter Rhelma's cold politeness. She showed Charles to his room and excused herself to attend to dinner preparations.

Geoffrey opened a cabinet to reveal assorted bottles and glasses. 'Scotch?' he asked, then turned to look at Charles with a grin. 'That might be an insult to a wine man — offering him whisky?'

Charles laughed. 'I'd enjoy a Scotch, thanks. And I'm by no means sure I'm a wine man.'

Geoffrey studied him for a few seconds. 'I see. Ice? Soda?'

'Just ice, thanks.'

'Funny, isn't it?' Geoffrey said, waving him to an armchair. 'I guess you know me a little — maybe more than I'd want you to — but I sit here looking at you and realizing I don't know you at all.'

Charles nodded. 'We're barely more than casual acquaintances, since I grew up, anyway. I don't even know your line of business. Are you in business for yourself, or in a partnership, or what?'

'It's my own thing, not a partnership. Menswear — formal, business and casual, in one of the big shopping centres. Thumping big rent in those places, of course, but that's where the customers are. It's a small business, but sound.'

'Good.' Well, well, thought Charles: my father running a sound business? He must have grown up at last. 'How many staff do you have?' he asked casually.

'Oh, just one fellow works with me. But

227

I recently opened another store on the other side of town, so of course I had to put in a manager there. But what about you, Charles? Your work in Canada, I mean. What was your line of geological work — mining? Construction?'

'I was working for a company that was involved in oil and mineral exploration.' Charles was faintly surprised at how long ago it seemed, but he and Geoffrey talked comfortably about his work until Rhelma came to say dinner was ready. Geoffrey went at once to help her serve the meal, with unfussed competence which showed he normally did this, which gave Charles another small surprise.

Geoffrey kept conversation flowing comfortably through the meal, with Rhelma neither contributing much nor remaining too noticeably silent, the cool reserve intact without discourtesy. Charles began to feel it was a pose — some kind of defence which covered the real woman. Had it not been so, she would not have appealed to Geoffrey Waring in the first place, let alone kept his devotion as she appeared to have done. When Charles complimented her on the dinner, she smiled with the nearest thing to warmth he had seen in her.

'Cooking is almost my only contribution to

running the household,' she said. 'The time I have to give to my work means I have to have someone come in to do cleaning and so on. Cooking is a kind of relaxation — a hobby I enjoy.'

When the table had been cleared and the dishes stacked in the dishwasher, Geoffrey suggested Charles and he might go into the study for a chat.

'Rhelma usually likes to unwind with some music after dinner,' he said, smiling at her.

The study had a roll-top desk in silky oak, shelves of books, an executive-style chair drawn up to the desk, and a couple of easy chairs. Charles sat down and Geoffrey wandered about the room chatting about books, but in a manner which suggested his mind was on something else.

Presently Charles said almost casually, 'Am I right in thinking you and Rhelma are pretty happily married?'

Geoffrey swung around from looking at books on a shelf, startled, as Charles had intended him to be.

'Well — yes. Yes, very,' he said. He looked at his son for a long moment in silence. 'Sorry, Charles.' His voice was quiet. 'I wasn't a very good husband to your mother. I guess — well, it took me a long time to grow up. It's not that I wasn't fond of Ursula. I was. But Rhelma — well, it's different. I-I hope Ursula was happy with Anthony Erskine. She deserved something better than I gave her.'

'Why did you quarrel with her?' Charles asked abruptly.

'Oh, I don't know that we quarrelled, exactly. It was more a sort of drifting apart, an incompatability mostly my fault. It wasn't — '

'I don't mean over the span of your marriage,' Charles interrupted. 'I mean at Glenlodge, in the winery office just before she was killed.'

Geoffrey stared. 'What?'

'You went to see her. Apparently whatever it was you wanted she wouldn't do. You were furious. Shouting.'

Geoffrey sighed. 'I see. Someone overheard. Did whoever it was know what it was about?'

Charles shook his head. 'No. But knowing you I'd guess it was that you wanted money.'

Geoffrey sat down slowly, and for a little while didn't answer. 'I was desperate,' he said eventually. 'Charles, I am still desperate. I . . . need your help.'

'Tell me: what sort of trouble you're in, and why you went to Glenlodge for help. And what happened.'

'I guess I've spent most of my life being a failure,' Geoffrey muttered. 'Like I said earlier, it took me a long time to grow up. You know that; Ursula knew that. But I've always tried to hide it and play the clever fellow. At Glenlodge I wouldn't have made a crust if I'd been left to my own devices. It wasn't just a lack of interest. It would have been the same whatever the business was. I was too busy enjoying life. Ursula ran Glenlodge. Not only because she loved it, but because she had to.'

He paused, and Charles guessed he found it bitterly humiliating to admit his failure to anyone, let alone his son.

'After we separated,' Geoffrey went on, 'I lived it up for a while. Then I met Rhelma, and I fell in love with her. We weren't, either of us, young any more. I knew she wouldn't tolerate an irresponsible husband. Young love was long gone. This time it had to be tempered with common sense. I had to win her respect. I had just enough to put a down-payment on a menswear business, and I worked. For the first time in my life, I really worked. I built it into something successful. On my own. I'd finally done something right.'

He ran his fingers through his hair. 'But just having a nice solid little business wasn't impressive enough. I still wanted to show Rhelma what a smart chap she'd married. I wanted her admiration, I suppose. So I borrowed to buy a second business — borrowed too heavily. I've overreached and I'm in financial trouble. I'll lose the business. I can't let Rhelma know,' he said with a note of desperation. 'I couldn't stand for her to despise me for a fool. I couldn't, Charles!'

The sound of a Mozart piano concerto, muted by the study's solid timber door, danced joyously somewhere in the house. Charles said nothing.

'So, I went to see Ursula. I knew Anthony must have left her pretty well off. I thought a loan wouldn't — '

Charles said sharply, 'My God! You never will grow up, will you? All the time you were married to Mum you leaned on her, and then all those years after the marriage ended, when you hit trouble, you went running back!' The anger was harsh in his voice and Geoffrey seemed to wilt.

'Sorry, Charles. Yes, I know. I guess that's why I lost my temper and shouted at her. I wasn't really angry with her. I was angry with myself.'

After a moment Charles said more quietly, 'God knows whether she'd have lent you the money if she'd been able to. Probably she would have. But she didn't have any money, or none that she felt was hers.'

'I know.' Geoffrey nodded. 'She told me she wouldn't touch Anthony's money — said it belonged to his children. I guess that was just Ursula's way of looking at things.'

'I guess it was.' Charles leaned back in his chair. 'And now you hope you can borrow it from me. Right?'

'Well — '

'Sorry. You've come to another dry well. Any savings I have — and they're not extensive, to put it mildly — will be needed, if I keep Glenlodge.'

Geoffrey stared at him. 'She kept her word, then? Ursula, I mean. She didn't leave you any money?'

'Not a cent. She told me years ago that she wouldn't touch what she regarded as Erskine money. It would all go back to Anthony's family. I understood how she felt. I didn't care then about the money, and I don't care now.'

Geoffrey's shoulders sagged. 'I simply don't know what to do.'

'Would Rhelma have enough cash reserves to help you?'

Geoffrey shook his head. 'I have to work this through on my own, somehow.' He shot a glance at Charles. 'Yes, I know that sounds hypocritical because I asked Ursula and you for help. But not Rhelma. I can't.'

'Then you have to sell the second business to clear the debt. Will it?'

'Just about. But that's an admission of failure.'

'Oh, for God's sake!' Charles snapped. 'If you're on the financial skids you'll be forced into liquidation and it'll be perfectly obvious to the whole world — if it's interested — that you've failed in the second business. You say the first one's sound?'

Geoffrey nodded.

'Right. So you took a chance and expanded too lavishly or too soon. It happens all the time. It's hardly the end of the world. Get out of the second business before it pulls the first one down. And for pity's sake, *tell* Rhelma. Talk to her. If she offers you money, just tell her you have to do this on your own. If she's worth a split biscuit she won't despise you. If she's half the person you say, she'll be glad you talked to her. Can't you understand that?'

Geoffrey looked doubtful. 'But — '

Charles shook his head. 'No buts. Just do it.' He grinned suddenly. 'Trust Uncle Charles, boy.'

His father smiled ruefully. 'I just so badly

wanted her to admire me.'

'Do you think she wouldn't admire honesty and common sense and a willingness to confide in her more than she'd admire business success?'

Geoffrey was silent for a moment. 'Maybe,' he said, looking up. 'Maybe you're right about that, too, Uncle Charles.' He smiled. 'I'm still in a funk about telling her, though.'

'Just do it,' Charles said again. 'It's the way to go. Bet you.' He stood up and said cheerfully, 'Is there another drink on offer?'

'Good thinking,' Geoffrey agreed, and they went back into the lounge as Mozart's concerto sparkled through its final flourish.

Rhelma smiled at them with a moment of almost dreamy relaxed contentment as if she had been in another, happier world for a moment. Then she flicked off the stereo system and the chill, polite shutter came down again. She can't really be like that, Charles thought as he had before, or she wouldn't be so special to Geoffrey.

But the remainder of the evening passed pleasantly enough, as Geoffrey — no hint of his problems showing — carried the conversation with his easy, unconscious charm. Rhelma made coffee, and presently took Charles completely by surprise by saying,

'Geoffrey, you look very tired. Why don't you go along to bed? I'd like to talk to Charles for a while.'

Geoffrey looked almost as surprised as Charles felt, and she added, 'Charles and I scarcely know each other, and he is your son.'

Geoffrey smiled and nodded. 'Good idea. Guess I do tend to hog the conversation, and I am a bit weary.' He stood up and kissed his wife. 'Goodnight, my dear. 'Night, Charles. Don't try eloping with my girl, will you?'

'I wouldn't stand the least chance against the competition,' Charles smiled. ' 'Night, Dad.'

He helped Rhelma clear away the coffee things and washed them in the kitchen sink, brushing off her protest with a cheerful, 'No problem. Bachelors like me learn to do domestic chores at an early age.'

He watched her put things away in cupboards and reflected that there was an unstudied gracefulness in the way she moved about the most ordinary tasks. She turned suddenly and caught him watching her, and stepped back against the cupboard almost like a cornered animal, the movement startling him almost as much as the intensity of the blue eyes that studied him.

236

'Do you know, or is it just that you intend to find out?'

He shook his head, bewildered. 'Know what? Find out what?'

'About me. About who I am. For God's sake don't play games with me.' She kept her voice down, but there was a fierce intensity of emotion in every syllable.

'I'm sorry,' Charles said. 'I don't know what you mean.'

'You don't believe your mother's death was an accident; you think she was murdered. You said as much the day of her funeral.'

Charles felt a jolt of tension. For several seconds he looked at his father's wife without answering, wondering what thoughts were running through her mind. 'I'm not quite sure what I was thinking that day,' he said carefully. 'I simply felt something was wrong — that the accident theory didn't make sense unless there had been some awful medical reason for her to collapse at the wheel — and an autopsy found there was none — or some drastic mechanical fault in the vehicle, and the police investigators found none. I'm not sure I had actually gone as far as thinking she had been murdered.'

'But now you do.'

'Now I'm totally certain.'

'And you have been investigating, looking

237

into the background of your stepfamily, looking for motives. Maybe even wondering about your father.'

Charles blinked. 'Why do you say that?'

'About your stepbrother and sisters I know — never mind how, but I know people who know them. About your father I can only guess, but if you are to be thorough you can't assume anything about anyone, so no doubt you have at least wondered about him. But I can tell you one thing: your father did not kill your mother. Geoffrey — ' She smiled faintly. 'Geoffrey has many faults. But violence, cruelty, are not among them.'

Charles nodded. 'I agree with you. He isn't capable of murder.'

Rhelma's face became shuttered and blank again. 'But I am.'

'Pardon?'

'I am. Capable of murder. If you don't already know, you'll find out. And you'll begin to wonder if Ursula knew, and I silenced her to stop Geoffrey from knowing.'

Her expression lost nothing of its guarded blankness, but a great shudder swept over her whole body as Charles stared at her in shocked silence, and she put her face in her hands.

Charles had no idea how long the silence lasted, but presently she dropped her hands to her sides and said very quietly, 'I didn't kill her, Charles. I have no alibi for that day, that time, as it happens. But I didn't kill her. As far as I know she knew nothing about me — cared nothing, probably. I didn't ever meet her. But no matter what, I would never have harmed her. I can't prove it, but it's the truth.'

He waited for a moment. 'But — you did kill someone, sometime? Is that what you're telling me?'

'I killed my first husband. They charged me with murder. A merciful jury found it was justifiable homicide, that I killed in self-defence.'

Charles felt a curious sense of unreality — standing in a spotless, well-equipped modern kitchen, listening to this attractive, elegant woman quietly telling him she had killed her husband.

'Was it?' he asked. 'Justifiable homicide?'

'That,' she said, 'is the nightmare I will always have to live with. How can I be certain there was no other way?'

She shook her head. 'It's the old, sordid story. He wasn't the sort of man I thought he was before I married him. I'd never guessed his drunken, black rages. Almost from the day we were married he was violently abusive — hitting me, kicking me if the least thing upset him when he was drunk. I left him twice. Each time he found me. The first time he coaxed me back with promises; the second time he threatened to kill me if I didn't go back. I was young, and at first I was idealistic, and then I was afraid. I went back. Then one day I was in the car, about to go to work, and he came rushing out of the house with the poker in his hands. I hadn't made breakfast for him because he'd been sleeping off a hangover. He was screaming abuse and he smashed the side window of the car, yelling that he'd smash my head in.'

She paused, her eyes dark with the memory.

'I reversed down the driveway. He ran after me. We had a gate at the end of the driveway and I would have to get out of the car to open it. He was squarely in front of the car and running towards me. I slammed the gear lever into first and stamped on the accelerator. The radiator grille hit him about waist-high and threw him backwards and I drove over him.'

She shuddered again. 'I went into the house and called the ambulance and the police. He was dead before the ambulance came. I told the police what had happened. There were neighbours, family — people who knew much of how he had treated me.

The jury listened. They believed my defence counsel's claim that I had acted on the spur of the moment without stopping to think whether I might kill him. But that wasn't true. Not that part. I meant to kill him.'

'My God,' Charles said softly. A kaleidoscope of thoughts tumbled through his mind, and settled into a picture that made sense of what he had always seen as Rhelma's withdrawn coldness. He had wondered if it was a barrier against intense shyness, but now he understood it was a shield against fear of discovery of the past. Then something she had said about Geoffrey registered.

'Rhelma,' he said hollowly, 'do you mean my father doesn't *know*?'

She shook her head. 'It happened in another state, many years ago. There seemed no likelihood he would ever find out. And if he knew, I believe it would damage our relationship beyond repair. I would probably lose him altogether. How could he trust a woman who had killed her husband?'

Her voice shook for a moment, and then she was in control of herself again. 'I don't think I could bear to lose him like that.'

'I think you totally underestimate his feelings for you. I don't believe that jury did you any special favours. I think they

241

simply used common sense. I agree with them. So will Geoffrey Waring. He loves you. I've never been more certain of anything. You love him. Talk to each other — prove you trust each other with things you wish had never happened, but in cold hard fact have no actual bearing on your relationship. Talk to each other. Now. Tonight. Please.'

She was staring at him. 'Tonight?'

'Yes. It'll be harder tomorrow. He won't be asleep yet. He has things on his mind, too.'

She closed her eyes for a moment, then looked up at him, suddenly looking more vulnerable than he would have dreamt she ever would, and managed a faint smile. 'All right.'

Moved by a quick awareness that she was close to tears, Charles stepped forward and put his arms protectively around her. She clung to him and cried with a quiet intensity, seeming to find some release from the years of fear of discovery.

Presently she stepped away and fumbled for a handkerchief to dab at her face. She said unsteadily, 'You are a very kind man, Charles. And I guess a wise one.'

Charles smiled. 'Kind to some extent, I hope. But wise? Oh, no, unfortunately. Rhelma, I'll leave very early in the morning, before anyone else is up.' He shook his head as she was about to protest. 'You and Dad have things to sort out, and you don't need a distraction. You need time alone together. I'll come back another time, if I may.'

She hesitated, then nodded and reached up quickly to kiss his cheek. 'Promise to come back. Goodnight, Charles.'

He slept surprisingly well, and left as silently as possible just before dawn. As he drove through the gradually waking city and headed west, he thought ruefully of Rhelma's words: 'You are a very kind man, and I guess a wise one.'

Wise! he thought grimly; all I do is blunder around in my stepfamily's lives and God only knows whether I'm helping or doing something hopelessly wrong. Why do they have to dump their problems on me? Do they imagine I'm some kind of two-bit psychiatrist?

Then he thought contritely that he was being unfair: after all, he had set out to find their secrets, if they had any.

But he said aloud to the empty car: 'If I turn up any scandals in Sandford and Netty's life, I think I'll pack up and go back to Canada next flight.'

11

However, when he had dinner with them a few evenings later, as far as he could tell they were an ordinary, well-adjusted couple with two perfectly normal children, and he came away considerably cheered, especially as he found Sandford the kind of man he would like to have for a friend. Obviously successful in his business, he was completely lacking in self-importance, and clearly regarded his family as his first priority, all in a relaxed, happy-go-lucky manner.

For Charles, the business of learning to run the winery and orchard absorbed his time and interest more and more, even though the more he learned, the more he realized how much more there was to learn.

He came in one day from walking through the vines alone, trying to remember at least some of what Giovanni Petroni had been teaching him about the characteristics of the different varieties, and how to judge how the fruit was developing and what sort of crop they could expect, barring some natural disaster such as a hailstorm. Pip was waiting in the office, and he felt the now-familiar leap of his spirits at seeing her.

'You looked,' she told him with a smile, 'like a grower absorbed in his work.'

He grinned. 'I felt like a schoolboy desperately trying to remember his last algebra lesson.'

Her eyes searched his face, serious in spite of her bantering tone. 'Is it important, then? To remember how X plus Y over C times B squared equals a good vintage?'

'It seems to have become so.'

'Enough to cash in your return ticket to Canada?'

'I haven't done it yet.'

'Nor moved into Glenlodge homestead.'

'No.'

'Have you been inside since the Rushtons left?'

He shook his head. 'It's a decision I'll have to make soon. For one thing, the Erskines want to put the house on the market. It will carry a good-sized price-tag, I imagine, so it may not sell very quickly. But in fairness to them, and to everyone, I have to move out soon. If I come here — well, it will be because I've made the commitment to Glenlodge.' He put out both hands to her. 'And to you, if you'll have me.'

Pip took his hands and went into his arms as naturally as if it was a lifetime habit.

245

After a very long time when words were both impossible and unnecessary, she said a little shakily, 'I've heard of more romantic proposals, but it'll do.'

He laughed and kissed her again. Then he looked down at her and said gently, 'You don't want to go to Canada, do you?'

'You silly dope, I'd live in a tent in the Sahara if it meant being with you. If you stay here, it has to be because it's what you really want to do more than any other work. Anything less would be unfair to yourself, Glenlodge, and me. Because you wouldn't be happy.'

'Mmm. Well, we can't have you married to a grumpy old man, so I have to do some very serious soul-searching to find which decision to take.'

She smiled. 'Well, you can do it without any distractions, too. I came to tell you I'm going to New Zealand tomorrow for three weeks, with a friend from work. Female, if you're interested to know.'

'Thank you. I felt a few grey hairs coming on there for a minute. You didn't mention going on a trip.'

'No. This other girl had someone else teed up to go with her, and she pulled out at the last minute, and I already had a passport from a trip to Norfolk Island a couple of years ago, so as I'm due for holidays anyway and the boss was agreeable, I said I'd go.' She untangled herself from his arms. 'And now I have to go back to work. I've a mountain of ends to tie up, and our bookings are on an early flight.'

He caught her wrist. 'Pip,' he said, his face quickly grave, 'I haven't misunderstood, or been dreaming, or anything, have I? You will marry me?'

'Just try wriggling out of it. See you in three weeks.' She headed for the car, half-turning, laughing, to blow him a kiss. Then she turned and ran back to fling herself into his arms and hold him fiercely. 'Oh, dear God, Charles,' she whispered. 'I love you.'

Then she was gone without a backward glance.

He stood for a long time, at first just letting himself be swamped by emotion, and then when the fireworks stopped fizzing around his bloodstream, he began seriously thinking.

Now, more than ever, they both knew he had to be sure that he was choosing the work where he would best feel fulfilled. Both possible careers — his work as a geologist and the management of Glenlodge — were challenging. Both involved, in very different ways, working with the earth beneath humanity's feet.

The difference was, he was trained for the first option, experienced in it and confirmed in his skills in it. The second option demanded many skills of an entirely different nature, and he was aware that some of them could scarcely be learned in a life-time.

There was no doubt that he had found the orchard, the vineyard, the winery, far more interesting than he could have imagined. Certainly there was modern technology, but underneath that was the feel of continuity in the ancient arts of nurturing a crop, of wine-making, and of working with the soil.

He smiled ruefully at himself. You're being sentimental and indecisive, Charles Waring, and it isn't good enough, he told himself sternly; what are you waiting for — some as yet unknown small factor to tip the scales and make your choice?

He had no premonition of how soon that factor would come. And when it came, it was not small.

★ ★ ★

It came four nights after Pip had gone to New Zealand. Early in the night she had phoned him from Mount Cook, sounding excited and happy with the world.

'I can look out of my window and see the moonlight on the snow on this great whacking mountain just outside. Well, actually it's probably several miles away, but it *looks* to be just outside. It's marvellous, Charles. Oh, I know it's nothing to you — you've seen hordes of great hunks of mountains with snow on them, but I've never seen one before, and — I know mountains are cruel in a way, like our desert country — unforgiving of mistakes. But it's beautiful, so beautiful I want to cry. And I suppose you're laughing your head off at me.'

Charles was smiling. 'I'm certainly not laughing at you. A mountain is beautiful, no matter how many you've seen. And the only time you should worry about your reaction to beauty is when you stop caring about it.'

There was a little silence at the other end of the line, and then Pip said softly, 'It's not surprising that I fell in love with you. You're so — *nice*. Oh, what a dreadfully inadequate word!'

'It'll do for now,' he told her. 'In fact, I think you're nice, too.'

'Mmm. Well, after that exchange of romantic extravagances, tell me, is it moonlight over there?'

'Yes, of course. We are on the same planet, you know.'

'Yes, I know, but it must rise a couple of hours later over there, that's what I meant, you ass.'

'Well,' Charles said cheerfully, 'later it may be, but it has risen. I just confirmed it with a look out of the window. Actually, it's around full moon, I believe.'

They talked trivialities for a few more minutes, laughing and content in the knowledge that they didn't need to say the things they really meant, especially with Pip's friend obviously in the same room with her.

After the call, Charles read for a while before going to bed, and for a while he lay drowsily, the memory of Pip's voice a warmth in his mind. He calculated afterwards that he had probably been asleep about an hour — still in that deep, early sleep which makes waking feel like trying to swim up from the bottom of a deep black pool of something thick like treacle.

He was vaguely aware that a noise of some kind had wakened him, and a different noise — a thinly harsh persistent noise — was being constantly repeated. He didn't want to bother about it. He sighed and rolled over to go back to the sleep from which he hadn't fully wakened, when Marmaduke the cat, who recently had taken to sleeping trustingly on his bed, sat up sharply and growled.

Charles snapped awake and put a reassuring hand on Marmaduke, and lay tensely, listening. A car started up — not close, but too close to be out on the main road. And he recognized the persistently repeated sound: Aristotle, the galah, calling: 'Hello, larrikin. Hello, larrikin.'

Charles sat up, instinctively keeping hold of the cat, while he flicked on the switch of the bedside lamp. There was no responding light from it; but there was a light he could see through the open door of his bedroom and through his window — a light that was not moonlight. A dancing orange glow, brightening by the second.

The house was on fire.

Fighting down the automatic surge of panic, he tucked Marmaduke under his left arm, keeping a firm grip around the cat's chest and front legs, and slid out of bed.

'It's all right, old chap. Just relax. We've got to get out of here, and if I let go of you, you're going to bolt off and hide somewhere in the house because you think of it as a refuge. And I won't be able to find you, and your home isn't a refuge any more. It's a death-trap.'

He tried to keep his voice soothing and unhurried, but he could feel the cat's muscles tensing as he realized only too well that something was terribly wrong. Charles opened the wardrobe and reached up to a high shelf where he had tossed his airline cabin-bag. It was a sturdy canvas carry-all with a zippered top and he sent up a flicker of prayer that the zip was open.

It was. Holding the bag between his feet he pulled the zip two-thirds closed with his free hand, and with a sharp movement he shoved Marmaduke head-first into the bag and jerked the zip closed, except a couple of centimetres for ventilation. Marmaduke's frantic scramble of terror was just too late for him to get free.

'Sorry, mate,' Charles said. 'You won't like it, but we'll make it out that way. Hang in there.'

He grabbed trousers and a jacket, snatching up his wallet from the bedside table, picked up the cabin-bag with Marmaduke meowing in outraged terror, and started toward the living-room and its telephone and its door to the garden.

One glance down the hall told him not to try that route. The front rooms were fiercely alight and smoke and heaven alone knew what deadly gases were billowing into the hall. He ran into his mother's bedroom, the fire lighting his way, and punched three zeros on the telephone beside the bed.

'Fire,' he told the voice which instantly asked which emergency service he required. He knew, even before he told the swiftly answering fire officer the location that already the house was beyond saving, and before the fire-units could arrive the fine house Anthony Erskine had built for his wife would be nothing but a collapsed ruin.

Banging down the phone again he picked up the cat and unlatched the window, thankful that it was a single-storeyed house and all he had to do to escape was to open the window and scramble out over the sill.

That was when he realized to his horror that the garden was on fire, right around the house. Mercifully, here under the window there was a concrete path against the house, and only low shrubs edging it, with open lawn beyond. He scrambled out on to the path, put the arm holding his clothes up in front of his face, and plunged through the burning shrubs.

The bottom of his pyjama coat was burning and there were bits of burning leaves on his hair, but nothing he couldn't quickly slap out with his hands.

Coughing from the smoke, he told Marmaduke, 'They haven't beaten us, Duke.' Afterwards he recalled with a kind of grim amusement that he had kept up a running commentary to the cat through the whole incident, and he wondered whether it had been a conscious effort to reassure his furry friend or a way of steadying his own nerves. He hadn't at that point even begun to consciously suspect someone had actually *tried* to beat them in the cruellest way.

He ran out to the middle of the clear space of the lawn and set down the bag and his jacket and trousers.

'It's all right, mate,' he said. 'Sit tight. I'll be right back.'

Shading his face with one arm from the growing heat, he ran around to the far side of the house, where Aristotle, the galah, was in his cage on the veranda. Charles could no longer hear the bird above the roar of flames and he found himself shouting, 'I'm coming, Risto, I'm coming!' He hadn't realized he even remembered Ursula's pet name for the bird.

He couldn't see the cage because of the glare of the fire. 'You *bastard*!' he sobbed with rage. 'If that bird's dead I'll *kill* you!'

Afterwards, he remembered saying it, and understood that he had known from the beginning that the fire was no accident.

All the pent-up fury that had lain below his grief at his mother's death surged up in him and found its expression in his blinding rage that her helpless pets had been left to die in an inferno that doubtless was meant for him. To others, his bitter outrage over the death of a crippled bird might make no sense, but to him it was a totally logical reaction to an act of cruel cowardice, and because of the animals' total defencelessness it enraged him more than the attempt to incinerate him.

He groped his way along the edge of the veranda, trying to shield his face from the searing heat as the windows began to give way and let sheets of flame lick out. He would have to give up. The bird must be dead anyway.

Then he saw the outline of the cage. Against the solid wall and away from the direct heat blasting out of the windows, it was protected for the moment from the worst. Whether Aristotle still survived he didn't know. The cage itself was a large affair of timber and close-mesh wire. Ursula had had it specially made to give the galah room to climb about, since it wasn't able to fly, and the frame was made on the principle of a wheelbarrow, except that it had two wheels in front instead of one. It had two fixed legs at the back to stabilize it, and a pair of handles, so that once the back legs were lifted clear of the ground the cage could quite readily be moved out of cold winds in winter and into shady places in summer.

Half blinded by the heat and smoke, Charles couldn't see the bird and didn't wait to try. He grabbed the handles and trundled the cage out on to the lawn beside the bag with Marmaduke, now gone still and silent with fear, inside. It was hot there, but not dangerously so.

Choking on the smoke and coughing rackingly, Charles felt in the pockets of the trousers he had carried out of the house and dropped beside Marmaduke's carry-all. His fingers found his key-ring and he ran for the garage. He just might, he calculated, have time to save the car.

Because of the paved driveway, the arsonist hadn't been able to complete the ring of fire around the house, and the roll-up door still felt cool enough when Charles put his hand on it to check if it was safe to open it. He unlocked it and cautiously raised it a few inches. There was no rush of fire, no flash-over where everything inside was at flash-point, just waiting for a rush of air to light it. He shoved the door fully up.

Already there was smoke seeping in, and the air was threateningly warm. His hands were shaking as he unlocked the BMW and slid behind the wheel. The splendid motor responded instantly to the twist of the key in the ignition, though above the roar of the fire it wasn't audible. He reversed down the driveway some twenty metres, then ran back and pulled the garage door closed again, even though he knew it was a futile gesture in an effort to slow the advance of the fire by denying it the extra air it would suck in through the big open door.

He ran back to the cabin-bag and the bird-cage. 'Are you all right, Marmaduke?' he panted, coughing. 'Good boy!' he added as a faint meow of anxiety and protest rose from the small opening he'd left in the zippered top of the bag.

'You're safe now, Duke, honest. You'll be all right. I know it's cramped and scary, but we'll have you out presently.'

'Hello, larrikin,' croaked a hoarse voice.

'Risto! You made it!'

The galah, pink and grey feathers showing strange colours in the fierce light of the fire, was panting and clearly disturbed, but he had emerged from his shelter-box inside the cage and was standing firmly on his perch and watching everything with bright black eyes.

'You old devil! Good for you! We beat him, fellers, we all beat him!'

He supposed when he thought about it later that there was a large element of hysteria about it, but he stood in the middle of the lawn, barefoot, in singed and filthy pyjamas, with his eyebrows and much of his hair singed off, while a fine house and all its fine furnishings and all his personal possessions were engulfed in a searing inferno, and he laughed in sheer delighted triumph.

He had escaped with his life and he had rescued a cat, and a bird who couldn't fly, and at that moment everything else was insignificant.

He put Marmaduke, still in his carry-all, on the back seat of the BMW and drove it further away, pulling off the roadway to clear it for the emergency vehicles. Then he ran back and wheeled Aristotle's cage away, across the lawn and down the driveway till it was beside the car and away from the heat.

Slowly, then, he turned and walked a little way back toward the house, and stood transfixed, staring at the blazing, tearing destruction. The moment of euphoria at having escaped was gone.

Even the explosion of rage that had driven him in those first minutes had subsided. The

258

anger was still there, deep and bitter, but it was partly numbed now by the onset of shock. He had never before seen at close quarters a house destroyed by fire, and this was not a stranger's house: this had been his mother's home. He had lived in it now for a good many weeks and grown to know it and appreciate its gracious qualities even though he felt no close personal ties with it. But much of the furniture was part of his childhood memories of the house at Glenlodge which had been his home.

There was his mother's desk of lovely polished timber; some antique chairs that had belonged to Ursula's grandmother; a solid cedar dining-suite; a small crystal vase which at age twelve he had carefully hoarded his pocket money to buy for Ursula's birthday and which, he had noted with an odd little twist somewhere inside, she had kept in pride of place on the mantel above the sitting-room fireplace.

All gone.

The local volunteer Rural Fire Brigade was first to arrive, a handful of men and women from varied occupations manning a medium-sized fire unit when emergencies like this arose, leaving their work or in this case their warm beds, to turn out in yellow overalls and safety helmets, leaping from the fire-unit and a couple of private cars to quickly roll out hoses and begin pumping water from the limited supply in the tank the fire-unit carried.

One man ran to Charles and said, 'You all right, mate?' Charles nodded and the man said urgently, 'Anyone else in the house?'

'No,' Charles said.

'Thank God for that,' the fireman said fervently. 'The town brigade's on its way; they called us, because we're closer.'

He looked hard at Charles. 'Did you get anything out? Clothes?'

'I got the cat and the bird, and the car. Oh, I did grab a jacket. And trousers. I put them down somewhere. Over there, on the grass.'

'Good. You get 'em on, mate, and you sit in the cabin of the fire-truck. Nothing you can do except wait for the professionals and the cops. And you're getting a good whack of the shakes.'

He patted Charles on the shoulder. 'You did damn well to get out.' He hurried off to the others, shouting, 'Stay up-wind of that fire! God knows what fumes are coming off it, and we don't have breathing gear, you know.'

On legs that felt oddly detached from his brain Charles walked over to his discarded clothes and pulled them on over his pyjamas, suddenly realizing that the fireman was right: he was shivering violently from a mixture of shock and chill. Away from the furnace-blast of the fire it was a chilly night. He didn't take the rest of the fireman's advice, and was still standing staring at the fire when the police and the urban fire-unit arrived closely followed by a vehicle from the electricity authority, with technicians to cut off the power in case of fallen electrical wires.

A senior constable asked if he'd been alone in the house, and when Charles said yes, echoed the volunteer fireman's, 'Thank God for that,' before he hurried off to survey the devastation.

The firemen, professional and volunteer alike, worked on the perimeter of the fire to try to check its spread. Someone asked Charles if there was a swimming pool, or a dam nearby where they could get more water, since this was well beyond any reticulated water supply. 'We should be able to save the shed at the back, with more water,' he said.

Charles shook his head. 'No pool,' he said, 'but there are a couple of big rainwater tanks underground. I'll show you.'

It was better to be doing something. He took the fireman to where the big circular sheets of concrete almost flush with the lawn formed the tops of the buried tanks, and helped the man lift the heavy concrete manhole covers. The fireman said, 'Don't get near the fire, mate, and certainly not in bare feet. Windows tend to explode outward sometimes and scatter broken glass and stuff. And the roof's about to come down.'

Charles looked down at his feet almost in surprise. 'Oh,' he said flatly. 'I hadn't even noticed. Guess I just forgot to pick up boots. There wasn't much time.'

The fireman nodded, seeing in Charles's face the numbed shock he must have seen too often before. 'Sorry there wasn't anything we could do. It was just — much too late.'

'I know,' Charles said bitterly. 'Thanks. For trying. But it was too late five minutes after the slime lit the match.'

The fireman looked at Charles for a couple of seconds. 'Ah,' he said neutrally. Then he was all business again, shouting for his men to bring a couple of suction hoses.

A major portion of the roof sagged and crashed in on the flames, sending them licking up even more wildly into the night sky. There was something so final about it that Charles turned and walked away to check on Marmaduke and Aristotle, murmur soothing words to them, and make sure

262

Marmaduke had adequate ventilation in the hold-all.

The partly open zip-fastener gave safe access to air, and Marmaduke, apart from a puzzled-sounding small meow when Charles spoke to him, seemed more or less resigned to the situation. 'It'll be all right, feller,' Charles said. 'I'll get you into somewhere more comfortable as soon as I can.'

The galah had lost interest in the strange events and had retreated into the wooden shelter-box where he often slept. Designed to give him protection from cold winter nights, it no doubt had protected him from the heat of the fire sufficiently to allow him to survive long enough for Charles to get to him.

Charles went back towards the ruins of the house, the flames dying down under the deluge of water and foam being sprayed on them. But their fury was mainly spent because they had consumed almost everything combustible.

The senior constable came over to Charles and said amiably, 'One of the fire officers reported that you had alleged the fire was in fact arson. Is that correct?'

'Yes.'

'Why do you believe that, sir?'

Charles tried to take a deep breath, and coughed heavily. 'I rather think both you and

263

the firemen must know it was arson.'

'I'd like you to tell me why *you* think it was, Mr Waring.'

'I was wakened by a noise. A crashing noise, rather like glass being smashed. I'd not so long gone to sleep, and I was half-asleep still, thinking I must have been dreaming. Then I heard Aristotle.'

The policeman stopped making notes and looked up. 'Pardon?'

Charles smiled faintly. 'My mother's pet galah. He had a cage on the veranda. He was calling out.' Charles felt it was better not to explain what Aristotle was saying.

'I could see the glow of fire,' he went on, 'and I grabbed the cat and some clothes and my wallet and called the emergency number. There was smoke in the hallway and the living area was well and truly on fire, so I got out by the bedroom window. I found the garden was alight all around the house — not just in the front where the house was burning. That couldn't have happened unless someone had gone right around the house lighting fires — with the help of something like petrol, I'd guess. And even inside the house — the whole front area went up as though a bomb had hit it.'

'I see.' The policeman nodded. 'Well, no doubt the arson squad will be called in

264

to investigate, but the fire officers tell me there's no doubt that a twenty-litre fuel can was thrown into the front of the house, and they believe that a considerable amount of flammable liquid was spread around the outside, just as you say.'

'He meant to make a job of it, didn't he?' Charles said bitterly.

'Do you have any idea who might have done this, sir?'

Charles shook his head. 'Someone who wants me out of the way. I only wish I knew who.'

The policeman looked at him curiously. 'You think your death was the objective?'

'That seems the most obvious thing, doesn't it?'

'Mmm. Sometimes people just like to burn things so they can watch the fire.'

'This one didn't stay to watch,' Charles said drily. 'He bolted.'

'How do you know that? Did you see someone?'

'No. But a few moments after I woke I heard a car start up and drive off in a hurry.'

'I see.' The senior constable looked at the still-burning wreckage for a moment. 'You know, setting fire to a low-set house like this wouldn't really be a very efficient way to try to murder someone.'

Charles shuddered suddenly. 'It wasn't all that far off being successful. If the cat hadn't growled, right beside me, I think I'd have gone back to sleep, and the chances then of waking in time wouldn't be good. Whoever the slime was who lit it didn't do it so he could stay around to see the fun. And no one could possibly gain anything by the fire, and it was always certain to be recognized as arson, so if murdering me wasn't the objective, what else — '

He stopped as another thought hit him.

'Yes?' the policeman prompted.

'Someone,' Charles said slowly, 'got into this house some time ago, apparently searching for something in particular, because nothing was stolen. Someone ransacked the office at the winery, apparently for the same reason. Maybe he didn't find it, and wanted to make sure no one else did either.'

'And you've no idea who this person might be?'

'None. I wish I had. Believe me, I wish I had.'

The policeman closed his notebook. 'Well, there'll be an ongoing investigation into the fire, of course. We'll have to ask you for a formal statement in the morning, sir, please.'

Charles nodded.

The policewoman who had come with the senior constable came away from speaking with one of the firemen.

'Are you all right?' she asked Charles. 'What about somewhere to sleep till morning? And how about transport?'

Her concern seemed real and beyond simple routine. Charles nodded. 'I can go to the winery — Glenlodge winery is mine. And the house there is empty. This isn't — wasn't — my house. It belongs to the Erskine family. I'll have to notify them. I was only staying here, more or less caretaking. I'm their stepbrother. I managed to get my car out of the garage before that section caught fire. But thanks — thank you very much.'

He looked at his watch. 'It's not all that far off morning anyway, and there'll be formalities with the fire brigade people. And I feel I should be here anyway. When it's daylight and there's nothing more happening here I'll go down to the winery and start telephoning the family, because — '

He stopped. 'Oh, my God!'

The shock in his voice was sharply clear and the police officers stared at him. 'What is it?' the senior constable demanded.

'The winery! He might have torched that

267

as well, just to make sure.'

'Make sure of what?' the policewoman asked, but Charles was already running towards his car.

'He thinks the house was torched to destroy some kind of incriminating evidence his mother had about someone. He doesn't know what it is or where she might have put it, but he thinks she was killed because of it. I'd forgotten, but I remember now he was telling the DI at the station.'

'Did the boss believe him?'

'I think he's been a bit uneasy all along.'

'Then if he's right it's possible whoever did this *might* have headed for the winery. Mrs Erskine ran it, didn't she? Maybe we'd better get down there.'

'Maybe. Can't do any harm. I'll just have a word with the fire boys.'

Charles drove as fast as he dared, conscious of Marmaduke complaining from his cramped quarters on the back seat, but trying to concentrate on driving while flinging anxious glances at the sky ahead for any sign of a tell-tale glow of fire. But the winery and the house were dark and quiet. Evidently the arsonist had convinced himself, the night he ransacked the office, that no dark secrets of his past were hidden there.

Charles felt faintly foolish when the police

car pulled up a few minutes behind him, but he was no less grateful for their coming.

They asked if he had keys and suggested they check inside — just in case, sir. They went briskly through both winery and house, finding nothing amiss, but assuring Charles it was no trouble and always better to look at the worst-case scenario than fail to take precautions. They drove away after reminding him to call in at the station later to make a formal statement about the arson allegations.

When they had gone, Charles stood looking at the house, the winery, the outbuildings, the rows of the vineyard bathed in the light of the full moon he and Pip had been lightheartedly chatting about only a few hours before. It seemed a year ago. He had turned on all the lights, feeling it was the best way to discourage any murderous arsonist from chancing his arm again.

'You won't win, you dirty bastard,' he said aloud. 'I'll stay and I'll run Glenlodge, and with the team I've got and the girl I'm going to marry, I'll make it work. And I'll find you, you hear me? You're not going to win. I'll run this place for Ursula Erskine and I'll run it for Pip, and I'll run it for me. And you can *rot*.'

Perhaps perturbed by the anger and

emotion in Charles's voice, Marmaduke produced a loud wail of distress which jarred Charles back to concentrating on the immediate problems.

'All right, Duke,' he said quietly. 'You've had the devil of a night, haven't you? Tell you what, I'll shut you in the garden shed behind the house here for the rest of the night. I don't think you'll come to any harm there, and in the morning I'll fix you up with everything you need here in the house. Because we're going to live here now — you and Aristotle and me.'

Having settled the frightened cat as well as he could in the garden shed, he drove back to the fire scene. Both the urban and the local volunteer brigades were still there, but preparing to leave. He thanked the rural volunteers and promised a donation to their brigade, and discussed payment arrangements with the senior urban officer.

'There's no question it was deliberate,' the officer told Charles. 'And whoever lit it didn't try to conceal the fact. Just chucked a can of petrol through one of the front glass doors and threw a match after it. It's a safe bet he'd sloshed a lot around outside as well. He sure meant the place to burn. Of course, there'll be police investigations and insurance company enquiries and all that, so don't touch anything in the wreckage, will you, sir?'

Charles assured him the ruins would be allowed to lie undisturbed, and gave a similar assurance to the police a few minutes later. Then they were all gone, and the first paling of the sky to the east announced it was dawn, and Charles thought of what he had to do, and what he had lost, and felt crushingly weary. He looked at the blackened, shapeless wreckage and thought of the total waste, but a flat numbness dulled the fierce rage he had felt earlier. It would come back, but for now it had to be put aside so he could focus on what must be done.

He first checked Aristotle and found him awake and obviously disturbed by finding himself in very different surroundings, but otherwise unharmed. Charles wheeled the cage against a tree for some sense of shelter, and realized he would have to ask one of the vineyard crew to bring the Glenlodge four-wheel-drive to collect bird and cage.

He drove back to the winery and let himself into the office to begin telephoning the family to explain that a part of their inheritance had just been reduced to rubble. He wondered grimly whether one of them was already well aware of it, and perhaps expected him to be a part of that blackened rubble.

They all sounded shocked, but that was natural enough, and he had no way of knowing whether the shock was because of the fire or because he had survived it. The house, which belonged to the Erskines, was insured, likewise the contents, which belonged to him. The fire itself, Charles knew only too well, had been someone's personal insurance against being found to be what Ursula had called 'evil'. Someone had taken out insurance by destroying something which pointed to that evil with an unerring finger. Evidence. But *what* had it been?

In terms of monetary loss to the family of Anthony Erskine, the fire was not too disastrous. Certainly a loss, but insurance would cover the bulk of it. But to do them justice, they all clearly felt a sharp emotion at the deliberate destruction. Except, perhaps, one of them only pretended. They all asked anxiously if Charles had been harmed at all, and how much time he'd had to escape. Jill had immediately asked after the cat and the bird, and then when Charles assured her they were safe, laughed a bit shakily and said, 'Sorry, Charles, for asking after them before I even asked if you'd been hurt; but I knew at least you were alive.'

He smiled for the first time since waking at the sound of smashing glass.

'That's all right. That was the only good thing — that I got them out. I thought I wasn't going to get Aristotle, but he was sheltered just enough from the fire by a part of the wall and the fact he must have been in his wooden sleeping-box.'

She said quietly, 'Thanks, Charles. You're a nice fellow to have for a stepbrother.'

They all asked where he would stay and when he told them, asked was he all right for necessities — bed, table, crockery, cutlery, blankets and so forth — all offering help. If someone among them wished he wasn't alive to receive it, it didn't show. Sandford asked if he needed cash, but Charles explained he'd been able to instinctively grab his wallet, which contained credit card, cash cards, driver's licence. He was touched by their instant, practical assessment of what his needs were, when he himself hadn't even begun to consider them. He was touched by their readiness to help. They all made him feel he really did have a family.

And he desperately hoped none of them was an arsonist and a murderer, even though he virtually knew that hope was a forlorn one.

He was still in the office making phone

calls when Cliff Barber, the orchard foreman now that Tom Rushton had left, came striding briskly in, whistling cheerfully.

'Hi, boss,' he grinned in greeting. 'You're an early starter.'

Then the grin vanished as he looked at Charles's unshaven, red-eyed weariness and singed hair. 'Hell, Charles, what's happened?'

Charles told him. 'Cliff, I'll need you to come with me in the utility to pick up the galah. His cage is too big for one chap to pick up, and I need to get him over here so he has some sense of security. Maybe that sounds silly, but I had the devil of a job to rescue him last night, and I don't want him dying of stress now.'

'What you need,' Cliff said firmly, 'is breakfast. Come on up to our place and Angie will fix you something. And you can have a shower and borrow my razor and some of my clothes — we're near enough the same size.'

'Thanks, Cliff, but I don't think I could eat.'

'You could, and you will. Come on. You're just about out on your feet, and' — raising a hand to check Charles's protest — 'you can stop worrying about the bird. I'll get Giovanni to come out with me in the ute and pick him

274

up. We'll put his cage on the veranda of the house here. Where's the cat?'

Charles explained. 'He'll be all right for the time being. I'll see to him later. He's in such a state of nerves I don't think he'd trust anyone for a bit. He'd bolt if he saw an open door. But honestly, I'm all right.'

'You're not. Angie 'd half murder me if I didn't take you home for her to fuss over.'

Charles smiled rueful gratitude, and found a shower, and a change of clothes that didn't reek of the bitter stench of smoke, made him feel able to face bacon and eggs and almost enjoy it. Cliff's cheerful wife plied him with food and coffee and refrained from asking any of the questions which must have been tumbling through her mind. Charles was grateful to be left unquestioned, but when he had eaten he found talking, reliving the fire, was a release for his tension and emotions.

Finally he looked up at Angie's concerned face and said quietly, 'I'm going to stay. I'm not going back to my job in Canada. I'm going to run Glenlodge.'

He added in some surprise, 'You're the first person I've told, actually. I think really that I made the decision weeks ago, but I hadn't consciously realized it.'

'Oh, Charles, that's great!' Angie's eyes were shining. 'Cliff will be so happy. So will the children,' she added with a laugh.

'The children? Why?'

'They think you're wonderful. Because you talk to them. When they asked once what you'd been doing in Canada you explained in terms they could understand. You got them all enthused about rocks, and how the earth is built of different layers of material. You took them to the river to look for topaz, and you told them about the tin that used to be found in the area.'

'I didn't do anything special. We didn't even find any topaz.' Charles shook his head. 'They're nice kids, your two. They often play around the winery and never cause any trouble. But surely Cliff would rather the place belonged to someone else — someone who knew what he was doing?'

Angela shook her head. 'All the men *like* you. They say you're — ' She hesitated, and then added quietly, 'They say you're as nice as your mother. Cliff says,' she went on in a more lighthearted tone, 'you hardly knew a grape from a nectarine when you first came, but you've never been afraid to admit it if you didn't know something and so you've learned quickly and worked jolly hard.'

She smiled. 'To quote Cliff: He's picked things up faster than a magnet in a packet of tacks.'

Charles laughed, and at once coughed in sharp reminder of the smoke he'd inhaled, and the memory of the devastation swept over him, bringing with it the awareness of all he had to do to deal with it.

'You should get at least a couple of hours sleep,' Angie urged. 'Drop down on the sofa, at least.'

He shook his head. 'I can't really spare the time. I'm all right, truly I am.'

The pressure of things which needed immediate attention kept him going through the day. He went to the police station to make a statement of the little he knew about the arson attack. He bought clothes. Sandford's wife Netty insisted on going with him to buy some essential furniture, and in the two hours they spent together choosing a bed, chairs, a table, a refrigerator, a washing machine, sheets and blankets, crockery, cutlery and cooking utensils, he came to realize why Sandford adored her. Quiet, softly spoken, she was highly intelligent, practical and with a delightful sense of humour.

Sandford provided one of his work-trucks and cheerfully helped load Charles's purchases, and drove them out to Glenlodge, where Cliff, Giovanni and Rob helped unload and carry things into the house, while Netty and Angela vacuumed and dusted and took care that the house was well-aired after having been closed for weeks, and helped Charles decide where everything should be placed. Jill took time off from her veterinary practice and came with Rex to bring cat food and bird seed, plus a litter-tray and a carry-cage for Marmaduke.

'Rex just came up from Brisbane this morning,' Jill said, 'and he said he'd be willing to bet there were a couple of things you wouldn't have thought to replace.'

Rex smiled at Charles and held out a package, which proved to contain a razor, soap, shaving cream, toothpaste and toothbrush. 'I guess,' Rex said quietly, 'you're lucky you still need them. Hell of a thing to happen.'

Charles stared at the simple items and felt the crushing meaning behind the often-read newspaper words reporting fires: The occupants lost everything.

In that moment he understood what 'everything' meant. He looked at Rex. 'You were right,' he said a trifle huskily. 'They're the simple things I didn't think of. And yes, I'm lucky I still need them.' He put his hand on the other man's shoulder. 'Thanks,' was suddenly all he could say.

He arranged for an intruder-alarm system for both winery and house to be installed urgently, and managed to get an electrician to install sensor flood-lights which came on when anyone came within twenty metres of either the house or the winery. He reflected that a week ago he would have thought such precautions almost absurd. Now he didn't.

Miriam phoned and offered to come over to help. 'I'll come today if you need me, otherwise tomorrow.' Charles assured her everything was being dealt with and there was no need for her to make the two-hour drive.

And he constantly thought achingly: I don't want it to be any of them. They're my family. I don't want it to be any one of them.

And as always he knew that that was a fairly hopeless hope.

When, late in the day, everyone had gone and all was quiet, he used Jill's carry-cage to transfer Marmaduke from the garden shed to the laundry, where he mightn't feel so fearful, though clearly it would take quite some days for him to adjust to new surroundings. Then Charles cooked himself a piece of steak, found to his surprise he could barely eat it, and lay down fully dressed on his new bed, and slept for twelve hours.

12

A sound woke him, and he sprang instantly out of bed, a memory of leaping flames vivid in his brain, until he realized it was broad daylight and someone was knocking at the front door.

He opened it to find a shocked-looking Jack Henty.

'Charles!' he said. 'My God, man, are you all right?'

Charles rubbed his hand over two days' stubble on his face. 'I could use a shave,' he said, with a rueful smile. 'And breakfast, come to think of it. Care to join me? Bet you haven't had any, this time of day.'

Jack came in. 'Well, no. Charles, I hadn't heard — I didn't know about the fire. Pip phoned me before daylight — guess it *was* daylight in New Zealand. She was worried because she'd tried to phone you last night and the line was dead. So I drove out to the house.'

He shook his head and shuddered. 'When I first saw it, I thought maybe it had just happened last night — thought perhaps — ' He didn't finish the sentence. 'Then I realized everything had been hosed down and it was all cold, so it hadn't just happened, and I'd have heard if . . . you hadn't made it out. So I came here. Charles, when did it happen? What caused it?'

Charles found eggs and bacon and a frying pan. 'It happened in the very early hours of yesterday morning. As for what caused it, it was some two-legged piece of filth with a couple of cans of petrol. One egg or two?'

'One.' Jack opened cupboards and drawers and produced cups and plates and cutlery, and switched on the electric kettle. 'Do you think,' he asked quietly, 'it was meant for you?'

'Not specifically,' Charles said, repeating what he had discussed with the police. 'I'd agree that setting fire to a single-storey house, even if you've ringed it with petrol so there'll be fire everywhere, is a pretty hit-and-miss way to try to kill someone. I think it was meant to destroy whatever it was that my mother had, and which was such damning evidence against someone that he or she is perfectly prepared to kill to hide it. I guess if the fire wiped me out as well, that was just a bonus.'

Jack made toast while Charles made tea, and they sat at the only table to eat, the simple routine of having breakfast somehow bringing some kind of sanity to a discussion of arson and murder.

'Do you think,' Jack asked, 'he — or she — will be satisfied they've succeeded? There's no further danger?'

'Maybe. For the moment. Whatever it was, it couldn't have been simply something Mum *knew*. She must have had actual evidence. Otherwise, silencing her would have been enough. It wasn't, obviously. The house was searched. Then the winery office was so thoroughly trashed that the searcher must have been convinced that the evidence, whatever it was, must have been hidden in the house. I'd have to agree, unfortunately. The office was pretty easy to go over thoroughly, because there aren't many places there you could hide anything. But in a big, fully furnished house there'd be dozens of places to hide things. But if you burn it down, making sure it's a good hot fire — well, everything's gone for good.'

There was a little silence, into which a raspy voice said, 'Silly old bird.'

Jack looked at Charles in clear delight. 'That's your mother's galah! You got him out! I wasn't game to ask about him and . . . her cat? Did he — '

Charles nodded, smiling. 'He'd taken to sleeping on my bed, so I was able to grab him. In fact, I guess he saved my life.'

He told Jack briefly about the fire, and the fire-fighters' valiant efforts which had saved the garden shed. 'It mightn't sound much, but there were quite a lot of tools in there, and a lawn-mower and stuff like that. They did a good job to save it.'

Presently Jack said thoughtfully, 'You said a while ago that the arsonist might think he was safe for the moment. Why did you say 'for the moment'?'

'Because,' Charles said grimly, 'I don't intend him to go on feeling safe.'

'Charles! For God's sake! This creature will stop at nothing. Don't stick your neck out.'

'I'll give the police a bit of time to see if they can pick up any evidence from the fire. If not, the only way to flush this vermin out of the woodwork is to make him think there's a snare tightening around him. What other way is there?'

'Let the police deal with it. Surely they're convinced now that your mother was murdered; and why.'

'Very likely. Yes, all right, maybe they do believe it. But what can they do? Unless there's something left from the fire that gives them a clue, what under heaven can they do? Because if the killer believes he's now safe, he'll just go quietly about his everyday affairs and no one will have any reason to suspect him. Or her. But if I start tossing out hints that I know a way to get the information my mother had, he has to try stopping me. He has to risk coming into the open. I'm the tethered goat that's the bait for the tiger. Only I'm not quite so helpless.'

'Don't be mad! You can't be safely on your guard against a determined murderer.'

'Jack,' Charles said quietly, 'my mother described this person to Pip as 'evil'. Everything shows she was right. I can't simply walk away from everything and pretend it won't matter now if this person is left on the loose.'

Jack Henty sat for a moment with his elbows on the table and his head in his hands. Then he looked up. 'Pip told me you and she are going to be married. I think she loves you very much, Charles. Don't get yourself killed.'

Charles smiled wryly. 'I sure don't intend to. But, Jack, Pip wouldn't want me to walk away and play safe, even if there is such a thing as 'safe'. Remember she took a pretty solid risk herself to try to make me stay because I seemed to be the only chance Mum's death wouldn't just go on being regarded as an accident.'

Jack sighed. 'That day by the river. Oh, yes, I know. You're a good pair — one as damn reckless as the other, when you think there's injustice somewhere. But Charles, I quite fancy having you for a son-in-law. Don't deprive me.'

Charles grinned. 'Thanks, Jack. I'll do my damnedest.'

★ ★ ★

Two weeks passed, in which investigations into the fire yielded no clues to the arsonist's identity, Charles had great difficulty in persuading Pip over the phone not to cut short her visit to New Zealand and come home, and Ursula's cat and bird settled contentedly into their new surroundings.

Geoffrey and Rhelma drove up from Brisbane one day to visit. Neither made any reference to the confidences they had unburdened on Charles the night he had stayed in their home, but Geoffrey was in high spirits and Rhelma, though by nature a quiet person, was very different from the 'ice-maiden' label Charles had once mentally applied to her, so he gathered they had finally confided in each other and found the trust and acceptance they had feared would not be there.

Charles involved himself intensively in every facet of the operation of Glenlodge, feeling his way carefully in the marketing side of the winery which had been Ursula's special field, and one where the rest of the Glenlodge team could not help or advise him. He found most people, from other growers to wholesalers and retailers, were gratifyingly willing to give him advice. His own staff worked with renewed sense of purpose since he had announced his intention to stay, and he felt the shared sense of anticipation as the grapes slowly filled on the vines and the stone-fruit grew toward maturity. There was a shared anxiety, too, as eyes scanned the sky for signs of early storms which could bring either welcome rain or disastrous hail which could strip trees and vines in a few hammering minutes.

'Still a bit early to worry about hail, with luck,' Cliff said.

'Can't be too sure there won't be a late frost,' Giovanni warned.

'Which is worse?' Charles asked.

Giovanni shrugged. 'Hard to say. Very late frost — say late October — can be real bad for the grapes. But with luck we won't get either.'

Pip came home, and was ecstatic that Charles was staying. 'Oh, I'd have loved

286

Canada, too,' she said. 'I know that. But this is home for me, and I've always felt it was where you belonged also. Silly, isn't it? You can't choose for someone else where they want to live or the work they want to do.'

'What about you?' he asked. 'What about the work you want to do?'

'Real estate? Well, of course I like my work, but — Beast!' she said, wrinkling her nose at him. 'You're teasing. You've always known that this is what I've always really wanted to do. Haven't you?'

He was smiling. 'I did rather guess. But I didn't let it influence me in my decision. I'm glad, just the same.'

Pip studied his face gravely. 'Charles — you're sure, aren't you? I mean, this is a very different career: are you certain you're not just taking it on from sentiment?'

He nodded. 'I've thought long and hard, and I'm certain. When I was a child — even in early teens, I suppose — I took it for granted that this would be my career, here. But everything between my parents was unhappy, so I turned away and wanted no part of it. But evidently, underneath, I hadn't turned away from free choice, as I'd always told myself I had. Even when I came back this time the place itself seemed to embody all the past conflicts. It took me a long time to realize the old ties had outlived the old conflicts. Oh, yes, I'm quite sure this is what I want.'

Pip sighed contentedly. 'I've always been fascinated by the wine-making. Ursula was so wrapped in it, and being such good friends, I guess it was a contagious enthusiasm, and I caught it. And I hardly ever drink any alcohol at all. I know it has a down side. Everything has, if it's misused. But it fascinates me — *growing* things fascinates me. Sorry. I'm babbling.'

He wrapped his arms gently around her. 'No. You're happy, that's all.'

She was very still for so long he said, 'What is it?'

'Happiness,' she said quietly. 'It's so fragile. It can be torn away just as fast as a hailstorm can shred an orchard. And — he's still out there. And we can't be completely happy because of him. You won't stop trying to find him, and he might kill you so you can't succeed.'

'I can't stop,' Charles said. 'Because it's just as you said: he's still out there; and while he is, we can't rest and we can't be safe.'

'Someone we know,' she said slowly.

'Almost certainly. Yes.'

'Dad said you were going to start spreading a rumour that you know something.'

'Mmm. I have been dropping a few guarded hints that I'm on to a line of investigation — nothing solid enough to take to the police, but *something*, just the same.'

'Oh, Charles, for God's sake, be careful. If only we *did* know something, however slender.'

And two days later, they did.

★ ★ ★

It was a Saturday afternoon and the men were off for the weekend, but Charles had gone across to the office to deal with accounts, and Pip had driven out and found him there, and she was perched on the end of the desk while Charles had put down a sheaf of papers and suggested they go up to the house for coffee.

Cliff and Angela Barber's two boys had been playing outside and around the winery and now Roddy, five years tall, with a sprinkle of freckles, came to the office door and whispered with disarming courtesy, 'Mr Waring, Paul and me are playing hide and seek. Can I please hide under your desk? If you sit there he'll never see me. He's been finding me all afternoon and I would like to win once.'

Charles grinned and turned sideways to give Roddy room to duck under the space which was the knee-hole of the big timber desk. 'Don't sneeze, now, and give the show away,' he whispered back.

He and Pip resumed a chat, and Charles said seriously, 'There's something I want you to think about. I need to give it heaps more thought myself, and I need to get professional advice — accountant and solicitor, I guess. I've been thinking of introducing some kind of profit-sharing scheme for the staff here. I haven't got around to detail, and since you're going to be a partner in this establishment you must approve or otherwise as you see fit. But I couldn't run Glenlodge without the team. They give the job one hundred per cent. I'd like to think they had a real involvement, a share of some kind. All of them, but especially Rob Carlyle. His skill is vital to us.'

Pip nodded thoughtfully. 'That sounds an excellent idea to me. As you say, all the legal bits have to be considered. But, yes, I — '

There was a knock at the door, and Paul Barber stood there. 'Excuse me, Mr Waring,' he said with the same politeness his younger brother had shown, 'but have you seen Roddy?'

'Yes,' Charles said, imagining the consternation under the desk at this seeming betrayal. 'I saw him pass the door — oh, five minutes — ten minutes ago. Did you see him, Pip?'

'That's right, I did,' she said solemnly. 'Can't say which way he went, though. Did you want him?'

'Oh, we're just playing hide and seek and usually he's real easy, but not this time. I'm stumped.'

'Give up?' asked an eager voice from around Charles's ankles, and everyone burst out laughing.

Roddy emerged from under the desk, flushed with excitement. 'Mr Waring, is that a treasure-map under your desk? Does it show where you can find topaz or something?'

'What map is that, Rod?'

'Well, I don't know that it *is* a map, really, 'cause it's in an envelope. But I mean the one you've stuck to the underneath of your desk.'

Charles felt a prickling feeling run down his spine like a trickle of iced water. For a string of seconds he simply sat without moving, conscious that Pip also was perfectly still.

Roddy said anxiously, 'I never touched it or anything, honest. I didn't!'

'No,' Charles said, feeling the inside of his mouth suddenly dry. 'No, of course you didn't. That's fine. No, it's not a treasure-map, I'm afraid — nothing exciting at all, really. It's only — ' He hesitated and racked his brain hastily for something to say. 'You remember a burglar broke in here once? Well, one day I had some money in fifty-dollar notes, and I put them in an envelope and hid them in case the burglar came back. And do you know, I'd clean forgotten them.'

He patted Roddy on the shoulder. 'Good man! You found them for me. So it is a kind of treasure, after all. And we treasure-hunters have to stick together, don't we? And if Paul hadn't been looking for you, you wouldn't have found it, so he's part of it.'

He took out his wallet and pulled two five-dollar notes and solemnly handed one to each of the boys. 'So this is your reward money. I might never have found the envelope but for you. Thanks, fellers.'

They darted off with whoops of delight.

Pip said slowly, 'Charles — '

He shook his head. 'I lied. One shouldn't. But maybe this time.'

He lay on his back on the floor and slid his

head and shoulders under the desk. A brown envelope was taped to the underside of the desk-top, at the back.

'An obvious place to look for something hidden, I suppose,' he said. 'Only I didn't think of it, and neither did our murdering friend.'

He carefully pulled the heavy insulation tape from the timber underside of the desk, and slid out and stood up. 'Shut the door, Pip,' he said in a tight, strained voice. 'And lock it, would you, please.'

He laid the envelope on the desk and, for a moment, they both stood looking at it in silence.

Then Pip said, 'It might be something else altogether, you know.'

'Yes,' he said. 'It might. But you don't think that, and neither do I. And if we're right, the contents of this ordinary-looking envelope are about to tell us who killed Ursula Erskine.'

He picked it up and added, 'And no doubt also killed a nice, ordinary garage attendant named Joe Franklin who somehow got in the way.'

'And,' Pip said gently, 'suddenly you don't want to know, do you?'

He swallowed hard. 'Oh, yes, I want to know, all right. But I think *knowing* is going to make me feel sickened, because it — it has to be one of them.'

'An Erskine family member. And you like them all.'

He nodded. 'And I like them all.'

He picked up a paper-knife, slit open the envelope, and carefully tipped the contents on to the desk.

They looked ordinary enough.

There were two photographs, a letter which was not in an envelope, and a photocopy of a newspaper clipping. One photograph was of a small boy in bathing-trunks and a floppy hat which shaded his face. He was seven or eight years old and he was standing on an anonymous beach — just a curve of sand and a fairly gentle surf — no landmarks showing. The second photograph was a selective enlargement of the first, in which only the boy showed.

Because of the hat and the way it shadowed his face, the photograph offered nothing in the way of possible recognition, even hair-colour being concealed.

But on his left arm, just below the shoulder, an oddly shaped mark was clearly discernible in the enlargement. About eight centimetres long and showing dark against the pale skin of his upper arm, it resembled two linked crescents, one facing forward and the other turned backward. Charles and Pip both looked at the photograph for a lengthy silence. Then Charles said: 'Ever seen anyone with that mark?'

Pip shook her head. 'If I had, I'm sure I'd remember. Of course, you couldn't see it unless he took off his shirt.'

'What do you suppose it is? Birth-mark? Scar?'

'Could be either, but I'd guess it's a scar. Whatever it is — ' She stopped.

'Whatever it is,' Charles said grimly, 'that little boy who now presumably is a man, will carry it forever. An unmistakeable identification. And since my mother hid the photographs and he tried so desperately to destroy them, it must link him inextricably with something he daren't allow to become known. Maybe these other things will tell us why.'

He picked up the letter. There was no sender's address, but it was dated a month before Ursula's car had crashed off the road. It was hand-written and he spread it out on the desk and they sat side by side to read it.

Dear Ursula,' a neat, crisp handwriting said, *I am sorry there has been a little delay in my replying to your letter but*

295

as you see from the return address on the back of the envelope, we had moved from our previous address.

I was delighted to receive a letter from you but somewhat concerned at its contents. I can well believe you would get a tremendous shock at seeing someone you believe to be Rupert. As you say, that scar is such a strange shape it's virtually impossible there would be two the same, though I was surprised you still remembered it from just seeing that photograph which I showed you all those years ago. Still, of course, the tragedy was so awful that everything about it was impressed on our minds — my family's especially, of course, living next door to Rupert's family as we did. The scar, you may remember, resulted from his climbing on to a table when he was about four, knocking a tray of glasses to the floor and overbalancing and falling on to the broken glass — very damaging gashes to his arm resulting. Better to have severed an artery and died, as things turned out.

I am enclosing copies of the photos you remembered, also a copy of a newspaper cutting at the time of the tragedy. I sincerely hope the person you know is not Rupert. The family, naturally enough, *changed their name and moved interstate — where, I don't know — and of course we had no further contact with them, as they wanted to totally sever all previous associations. Poor people. The other two children seemed perfectly normal. The parents were utterly devastated. I think it was really much worse for all of them than for Billy Macfarlane's family.*

We did hear that Rupert had done other pretty awful things with animals and even other children, both before and after Billy, but nothing to quite match that, thank God. Though one wonders whether he would ever change.

What a gloomy letter! I'll write more cheerfully next time.

Sincerely,

Elaine.

Charles put down the letter wordlessly, and unfolded the copy of the newspaper clipping. It was undated and without any indication of which newspaper it had come from. Blackly headed: SHOCK KILLING OF TODDLER, it read:

Even the most seasoned police investigating the death of two-year-old Billy Macfarlane have been clearly distressed as the circumstances have come to light. The seven-year-old son of family friends has been identified as the killer, having lured the toddler from his home yesterday and taken him to a nearby pedestrian overpass, where he helped the little boy climb on to the safety rail before pushing him so that he fell into the path of a semi-trailer.

Two witnesses who saw the children ran to try to take the toddler off the rail, at first simply believing he was in danger of overbalancing. Both declined to be identified, but one, a shaken teenager, said 'I thought the little kid might fall, but it never entered my head that the older bloke was going to shove him off, deliberate as could be. Then I'm blowed if the little s — didn't watch the semi-trailer run over the poor baby, and laugh like anything. I'm telling you, mate, he laughed. I was sick.'

Police said the older child had told them and his distraught parents he had decided to kill Billy 'Because he broke my toy train and nobody's going to spoil my things and get away with it'; and had earlier gone on to the overpass and dropped stones in front of approaching vehicles so that he would know just when to push the toddler over.

The driver of the semi-trailer was treated for shock.

Police said because of the older child's age, no criminal charges could be laid.

When they had finished reading, Charles and Pip sat for a long minute in silence, just staring at the piece of paper. Then Pip whispered, 'Dear God in Heaven.'

'Evil,' Charles said. 'Mum used the word 'evil'. She wasn't wrong.'

'How-how do you suppose he found out what she knew? He must have found out.'

Charles shook his head. 'I don't know. But I guess she must have confronted him with it. And he certainly wouldn't want his secret to get out. I don't know why she would tell him. She must have had a very good reason. She must have known it was a dangerous thing to do. She *must* have.'

'That obviously was what she was agonizing about,' Pip said. 'When she became pale and looked ill. When she asked me if I thought people — evil people — changed. I suppose this person — this creature — seemed just an ordinary human being. It happens like that, doesn't it? Even a serial killer can behave like a normal person. People say afterwards that he was just a nice quiet fellow, never made enemies, just a pleasant, polite — Oh, God,

Charles, it's horrible.'

She turned to him and he put his arms around her and held her tightly.

Presently he said, 'I've been wrong all along.'

She stepped back and looked at him. 'What do you mean?'

'Because it isn't one of the Erskine family.'

'Not — How do you know?'

'Because, remember, the police checked them all out for any criminal background. Changed name or not, they would have been able to trace right back. I mean, you and I couldn't because we haven't the resources, but the police have.' He frowned. 'Now we've run into a blank wall. Except, of course, I can take this to the police. It will certainly give them something to work on.'

'I wonder,' Pip said, 'why Ursula didn't do that?'

'Do what?'

'Take this to the police.'

'Well, for one thing, I don't suppose this fellow had done anything criminal — since Mum knew him, I mean. There was no occasion to bring in the police. The child couldn't be charged. The man couldn't be charged for what he'd done as a child.'

'Now that,' Pip said thoughtfully, 'may just be why there was no criminal record to find against any of the family: Rupert, whoever he was in later life, had no charges laid, no conviction recorded, because of his age. Maybe officially there was nothing to find.'

Charles rubbed his chin. 'Mmm. That may be right. But of course they can readily find out what all this is about.' He touched the papers on the desk. 'The catch is, of course, it still isn't *proof*. It may mean we *know* who killed my mother, who searched the Erskine house, ransacked this office and bashed me over the head, and finally turned to arson to cover his past. But none of this is a shred of evidence that could warrant his arrest. Knowing who committed a crime and producing evidence to prove it are two very different things.'

Pip picked up the photograph of the little boy and stared at it for a moment, then put it down with an involuntary shudder.

'At least,' she said, 'knowing would be worth a great deal. It would mean not only knowing who was guilty, it would mean knowing who was innocent.'

He nodded. 'That,' he agreed, 'would matter a great deal.'

'But even when the police find out, will they tell us?'

Charles shook his head. 'I hadn't wondered about that. I don't know. Rogerson might — the inspector. He's a pretty human sort of fellow, even though I wasn't his favourite person for a while. But I don't know what the official line would be in the circumstances. It'd probably be against regulations, so I doubt if anyone else would be prepared to tell us anything. I think maybe I won't give this stuff to anyone but him.'

He opened the telephone directory on the desk with a small smile. 'Better find the station's regular number and not use the emergency call.'

He punched the numbers and asked if it was possible to speak to Inspector Rogerson. 'I know it's a Saturday afternoon,' he said, 'but this is important.'

'I'm sorry, sir,' the voice which identified itself as belonging to Constable Evans said pleasantly but firmly. 'The inspector is on a week's leave and won't be back until Wednesday. May I help you, sir? If it's urgent I can put you in contact with Sergeant Blakely if necessary.'

Charles hesitated. 'No, it's not so urgent, I guess. I think I'd prefer to wait and speak to Inspector Rogerson. Thanks, anyway.'

'Nothing else gone wrong, I hope, Charles?' Sandford Erskine asked from the open window.

Charles and Pip both turned in a startled

302

movement and Sandford said quickly, 'Sorry! I shouldn't have gone blurting out questions like that. Just as I passed the window I couldn't help hearing you saying you wanted to speak to Inspector Rogerson and — well, I guess everyone's on edge after the things that have been happening. I didn't mean to be an eavesdropper.'

Charles smiled and shook his head. 'It's all right, Ford. We didn't hear your car come. No, there hasn't been any new criminal activity, I'm glad to say. But I have been told something that could prove very useful to the police in tracing the arsonist, though it's not a thing I can follow up myself, and I don't want to talk to anyone but Rogerson about it. Not even to Pip, much to her frustration.'

Sandford looked embarrassed. 'Hell, Charles, I don't want to pry. But if you've got anything that'll help nail the guy who torched Ursula's house, I sure hope it works. Dad was really proud of that house, just the way he was proud of your mother. It was such a damned *waste*, to see it destroyed, even if you could overlook the fact it nearly cost you your life.' He shook his head, his normally cheerful face shadowed with regret.

'Actually,' he added, 'I really came out to see if there's anything you'd like done here — in the old house, I mean. Any repairs, or renovations or anything. I'm quite happy to give you a few hours at weekends.'

He grinned his disarming boyish grin. 'I spend most of my time supervising other people working these days. I don't get much time at hands-on building any more, and I still enjoy it. So, if there's anything?'

Charles was touched. 'Thanks, Ford. That's awfully good of you, and I would appreciate your advice about something Pip and I were thinking of doing to the kitchen.'

Pip had unobtrusively gathered up the papers off the desk and slipped them back into their envelope, then casually tossed them into one of the desk drawers as if they were of no consequence.

They all walked up to the house, Sandford saying, 'Er, Charles, was there any significance in what you said about the kitchen? That you *and Pip* were thinking of doing something to it?'

Charles laughed. 'Only that we're going to share it. Stupid girl has agreed to marry me.'

Sandford let out a whoop of delight. 'Congratulations! Best news I've heard for ages. Netty predicted it would happen. I don't know how she can pick up these things. She'll be pleased — really pleased. It means you're staying, then? At Glenlodge?'

Charles nodded. 'I admit that when I came home I'd never considered this as my life's work, but I find I want it.'

The three of them spent an hour of plans and laughter in the old house, with Sandford agreeing with them that a few minor changes were all that were needed, the house having a character and charm which only needed some unobtrusive alterations to add convenience and efficiency.

As Sandford was leaving, he got into his car and started the motor, and then wound down the window and looked at Charles and Pip as they stood arm-in-arm waiting to wave him farewell, and suddenly the laughter was gone from his face and he looked at Charles with troubled eyes.

'Charles,' he said slowly, 'you said you'd heard something that might help the police identify the bloke who set fire to the house.'

Charles nodded. 'Yes.'

'But — you think the same person killed Ursula, don't you?'

'Yes.'

'Do the police?'

'I don't know.'

Sandford sat gravely still for a moment, and then slowly shook his head — whether in disagreement or distress there was no way of knowing. Then he smiled at them almost wistfully.

'Be happy, you two,' he said, and drove away.

They stood in silence, watching the car till it was out of sight. 'Oh, God, Ford,' Charles said softly, 'don't let it be you.'

For a moment Pip didn't speak, and then she said, 'Why did you tell him you had some information?'

'I want the killer to know. If it's not Sandford, he's bound to talk about it.'

'Charles, for God's sake, be careful! This person is — '

'Evil,' Charles finished grimly. 'I know. Why do you think I made a point of saying I wouldn't tell even you what it was that I'd learned?'

13

Forty-eight hours later, on the Monday afternoon, Charles had just come back into the winery after helping Cliff Barber replace a section of the trickle-irrigation system in the stone-fruit orchard, and as he walked in, the phone was ringing. The replacement work had taken longer than expected, and Cliff had gone directly back to his own house, and everyone else had gone home.

'Charles?' Jack Henty's voice said as Charles picked up the phone. 'I don't know what it's all about, but I've a second-hand message for you from Pip. Seems she couldn't raise you earlier and asked Hamish Stevens who works in the same office to try to get you or else call me — which he did.'

'I've been out in the orchard till just now. Is there anything wrong?'

Evil.

The word flicked into his mind as if projected on to a screen, and he couldn't keep the edge of anxiety out of his voice.

'Oh, no, apparently nothing like that,' Jack said. 'Only Pip told Hamish Stevens it was important. She wants you to drive out to

307

Donnelley's Castle.'

'Donnelley's Castle?' Charles echoed. '*Now*?'

'Apparently. Hamish said she told him she realized you wouldn't be there before dark, but it didn't matter. She'd wait there for you. I asked him had her car broken down or something, but he said no, she gave him the message before she left the office. She had to look at a property out that way, and then she was going there to wait for you, and to tell you there was something she needed you to see. And she said you were to bring the papers from under the desk — that was very important. Does that make sense?'

'Yes,' Charles said. 'That is, I know what papers she was talking about.' He frowned. 'I wonder why she didn't use her mobile phone to call you — or me — herself?'

'I asked Hamish that and he said her mobile was out of action.'

'I see. Well, she must have some reason for wanting me to meet her *there*, of all odd places. It's long after sundown now. It'll be well and truly dark by the time I get there, so I'd better get going.'

'You remember the way?' Jack asked. 'I guess it's a good many years since you were there. One of the service clubs set up picnic tables and things out there some years back.'

308

'Oh, I remember the way — or I will when I get out into the area.'

'You can't go in past that winery any more. It's closed to the public. But the other road's open, and there are signs for tourists to follow.'

'Right. Thanks, Jack.'

Charles put the phone down and stood for a moment, puzzled, but with a flicker of excitement that was almost apprehension.

He and Pip had not told Jack about finding Ursula's hidden papers, so it would be natural for Jack to assume that what Pip wanted to show Charles was something in connection with a piece of real estate she wanted his opinion on.

But to Charles, the only reason she could want to meet him urgently, with the papers, must have a direct bearing on that damning evidence which had cost Ursula her life.

Even so, Donnelley's Castle was an odd place to want to meet him. Odd, and isolated.

Belying its name, the castle was not a building at all, but a strange, jumbled pile of huge, grey granite boulders, some almost as big as a cottage, others more the size of an average room, tumbled together so that they made cave-like recesses, with narrow, rambling passages between. A marvellous place, he recalled, for children to play hide-and-seek in and out among the great rounded boulders; intriguing for adults as well, and in one part allowing a fairly wide view of the surrounding countryside for anyone who cared to make the easy scramble to the top, which was mostly only twelve or fifteen feet high; one boulder-height.

But although it was fairly close to the winery Jack had mentioned, neither it nor any other building was in sight or shouting-distance of the rocks. It was not, Charles thought, an ideal place for a woman to be alone at night, even sitting in a locked car. Obviously she wouldn't have expected him to be quite so late in getting there, but that didn't explain why she had chosen it, so whatever her reason, it must be somehow connected to those rocks, and it must be important. Very.

There was a torch always kept on the office desk, and he picked it up, collected the packet of damning evidence from where he had pushed it into the pocket of an old pair of overalls that hung on a peg in the winery.

He had calculated that no intruder would expect such a casual hiding-place. He locked up the office and went across to the house to get the car, and the sensor-lights, snapping on as he approached, revealed Marmaduke sitting on the veranda.

'Oh, hi, old chap,' Charles said. 'Waiting for dinner? Mine will be a bit late tonight, too. Better give you a snack, though, don't you think? I guess Pip won't mind waiting another two minutes, not when it's for you.'

He let himself into the house, poured some milk into one bowl and some dried cat-food from a packet into another, and drove away.

Out on the highway he turned north and put his foot down, watching the needle climb to the speed limit and resisting the urge to push it further. He didn't want to lose time by being stopped for speeding. The highway by-passed the town of Stanthorpe, and presently he began to keep watch for the once-familiar turn-off to his goal. He found it, swung on to a narrower sealed road which passed among orchards, the slash of his headlights showing their blossoms now mostly gone, with young fruit rapidly growing toward maturity, often, in the case of stone-fruit, under the protection of hail-netting stretched taut above the trees.

As Jack had said, a direction-sign presently pointed him left, and then another left again, on unsealed gravel this time. He drove into the park area over a cattle-grid and stopped, alarm jolting through him even while he told himself that what he saw might be either quite irrelevant or exactly what Pip had arranged.

His headlights showed Pip's white Mitsubishi Magna sedan, and beside it a blue Ford Falcon station-wagon. Alarm sharpened coldly to fear when he saw both were empty.

He pulled up and parked beside Pip's car, cut both motor and headlights and slid out of the car, torch in hand, and stood, listening.

The day had been quite hot, but now a stiff breeze, high in the eucalypts which dotted the area quite plentifully, made it hard to hear small sounds. A young moon slanting westward flung long shadows and soon as it slid down behind trees only its indirect glow would be left to light the park.

Charles simply stood still for a long minute. Regardless of the wind, if Pip was anywhere in the park she would have heard his car, seen the glow of the headlights.

She would come, or call to him.

She didn't.

Moving carefully now, but quickly, he went to her car. It was not locked and the keys were still in the ignition. There was a brief-case, some real-estate brochures with her agency's name on them, and a tailored jacket on the front seat. The rear seat was empty. Likewise, when he opened it with a sick, half-formed horror clutching somewhere in his gut, was the boot.

He dropped Pip's keys into his pocket with his own, and moved to the blue Ford. It was locked and, apart from sunglasses and an open packet of cigarettes on the dashboard, it was empty and anonymous.

And maybe its presence here was coincidental and innocent. Maybe.

He turned toward the shadowed bulk of the great boulders and shouted!, 'Pip! Phillipa! Where are you?' He did it again, and paused; and again; and with each futile shout, frail hope faded until it was gone, and terror came storming in.

Something unthinkable had happened. Whether the owner of the blue station-wagon had known Pip was coming, and had lain in wait, or whether some evil chance had brought him here to find her alone, he was involved in her disappearance. And — anything else was illogical — the answer was somewhere in that labyrinth of massive rocks. For the space of half a second he wondered whether he should go to the nearest house and telephone the police for help. He dismissed the idea as untenable. If Pip was alive, every second might count.

If Pip was alive. The thought seared

through his whole being with white-hot agony. Oh, God, let me find her in time. Oh, God.

He started swiftly towards the rocks, and his foot struck something on the ground. He stooped and picked it up and examined it in the moonlight, and he understood.

Not only had an ambush been set for Pip, but for him as well. Arrogant, stupid fool that he had been, he had believed he alone would be the target if the killer chose to try to silence him, and he had pulled Pip into the very danger he had thought he was shielding her from. He didn't know the means used for luring Pip here, but she had been the bait to set the trap for him.

Someone named Hamish Stevens — or who said he was Hamish Stevens — had telephoned Jack Henty with the message. And he had said Pip's mobile phone was out of order. That part, at least, was true. Charles held Pip's mobile phone in his hand, and it had been very effectively smashed.

He dropped the wrecked phone and moved swiftly towards the rocks. Very well, you foul slime, he thought, the mouse is coming to the trap; but at least the mouse knows the trap is set, and this mouse will fight.

He gritted his teeth. Whatever happened now, he must keep control of his terror and

314

agony over what may have happened to Pip. He must not let it blind him into rashness. He must *think* — must find depths of animal cunning in basic survival. For if he died, so did Pip. And if she was already dead, he didn't care if he died also, provided he could take the killer with him.

He walked straight towards the main path that led in among the boulders, shouting as he went, 'Pip! Where are you?' If the killer had a rifle, he reflected, he could pick Charles off quite easily in the moonlight. But somehow he didn't think that was the plan, and he didn't think a rifle would be the weapon. If that had been the intention, the killer could simply have sat in his car and waited for Charles to arrive, and blown him away and driven off. No. Something else was planned.

This killer enjoyed cruelty. He wanted to taunt Charles with the chance, however false, to rescue Pip. He wanted to play, unless Charles was mistaken, some deadly cat-and-mouse game among the boulders — always, of course, with the overwhelming confidence of his own success.

Certain that he was being watched — not from any sixth sense, but because it was simply logical — Charles walked the main path until he reached the long shadows the eucalypts threw. Then he abruptly dropped flat and crawled in the shadows of the trees around to the shadowed side of the castle itself. The years had long since erased any memory of any familiarity he might have once had with these rocks, but because of the very nature of the place, with the boulders leaning against each other, there would be more than one way into the labyrinth.

★ ★ ★

Jack Henty glanced at the time and decided he might as well begin preparing the vegetables for dinner. They could microwave some mixed vegetables and grill some steak or chops when Pip came home. Charles would very likely be with her, so he'd be as well to stay and eat with them rather than go home and have to begin preparing something for himself.

What on earth Pip could have wanted him to see out around Donnelley's Castle at this hour he couldn't imagine, but she must have wanted his advice about a property of some kind, though not for themselves, since they already had a fine property in Glenlodge.

Even Hamish Stevens had seemed amused by the whole thing. Jack took a paring-knife out of a drawer, and froze in mid-movement, literally feeling the blood drain from his face.

Pip had shown him a postcard about a week ago. A postcard with a photograph of the Tower of London. And Pip had said: 'That's nice of them! Hamish Stevens and his wife, from the office. They went overseas last month for two months of his long-service leave.'

He went to the letter-rack on the sideboard in the dining-room and with shaking fingers picked up the card. Dated two weeks ago, the note on the back read: *One more week in this marvellous city, then we hire a car for four weeks in England, Wales and Scotland. Hamish and June.*

Slamming the card down, he crossed to the telephone in three strides and delivered his message crisply and precisely, in a voice under rigid control. Then he went and unlocked a cupboard and took out a twelve-gauge shotgun and a box of shells, picked up a torch and car-keys and ran out of the house.

★ ★ ★

Charles edged carefully between two monstrous boulders which met above his head so that the stalker couldn't spring on him from above, which Charles felt would be the most likely form of ambush. Even though there was heavy shadow between the rocks the darkness wasn't complete, and his eyes were beginning to adjust. The moonlight still fell on the upper part of some of the rocks and created just enough reflection to fractionally lighten the gloom below except in the deeper recesses.

Thin grasses and shrubby plants grew except where people most frequently walked along the wider spaces which served as twisting paths, weaving in and out so that at every few paces the paths turned another blind corner.

The spot where Charles had chosen to edge his way into the maze-like jumble was an unused space where he had to bend almost double to get under the rock overhang, and there was dry vegetation underfoot so that he had to feel his way carefully with his feet at every step to avoid snapping a dead branch and revealing his whereabouts.

In a few slow, cautious paces he came to a more open space and stood up, still pressed back against the curve of the boulders he'd just crept between, and waited, listening with desperate intensity, cursing the wind for blocking out the chance to hear faint sounds like the rasp of a shoe on rock. Or a muffled moan.

He tried to steer his mind away from

hideous possibilities. He knew a man who had served in the army in Vietnam. 'If you're in a life-and-death confrontation,' that man had said, 'never let the enemy make you so angry you're blinded to danger. That's the quickest way to get killed, and then he's won. Because you're no use dead.'

Charles took a deep, slow breath. You're no use dead. The noise of the wind would cover his own footsteps, also; it wasn't entirely a disadvantage.

I have to move, he thought; right or left? Start searching.

'Welcome to the castle, Mr Waring,' a man's voice said. Not very close. With sound distorted among the rocks, direction was impossible to pinpoint, but certainly the speaker was deeper in the tumbled confusion of granite.

'Do come in,' the voice went on. 'I'm so sorry the lady isn't able to come to you, but I'm sure you can find her, if you just look.'

Whose voice?

Charles realized with a small shock that until this moment he hadn't even wondered who it was who was waiting for him. Not that it really mattered now.

Whoever he was, he wasn't within a few metres, so Charles moved quickly forward, around one boulder, into a small open space; around another boulder, back pressed against the reassuring solid mass that guaranteed no surprise attack from behind. A narrow, curving path disappeared to right and left, only a few metres of it visible before it curled around a globe-like rock perhaps four metres in diameter. And under every boulder was a dark recess, and many of those recesses were big enough to have a body pushed under, out of sight in the shadow.

'Come along, now, Charles,' the man said, the mocking taunt still in his voice. The certainty that he would win. He was enjoying himself. 'You want to kill me, don't you? After what I did to your mother? And I've got your girl. You want to know what I've done to her, don't you? Or maybe you'd rather not.'

Charles moved quickly to his left, trying to fix the direction of the voice, trying to ignore what it was saying. It was closer now, but he was sure it wasn't in the same place as at first.

The man laughed.

Damn the wind, and damn the way the rocks distorted the direction of sound. Now it seemed to come from still another direction. The man was ducking and weaving among the boulders. He must have memorized the place intimately, every rock-position, every space and path and overhang. Not that it would be very difficult if you spent an hour or two at it. Charles tried to visualize the area the jumbled rocks covered: not so enormous, as far as he could recall. Maybe as big as two or three good-sized houses. But the haphazard nature of the pathways, tiny open spaces, dead ends, cave-like shadowed under-spaces, made finding an armed intruder a nightmare.

'Charles,' the man said. Charles froze against the side of a boulder. The voice had come from above him, on top of the rocks, and very close.

'Charles, if you're wearing a watch, and I'm sure you are because I've not seen you without one, check the time. You've got ten minutes. You understand? Ten minutes.'

He was moving. He was further away.

'Ten minutes, and then I kill Pip. That's fair, isn't it? I'll keep talking to you. I'm going back near to her now. You find her and you'll find me. I'm playing fair, aren't I? Ten minutes, and then she's dead.'

Charles held his watch close to his face, checking the time. He didn't doubt this creature would keep his word. If Pip wasn't already dead.

'You hear me, Charles? You'd better answer.'

Charles took a ragged breath. 'I hear you, Rupert,' he shouted. And began stealthily to move.

There was a silence, and he could almost feel the killer working back through the rock-pile, his turn now to try to judge where Charles's voice had come from. Of course, Charles thought suddenly, I do know his name: he *is* Rupert, whatever he calls himself now.

'So,' the killer said, startlingly close again, 'you know it all, you smart sod. A lot of good it's done you.'

For the first time there was an edge of anger in his voice. The mockery was gone. Good, Charles thought grimly: get angry enough and you just might do something foolish.

He waited, motionless, every second a mounting agony as it ticked away. He strained desperately to hear a foot-step, but there was no chance above the noise of the wind.

'Time's getting away, Charles,' Rupert said. Still close. Too close to allow any further movement forward in the direction Charles had been going. Carefully he edged back the way he had come around two boulders, then turned right.

Whose voice? Abruptly he realized it did have some value to know who he was pitted against. If it came to a form of hand-to-hand combat he could be certain Rupert was armed with something — knife, hatchet, anything lethal; the only weapon Charles had was the torch, fortunately a long and fairly heavy type rather like a police torch, but as a weapon in a desperate fight it was pathetic. So the identity of his opponent did matter.

If, as Charles had always believed, the killer was part of the Erskine family, there were only two men, and now the women were eliminated. Sandford Erskine and Douglas Wentworth.

Of those two he would certainly prefer to be pitted against Douglas rather than the leanly muscular Sandford, toughened by the physical nature of his work. Then the chilling thought occurred that Douglas, as a doctor, could have access to some pretty lethal substances to fill a syringe with: the quick jab with a hypodermic loved by some writers of espionage fiction and not without foundation. Exactly what a general practitioner would have on hand to serve the purpose Charles didn't know, but certainly an overdose of certain things could be pretty

323

deadly. He had a memory of Douglas at the racecourse, white-faced and momentarily full of hate, saying with quiet intensity: 'I'll kill you'. And in that moment seeming perfectly capable of doing it.

Maybe it wasn't Douglas's voice. But it was a voice he knew, even though it was altered in tone by the effect of echoing among the rocks, and being muffled by the wind.

Sandford?

Even now, he didn't want it to be Sandford.

One of the staff at Glenlodge? Of them, only Rob Carlyle, because there was no slight Italian accent, so it was not one of the Petroni brothers, and Cliff Barber had been with Charles all afternoon.

He looked at his watch. Three minutes gone. Edged forward, close against the boulders, tightly aware that under some of their curving shapes Rupert could be crouched in shadow. And certainly under one of those recesses Pip was lying. Bound and gagged at best. Perhaps unconscious. Perhaps dead.

Shut out that thought. Hold the torch like a club, move sideways. Damn! A dead end; wasted seconds; nothing there. He'll be waiting where she is, in case I find her.

Charles could feel sweat trickling down between his shoulder blades. He stepped around a boulder into a tiny open space and shock jolted through him like an electric current as he came face to face with a staring figure in the half-light. He swung the torch up defensively, and then lowered it, and any other time would have laughed. Someone with a quirky sense of humour and little regard for leaving nature alone, had painted a life-sized picture of a humanoid creature on the rock opposite where Charles stood.

The monster Charles was stalking — and who was stalking him — was a deadly reality. His heart hammering with shock, he crossed the open space in a couple of quick strides, then cursed the path silently as he realized he was getting too near the outer edge of the rocky conglomeration. He had to turn back. Almost at once his tormentor called to him again.

'Five minutes. Come, Charles, you're not trying.'

The voice was above him again, of that he was certain; above and to the right. Suddenly he wondered whether in fact Rupert had Pip on top of the rocks, and not hidden under a shadowed overhang at all. And, equally suddenly, perhaps because the speaker was standing on top of the boulders and his voice was less distorted, Charles knew who he was dealing with.

Time was running out. Time for caution was gone. So was any time for regret.

Charles sought and found a place where he could scramble up far enough to see over the top of the rocks. Trying to keep his head as low as possible, he scanned the jumble of granite. Impossible to tell if Pip was there, but it seemed unlikely. But he saw Rupert. There was still enough moonlight.

He was standing perhaps twelve metres away, staring downward, his back half-turned to Charles so that he didn't see him. He held a long-bladed knife in his right hand, and there was something in his left hand also; probably a torch.

Charles dropped lightly to the ground and began working his way quickly through the maze of boulders. He felt the chances were that Pip was lying somewhere just under where Rupert was standing waiting, and if that were so, he would stay there, and wait, and be ready to carry out his threat of murder. If he hadn't already done so.

The time had almost run out, and so the time for stealth was over. Charles followed the gaps between the rocks at a run, not caring whether the stalker heard him. And then he saw something lying under the shadow of a boulder, and he didn't need to be able to see clearly to know what it was.

'Pip,' he said. 'Pip, I'm here.'

'Well done, Charles,' said the voice above him. 'Time almost beat you. Unfortunately you don't win, just the same.'

Torch gripped, every muscle tensed for battle, Charles snapped the light on and looked up at Rex Bartlett just as Rex raised his left arm and Charles saw he held a handgun, its muzzle steadied on his chest.

Charles had an instant of bitter awareness of defeat without even a fight, and then the crash of a gunshot boomed in echoes around the boulders.

For a second Charles thought it was curious: he didn't feel anything, not even the impact of the bullet. Then Rex Bartlett half-fell, half-jumped to the ground scarcely more than a metre away, and then lurched to his feet. His face in the dim light was contorted as if with rage, his left arm hung, oozing dark wetness, but his right hand still gripped the knife.

With barely a half-second to recover his balance, he lunged at Charles with deadly intent.

Reacting more from pure instinct than any faintest understanding of what had happened, Charles swung the torch with all his strength.

Rex saw the blow coming and in a flash of tigerish speed he lashed out with the knife. The blade grated across the torch and gashed Charles's arm, and then the torch flew somewhere away and went out.

But in the same moment the knife, jarred by striking the metal of the torch, dropped from Rex's fingers. Both men lunged for it as it lay on the ground, and Charles, perhaps out of the desperation that comes only from trying to save what one loves, snatched it up first in his left hand, only dimly aware of some damage to his right arm. Rex charged at him and Charles struck upwards with the knife.

The impact of Rex's headlong rush at him slammed Charles back against granite, and then Rex's grip dropped away, and he fell, slumped down in a strangely crumpled heap.

Charles went on leaning against the boulder for a few moments, desperately sucking air into his lungs and trying to clear his head of the buzzing in his ears. It was only next day when he found a tender egg-sized lump on the back of his head that he realized he had hit the boulder hard enough to be almost knocked out. A bright light seemed to be swamping him, and it took him a second to realize it was torchlight.

'Charles!' Jack Henty was saying urgently.

'Charles, are you all right? What — ?'

'Pip,' Charles said, dropping on his knees. 'Here, Jack. Torch.'

She was moving, and making stifled sounds, and Charles thought he had never seen or heard anything more beautiful in his life.

'Pip,' he said over and over. 'Oh, God. Pip.' Incoherent it may have been, but it was a fervent prayer of thankfulness.

She was bound cruelly tightly and savagely gagged, and there was an ugly bruise on her face, but there was life in her eyes. Charles tried to tug at the knots in the cords that bound her wrists and legs, but his right hand didn't function very well, and the knots were impossibly tight.

How long, he wondered in anguish, did limbs survive extreme restriction of circulation? Was it enough to cause irreversible damage? Please, he begged silently, let us have been in time.

He looked at Jack, kneeling beside him. 'A knife. Have you got a knife? We have to cut these cords, and quickly.'

Jack shook his head. 'No, I haven't got one with me. Usually have a pocket-knife, but I'd just showered and changed.'

Charles stood up. 'There is a knife,' he said grimly.

He dragged Rex Bartlett's crumpled form out straight and tugged the knife from its place where the blade was buried up under the rib-cage. With a sick feeling of repugnance he wiped the blade on Bartlett's shirt. The man didn't move and his eyes were glazing in the torchlight. Death must have been almost instant. Better than you deserved, Charles thought; and was instantly ashamed of the thought.

But there was no time for niceties. He handed the knife to Jack, who had watched him without comment. 'He cut my right arm,' Charles said. 'Your hand will be steadier than mine.'

Jack freed the gag first, and quickly cut the cords, and they both worked at rubbing the circulation back into blue hands and feet. Finding it hard at first to speak, or breathe normally, Pip whispered assurances that she was all right, except that Rex had punched her and knocked her out while he tied and gagged her.

As the fearful pain of restored circulation surged through her cramped limbs, there was a wail of sirens growing closer.

Charles looked at Jack, who nodded. 'Police. I called them. But I figured by the time they really understood what I'd said, I could get here sooner, because I know the way better, even to a shortcut. It's a long story. But Charles, before they come, about him . . . '

He nodded at the shape sprawled on the ground. 'I saw he had a handgun. I had a shot-gun. I fired. I think I meant — hoped — to kill him. Instead I just smashed his gun-arm. But he fell off the rock. And he fell on his knife.'

'But Jack — '

'I know, son. I know. But there'd be enquiries, charges that have to be levelled because the law says so. No cop would blame you. But they'd probably have to charge you. No jury would convict you. But you might have to stand up in court and defend what you did, and heaven knows what legal expenses you'd have. I saw what happened. He tried to kill you, and I wounded him. That's what the law calls reasonable force. But he died because he fell on his knife.'

'He's right, darling,' Pip said hoarsely, teeth gritted against the pain in her hands and feet. 'I certainly saw it all. He fell on that knife. It was an accident.'

'And how,' Charles said, still with a sense of unreality, 'do I explain this?'

He held out his arm. The sleeve of his flannelette shirt was ripped to reveal a four-inch gash still freely bleeding.

'You fought with him on top of the rocks,' Jack said. 'He gashed your arm and you overbalanced and fell. That's when I saw him aim the pistol, and I fired. Right?'

'They won't believe it.'

'Pip and I are witnesses. They have to believe it. And I guarantee you they'll be happy to believe it. Officially, anyway. What they think privately won't matter.'

Charles, still kneeling beside Pip and massaging her hands, looked at Jack with a rueful smile as a police loud-hailer echoed over the rocks.

'I don't know yet how you got here, Jack, but I'll tell you one thing: I sure am glad you're on my team.'

★ ★ ★

They sat in the lounge drinking coffee. Jack had lit a small fire in the grate, saying he thought everyone needed its companionable warmth, even though the night wasn't really cold. And in fact, Charles thought, as he sat with his bandaged arm around Pip, the fire and the warmth of the coffee were indeed a comfortable antidote for horrors.

The doctor in the casualty department of the hospital had reluctantly yielded to Pip's insistence that she wanted to go home, after she had been given treatment for shock and it had been confirmed that, apart from bruising to her face and some swelling and tenderness still in her hands and feet, she had not suffered any major damage.

'A long, hot bath and a long sleep,' had been the young doctor's smiling prescription, in addition to some pain-killers.

After stitching Charles's arm under a local anaesthetic he had given him some tablets also, and an anti-tetanus injection. 'That arm won't be very comfortable for a few days. And watch for any signs of infection,' he had said cheerfully. Then he had looked closely at Charles, and from him to Jack Henty, sitting quietly in the waiting-room.

'Your father?'

Charles shook his head. 'Miss Henty's.'

'Mmm.'

As the only doctor on duty it would have been this man's job, Charles reflected, to examine Rex Bartlett and pronounce officially that he was dead on arrival. Confirmation of the obvious, perhaps, but necessary, no doubt. Charles suspected that the police would have told this young man very little of what had happened, but he thought Dr Winthrop was quite capable of piecing things together for himself.

He looked from Jack back to Charles.

'He used a shot-gun?' It was almost a statement.

Charles nodded.

'And you and the d.o.a. got knifed.'

'The d.o. — ? Oh. Yes.'

'Miss Henty had been bashed, gagged and bound. Whose knife? And remember I haven't asked you any of these questions.'

'Of course you haven't. The dead-on-arrival's. And I haven't answered any questions.'

The doctor nodded. 'You've all had quite a night. My professional advice is to talk it out between yourselves. In the armed forces or the emergency services they call it debriefing, I guess. I'd call it unwinding.' Dr Winthrop smiled. 'Talk it out tonight, take some pain-killers and sleep half the day tomorrow.'

So they sat in the warmth of the lounge and talked. Pip had soaked in a hot bath while Jack and Charles made coffee and Jack produced some cake. 'I've read somewhere that carbohydrates are good for shock,' he said. Pip was wrapped in a towelling robe over pyjamas and a little colour had come back into her face, but the blue bruise streaked her cheek below her left temple.

The police had taken statements from them all, separately. A uniformed senior constable, a detective, dapper in a grey suit, and Inspector Rogerson — home from leave a day early and still in jeans and checked shirt which he'd been wearing during a quiet evening at home with his family when his phone had rung. The senior constable who had taken Jack Henty's urgent and demanding telephone call had told him, 'It's tied up with the Erskine case and it sounds as if it could be nasty. I know you're still on leave, sir, but I thought you should know.'

Rogerson had thought so, too. At the hospital, after listening to Charles's account of events, the inspector had looked at him steadily.

'You probably feel we haven't exactly covered ourselves with glory over this whole affair.'

Charles shook his head. 'I honestly don't know what more you could have done. There was simply no evidence to work with. I accept that. I felt I had to go blundering on, trying to stir up some reaction, and I almost brought about Miss Henty's death, and my own. I haven't exactly covered myself with glory, either.'

He put his hand over his face for a moment, wondering how long it would be for Pip before the horrors of the night faded. Then he said, 'But you never quite dismissed my concerns as nonsense, did you?'

The inspector smiled. 'I wanted to. But I was always uneasy about that accident. It's my suspicious nature. It seemed the sort of accident that might be very convenient for someone, and it was — as you said — the sort of accident that never should have happened. So I kept wondering *why*. Why there, on a straight, reasonably wide bit of road, in the only spot where driving over the edge could be guaranteed fatal? Mrs Erskine knew that road. Even a swerve to miss an animal, even a blown tyre — nothing should have caused her to drive off the road. I spent a lot of time there, the next morning when we were called after one of her employees went out to see why she hadn't come to work, and found her. It had rained, and there were no tyre marks to help us. You know all that.

'When you first raised your concerns over your mother's death, Mr Waring, I told you I had investigated the backgrounds of the Erskine family, including spouses. When I learned that Jill Erskine was engaged to a man named Rex Bartlett, I had his past looked into, and found nothing strange.

'Rex Bartlett was a real person and had no criminal record. Nor had he changed his name: he was born Rex Bartlett. There seemed no reason to suspect him of anything. If I remember correctly, he was a bit of a drifter, never keeping a job long, but no criminal factors known.'

Charles stared. 'But — that can't be.'

'Oh, I think it can,' the inspector said unemotionally. 'The man who died tonight does carry that very distinctive scar. *He* was not Rex Bartlett. It seems he told Miss Henty that he had met Mr Bartlett several years ago while Bartlett was hitch-hiking in north Queensland. They were the same age and apparently not unlike in appearance. So Rex Bartlett, who had no wife or family to raise a hue and cry, is buried somewhere in a lonely place, and Rupert took his identity.'

Charles felt numb. 'Poor Jill,' he said.

'Miss Erskine?' The inspector nodded. 'Yes. But I think you should tell her about the dog. And remember, if she had married that man the future could have been unthinkable.'

His tone indicated that he was soul-crushingly familiar with the unthinkable. He stood up. 'Perhaps it is far better that he should have met with a fatal accident.' There had been just the faintest emphasis on the last word. He smiled at Charles. 'Good night, Mr Waring.'

Remembering this now, Charles said to Pip, 'Inspector Rogerson said Rupert had told you about Rex Bartlett.'

Pip shivered. 'Yes. He . . . told me a lot of things.'

'Don't talk about it if you don't want to,' Charles said quickly. 'You've had to go over it once tonight, with the police. Leave it till you feel better.'

Pip shook her head. 'No. That doctor was right; it'll be better to talk it out.'

She took a deep breath and pressed against Charles more closely. 'He lured me out there,' she explained, speaking at first with flat weariness, 'by phoning me at the office. He said he was Cliff Barber. He disguised his voice by speaking as if he had a cold. He said Charles had received a phone call and left the winery in a great hurry, telling Cliff to call me at the office and tell me to go out to Donnelley's Castle straight after work; it was very important and I must tell no one where I was going. Charles might not be there when I arrived, but he'd be along soon after, and I'd be quite safe because Rex Bartlett would be there, and I could trust him.'

She shut her eyes for a moment. 'So I went, and he was there. I asked him if he

338

knew what it was all about, and he smiled and said, 'Most of it. Charles will have the last bits of the puzzle when he comes'.'

Animation in the form of anger came into her eyes and voice. 'Do you know, I remember thinking Jill had chosen a lovely fellow. He was so courteous and pleasant, as well as being a smashing looker. He helped me out of the car. Then he turned around, still smiling, and hit me a thumping whack on the side of the face and knocked me out.'

Instinctively she touched the bruise. 'When I came to, of course, I was gagged and tied up. He used my mobile phone to call Dad, then he smashed it. He made me tell about the letter and the photograph — made me tell by telling me — '

She caught her breath and looked at Charles. 'He told me the way he'd kill you if I didn't tell him.' She shivered. 'Never ask me to tell you that. When he had me tied up he talked. He seemed to want to be able to tell someone how clever he was, and since I wasn't ever going to be a witness against him, he felt quite safe in telling me everything. He told me Ursula had gone to him and told him she knew who he was and had the proof. If he broke his engagement to Jill and went away and never came back, she would keep his secret. But if he didn't, she would take the evidence to Jill. He laughed when he told me. Called her a silly old fool. He said marrying Jill was his chance to *be* someone. Her family had money; locally they were highly regarded, and he'd be part of that, and no one was going to stop him.

'He said almost exactly what he said after he killed that little boy: 'No one gets in my way and gets away with it'.

'He went over the border into New South Wales — telling Ursula he was going out of Jill's life. He had a very heavy bullbar fixed on his car and came back and waited, that evening, for Ursula to drive home from Glenlodge. He followed her and as she came to that bend in the road he accelerated and hit her car from behind and pushed it over the edge, just as Dad suggested it had been done.

'Then he went to a different motor body-works in New South Wales and had them take the bull-bar off. So there was no damage to his car and no bull-bar to show paint or scratches, or stir any kind of suspicion, because no one knew he'd ever had a bull-bar. But Joe Franklin happened to ask him why he'd had the bar taken off, and explained he'd noticed the car, parked as if it was waiting for someone, and he'd remembered it because of the number-plate letters — he'd made a funny phrase, apparently a hobby of his, using the letters as the first letters of words — you know, like NDP for No Damn Petrol. And Joe said it was imprinted on his mind because it was the day Mrs Erskine was killed in the accident.'

'So he killed Joe,' Jack Henty said bitterly.

'So he killed Joe. All the other things — searching the house, searching the winery office, then burning the house — they were all just as we guessed: to get rid of the evidence Ursula had, though he didn't know what it was.'

There was a silence while they all stared at the fire, and saw many other things.

'Poor Jill,' Pip said presently. 'It's worst for her.'

'Yes.' Charles tightened his arm around her. Then he remembered. 'The inspector said he thought we should tell Jill about the dog. What did he mean? Do you know?'

Pip nodded. 'You remember Rex — Rupert — found a dog with one of its front legs mutilated and took it to Jill? He told me he'd chopped the dog's leg off with a hatchet just to impress her by rushing this injured dog to her to show how kind he was. He laughed.'

'Dear God,' Jack murmured.

They talked a little longer, until Pip's eyelids began to grow heavy from the pills the doctor had given her to take, and her father and Charles helped her into bed, and she was asleep almost before they could draw the covers over her.

Charles drove home. As he drove, he thought of the things he had learned of the people who now were his family, and who had been virtual strangers not so long ago. Their weaknesses, tragedies, perils.

Those confidences they had entrusted to him were burdens he had never wanted. Yet that was the price of belonging in the family, and suddenly he knew he wouldn't want it any other way.

★ ★ ★

Pip and Charles went the next day to see Jill. White-faced and hollow-eyed with the agony of betrayal that was worse than grief, she was quiet and controlled. Or too numbed by shock to show any emotion.

Miriam and Douglas were there, and Sandford and Netty, and though they were all subdued with the awareness of the awfulness of the past night, they greeted Charles and Pip with the same warmth and concern they gave to Jill. Charles had not seen Douglas since the day at Corbould Park racecourse, but the doctor's attitude showed only what seemed genuine friendship. Whether he had done anything to seek help for his addiction Charles couldn't know; or whether he ever would.

'I will be all right,' Jill told Charles and Pip. 'Right now I don't know how to get through the next twenty-four hours. But I will. And I will deal with the rest of my life. I promise.'

She smiled faintly at Charles. 'I'm glad you're my brother, too.'

'Well,' Charles smiled back, 'only a sort-of brother.'

She put her hand on his arm and reached up to kiss his cheek. 'Sort-of isn't bad. And Charles, neither you nor anyone else will ever tell me, and it doesn't matter. But if you killed him, thank you. Miriam,' she said quietly, turning, 'let's go and make some coffee.'

They went out to the kitchen, and after a stunned silence Sandford said softly, 'That goes for all of us, Charles.'

Then he looked at his stepbrother and said with sudden curiosity, 'That day away back when you were nearly shot, down by the river: do you suppose that was Bartlett?'

'Oh, no,' Charles said, recovering his composure and gripping Pip's hand tightly. 'I'm sure that was just some harmless nut.'

THE END